Fall 2013, Issue Number 25, *www.DarkDiscoveries.com*

Publisher
JournalStone Publishing, LLC

Editor-in-Chief
James R. Beach

Assistant Editors
Aaron J. French
Elizabeth Reuter
Lacey Friedly (Submissions)

**Art Director,
Layout, and Design**
Cyrus Wraith Walker

Contributors

Nancy Kilpatrick
Elizabeth Massie
Yvonne Navarro
Chris Marrs
Rhodi Hawk
Nancy Holder
Steve Holetz
James R. Beach
John Palisano
Jason V Brock
William F. Nolan
Jonathan Maberry and David F. Kramer

Joe R. Lansdale
Stephen King
Jack Ketchum
Joel B. Kirkpatrick
Derek Botelho
Jim Smiley
Yvonne Navarro
Robert Morrish
Richard Dansky
Amy Shane
Michael R. Collin

Special Thanks
Cassandra Peterson
Lynn Lowry
Charlaine Harris
Asia Argento
Leah Jung
Kendare Blake
Alan Rodgers
Rocky Wood (for his assitance in obtaining the
the Stephen King/Matheson Tribute.)

**Contributing
Artists/Photographers**
(Cover Image) Christopher Vernale
Other Photographers (See Captions)

DARK DISCOVERIES
(ISSN 1548-6842) is published (Qtrly) by
JournalStone Publications, 1261 Peachwood
Court, San Bruno, CA 94066

Christopher C. Payne
JournalStone Publications
1261 Peachwood Court, San Bruno, CA 94066,
U.S.A.
christophercpayne@journalstone.com.

Please make check or money order payable to:
JournalStone Publishing and send to the address above.
Credit/Debit cards via Paypal at:
christophercpayne@journalstone.com. Advertising
rates available. Discounts for bulk and standing retail
orders.

I0683849

Fiction

Interviews

Features

Redheads

"A killer far worse than insane."

Redheads

Jonathan Moore

Chris Wilcox has been searching for years, so he knows a few things about his wife's killer. Cheryl Wilcox wasn't the first. All the victims were redheads. All eaten alive and left within a mile of the ocean. The trail of death crosses the globe and spans decades.

The cold trail catches fire when Chris and two other survivors find a trace of the killer's DNA. By hiring a cutting-edge lab to sequence it, they make a terrifying discovery. The killer is far more dangerous than they ever guessed. And now they're being hunted by their own prey.

"This is accomplished and exciting work, which at times seems to channel the best of Michael Crichton in its attention to believable, telling detail. Moore's a major new talent, I promise you."

--**Jack Ketchum**, author of *Off Season* and *The Girl Next Door*

SAMHAIN
PUBLISHING

samhainpublishing.com • samhainhorror.com

Updates
from the Dark Beach
GUEST EDITORIAL

Welcome to issue #25 of Dark Discoveries, our Femme Fatale theme, in which we explore the wonderful facets, perspectives, and angles of the human female—all of them fascinating, all of them interesting, and some of them horrific.

In short, we've done our best to hand over the content for this issue into the competent hands of our favorite female authors, artists, and personalities. True, one could argue that we, those beastly males, have maintained a presiding editorial kingship here, but after all someone's got to scrub the pages clean, and make sure the typos get rooted up.

I'm honored and excited to be doing the guest editorial for this particular theme. I attend many writing conventions during the year, and it was brought to my attention, through one elbow-rubbing or another, that DD appears to publish more male work than female; I'm not in a position to say whether or not this is true, but it did get me thinking about doing a theme composed largely of female content, or at least with spotlights on established female authors. I spoke with our Editor-in-Chief James Beach and he said he'd already been thinking of doing the same thing, only that he wanted to give it a unique slant, a variation on the theme, a version that had never before been done. Both of us were certain we didn't want to use the Women in Horror heading, a term that's been hackneyed and now runs trite. (Just ask Yvonne Navarro, our recurring columnist.)

James and I discussed possibilities, finally settling on Femme Fatale, a theme that retained the immediacy of "horror," but wasn't so limiting, allowing us to delve deeper into the magical realm of the female and shine a lens on her from all sides.

Hopefully, we succeeded. But you tell us. Talk amongst

yourselves, spread the word, and send us emails. Do what you do!

We have a stellar line up of original fiction by all female authors this time around. For the most part, DD is no longer accepting reprints (unless Stephen King calls us), and so the stories herein reflect this recent change. New fiction from genre mainstays Nancy Kilpatrick, Elizabeth Massie, Nancy Holder, Yvonne Navarro, and Rhodi Hawk. Plus an extremely twisted story from newcomer Chris Marrs. These include some of the best stories DD has had the privilege of publishing.

For nonfiction, we have articles studying the actresses of the Italian Giallo film genre, a look at Hammer Studios' Karnstein Trilogy, a focus on women in YA, and our regular stable of columns (including a new one from Jonathan Maberry and a new addition from Richard Dansky that will feature video games and horror). Also check out our great new interviews with Charlaine Harris, Elvira/Cassandra Peterson, Lynn Lowry, Asia Argento, and Leah Jung (our fantastic cover model).

On a sadder note, and a more masculine one, Legend of Literature Richard Matheson recently passed away on June 23rd of this year. We have pulled together several thoughts and remembrances in his honor, including pieces by Joe R. Lansdale, Jack Ketchum, William F. Nolan, Jason V Brock, John Palisano, and the one and only Stephen King. Matheson's contribution to the genre that we all here love is unprecedented, and indeed I would go so far as to say transcends it. His clear insights into the world, which he incorporated into his fiction, will surely be missed.

There you have it: Dark Discoveries offering its female-themed issue up for public consumption. Now, why did we call it the menacing Femme Fatale as opposed to Angelic Femmes, you may ask? Well come on, this is a horror magazine; we expect blood and violence from all of our contributors, and this demand is no less imposed upon the females.

Fabulous job, ladies. Enjoy your issue.

–Aaron J. French
Associate Editor
Dark Discoveries

CASSANDRA PETERSON ON ELVIRA, MOVIES, AND MUSIC

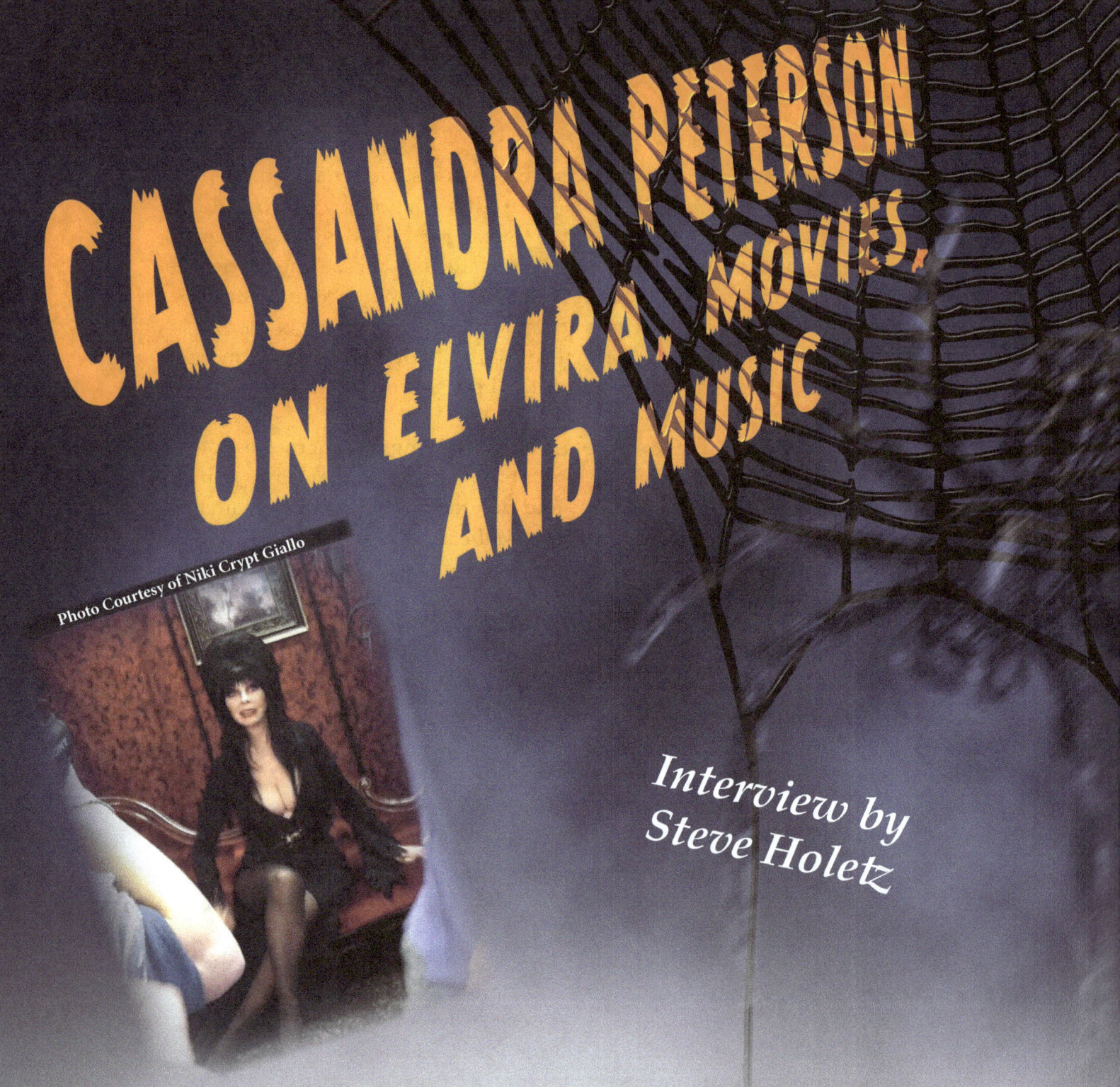

Photo Courtesy of Niki Crypt Giallo

Interview by
Steve Holetz

CASSANDRA PETERSON is most known to the public as her horror-host creation, Elvira "The Mistress of the Dark". Created in 1981, the larger than life figure has become a pop-culture icon all over the world. Starting out as a dancer in the James Bond film Diamonds Are Forever, Fellini's Roma and Stephanie Rothman's Working Girls, Cassandra eventually landed the part of the hostess of "Fright Night" on Los Angeles' KLJ-TV. Besides the TV series, she also hosted a couple different home video series, starred in two Elvira feature films, and made a number of other film and television appearances over the years – not to mention the comics, toys, video games and more featuring her likeness. Cassandra took the time recently at Crypticon Seattle to chat with me about her career and what's happening with her now.

STEVE HOLETZ: I've got a question for you. Now you've been "Mistress of the Dark" for a really long time. Are you happy with the relationship, or do you hope that one day The Dark will pop the question?

CASSANDRA PETERSON: (Laughs) I'm happy with the relationship the way it is now. I like to keep things kinda loose, you know what I'm saying, so yeah, I'm just gonna keep going just like I am for the next 30 years or so.

SH: Nice. Now, by my count you have hosted over 160 films in your horror-hosting career, and one of the things I have always appreciated about your work is that you come to it from a comedy writer/improv background. Were there any films that you were preparing for where you were like, "Oh, this is comedy gold! We're gonna kill this one!"

CP: Well, the crappier the film, the more comedy gold it is, I'll tell you that. I mean, sometimes you get a film that just does not lend itself to humor, and then you have to go off on a li'l tangent, not even talking about the film, and do something else, you know? But the crappier the

Photo Courtesy of Niki Crypt Giallo

film, yes, the funnier it always is. Something like *Plan 9 from Outer Space*? That's comedy gold. Something like *Attack of the Killer Tomatoes* is NOT comedy gold, because they have already made all the jokes in there, and you don't have anywhere to go. You know what I'm saying?

SH: Certainly. Now, was there an original *Movie Macabre* couch, and do you have it?

CP: There was an original *Movie Macabre* couch, I do have it. The really wacky thing about that couch is that the local station where I first started was renting that couch, because obviously the prop guy thought the show wouldn't last longer than a couple weeks. They rented it for 5 years, and by my estimation that couch is worth around $26,000! I bought it for $350, so I got quite a deal.

SH: At the end of the shoot? Very nice!

CP: Yes. World's most expensive couch!

Photo Courtesy of Niki Crypt Giallo

Photo Courtesy of Niki Crypt Giallo

SH: So you got a sweet deal.

CP: I got a sweet, SWEET deal. (Laughs)

SH: Everybody is aware of your 1988 film, *Mistress of the Dark,* but as champions of independent film, and hosts of our own independent film festival, we know what challenges there are in making your own independent film, and you did just that with *Elvira's Haunted Hills* (2001).

CP: Yeah, shoot me. Ha ha.

SH: Are you at the point where you can look back and laugh yet?

CP: No. I don't know if I'll ever look back and laugh about that. That was one of the most grueling, horrifying, terrifying things of my entire life. Knowing that your own money is on the line, you are in Romania, where they have none of the equipment, or the props, or anything you need, and having your producing

partner be your ex-husband, not a good scenario, the whole thing. Bad, Bad, Bad. I think that drove the nail in the coffin of our marriage for sure, so anyway…no, it'll be a while until I can laugh about that. Maybe never.

SH: In 2010 you revived *Movie Macabre* with 20 new episodes, featuring public domain films. Was your approach different this time?

CP: It was different. We were trying to make it a little more hip, and groovy, and edgy. I got a new writer who I started working with who I absolutely adore, a man named Ted Biaselli, and I think it was maybe a little bit saucier and edgier. We did a lot of things that we couldn't afford before, and we had the time and the money. We were able to bring in some actors that I could work with, and just expand the little vignettes in-between…

SH: …little mini-plots almost for each film, which was kinda of cool…

CP: Right! Those come in really handy when the movie sucks. And not sucks in a good way, but sucks in a bad way. So yeah, we did all kinds of things that I always wished I could do, but didn't have the time or money to do before.

SH: Is there any particular film that you've always had your eye on?

CP: Yeah, *Plan 9 from Outer Space,* but you know, we tried really hard to get it for this (last) series that I did, and could not get it. Somebody owns it, and they just aren't giving it out for the right amount of money. Not the amount of money that I could afford, anyway. But that would be my ultimate gem. I just love that movie to death.

SH: Absolutely. Are there any plans to do more *Movie Macabre*?

CP: Not at this moment. I would love to do it again, but if I do, I would definitely have somebody else pick up the tab.

SH: Fair enough. Now, I was looking over Twitter as I am wont to do, and I saw this: "Keep an eyeball out for a couple of groovy new Halloween tunes from me and my bud Fred Schneider." More info, please?

CP: Yeah! Well, I'm not really supposed to say, but I do have two songs coming out. Fred Schneider from the B-52s wrote them both. I love him, and he wrote some really funny songs and produced these. I'm going to tell you the titles, because they are just too funny. They are "The 13 Nights of Halloween," pretty classic, and the other one is called "My Two Big Pumpkins." I think people will enjoy those. My Two Big Pumpkins, anyway, ha!

SH: Nice! We will keep an ear out for those. This Hallowe'en?

CP: Yeah. They will be out in just a few weeks, so you've got the scoop!

SH: One final question we always ask our guests on *The BoneBat Show*, Cassandra: What pisses you off?

CP: Doing this interview pretty much does! (Laughs) I'm really mad now.

SH: Hahaha, yeah, I have that effect on people. It's weird. Thank you so much for spending this time with me, I appreciate it.

CP: You're welcome! It was fun. Thank you.

Photo Courtesy of Niki Crypt Giallo

Steve Holetz is producer and co-host of *The BoneBat Show*, a comedy, music and pop culture podcast that has been rocking the virtual airwaves since 2007. He is also director of Seattle's BoneBat *"Comedy of Horrors" Film Fest*, the world's ONLY dedicated Comedy/Horror event. When not interviewing independent creators for *The BoneBat Show*, manically watching horror comedy films for the festival, or sharing his favorite movies, comics and video games with his family, Steve can be found spinning independent metal, rock and punk music on the *Bonehand Heavy Half Hour*. All of Steve's projects can be found at www.bonehand.com.

⚜⚜⚜

Photo Courtesy of Josiah Duncan

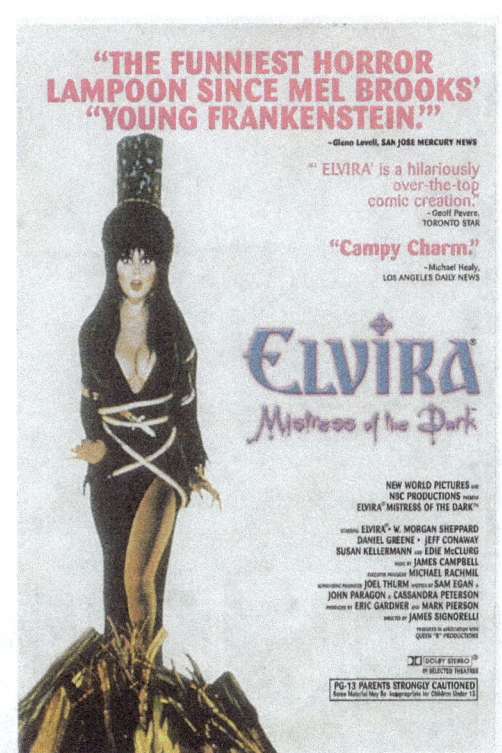

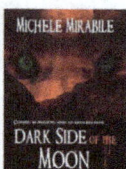

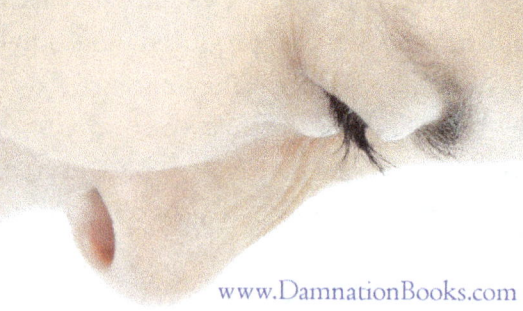

The Dames of Damnation Books

www.DamnationBooks.com

Collette Thomas
Deadly Games; Deadly Affairs

Angela Meadon
A Taste of You

Michele Mirabile
Dark Side of the Moon

Su Halfwerk
Zuphreen; Intricate Entanglement

Fiona Dodwell
The Banishing; Obsessed

Wendy Callahan
Dead Wrong; Hill Magick

A.O. Roland
Winterborn

K.C. Elliott
Dead Town

Raven Starr
Vampire's Embrace; Half Ghost

Sandy DeLuca
Into the Red

S.A. Bolich
Who Mourns for the Hangman?

Amy Grech
Blanket of White

Carrie Lynn Barker
Markheim Series: Sound & Fury; Blood & Ash

Jenny Ashford
Bellwether

Denise Broussard
Behind Bars

Jennifer Cloud
Magic Rising: Dragonfly

Kathleen O'Donnell
The Last Day for Rob Rhino

Dorothy Knight
Cannibal Man

Briana Lawrence
Treat Me Kindly

Naomi Clark
Afterlife; Demonized; Night and Chaos

Joanna Parypinski
Pandora

Kathryn Meyer-Griffith
A Time of Demons; The Last Vampire;
The Nameless One; Witches; Vampire Blood;
The Calling; Blood Forge; Evil Stalks the Night

Gretchen Elhassani
Volunteers for Literacy

Mimi Williams
Beautiful Monster

Sherry Decker
Hook House & Other Horrors

Angie Skelhorn
Severed Ties

Rose Mambert
The Muses

Yolanda Sfetsos
Alyce Kerr Faith Healer series:
Faithless; Careless; Boundless;
Better Off Alone; Damaged;
Sinful; Restless

Karina Fabian
Neeta Lyffe: I Left My Brains in San Francisco

Michele Acker
Blood & Ashes Series: Sacrifice; Betrayal;
Portal to Murder; Binding Ties

Laurencia Hoffman
Casting Stones

On this torturously bright Sunday morning, church bells screaming through the humid air of the preternaturally quiet city, jays shrieking annoyingly on the dead branches of the fungus-infested oak outside the bedroom window, Ash crawls around the fat body curled in a ball, straddles fleshy hips and then pulls back the head by the hair and slits the thick throat with the 12" butcher's knife.

Earlier, the meat—formerly known as Gerald—was lying on his back, snoring obnoxiously, sweating up the futon like a pig in the room they shared in his cheap and cheerless apartment these last three weeks. Gerald normally slept on his back, taking up most of the bed, arms extending crucifixion-style, like the blubbery savior-of-the-world he thought himself to be.

Ash stunned the creature, of course. Father deemed it necessary and always demanded such treatment before the kill.

Now, the damp sheet dampens further as blood seeps into the fabric. The meat makes a wet gurgling sound that, if its windpipe was not severed, might be a gasp of surprise. Vitae spurts from the carotid like water from a lawn-watering system, shoot/pause, shoot/pause, and Ash thinks it is the most beautiful fountain in the world. Crimson bathes the chest and arms and shoots down as far as its limp dick while the death throes puppet-jerk its body erect one last time. Futilely, its chubby fingers grab onto its torn throat to stem the flow. Ash is also coated in red, glorious red, the color of life and passion and fury, a color so different than the washed-out beiges and stark whites of this little life that has been shared for twenty-one progressively longer days which have finally, mercifully, been brought to an end. The blood is still warm, comforting. Familiar.

When the meat falls back and the glassy panic in its eyes fixes as life extinguishes, only then does Ash's gaze focus on the butcher's knife, honed so carefully the night before while Ash sat alone in the seedy kitchen waiting for the meat to come home from the bar stinking of beer, cigarettes and sex. The knife, also scarlet now, drips liquid onto the meat's still torso from the forged stainless-steel blade and Ash thinks it might be the most exquisite still-life ever—*The End of An Endormorph!*

The meat's lungs have stopped inflating and deflating, its flabby fifty-something stomach also ceasing movement. The meat is dead and that state fascinates Ash, who climbs off the carcass and perches beside it on the bed they shared for fornication and sleep and little else.

On impulse, Ash's tongue flicks along the flat side of the knife blade, careful to avoid the razor edge. The liquid is thick, silky, the taste sweet as candy. A finger runs down the meat's body and is quickly coated with red liquid and Ash's mouth opens in anticipation, eyes close, full lips sucking in this richness that forms fond memories...

Father's hand dug into the metal tub under the grinder and lifted out as a raw red hamburger glove. A finger went into Ash's mouth, sucking the blood, spitting out the meat. The blood, so sweet and juicy, Father's flesh salting it, made it earthy, lingering, the taste hopeful in an otherwise hopeless and unforgiving world.

The animals that Father killed and butchered left heavy carcasses dangling and spinning from hooks in the barn as they bled out. Father dipped a tin cup into the other tub under the animals that captured the blood that he used for sausages and other things. "Drink. The blood is life."

And Ash drank. Often. Father killed animals often...

Ash never tires of the blood. Bleeding is as natural as breathing. As close to the divine as...as a dead Jesus.

The knife makes quick work of the dangling part, the one the meat was obsessed with, the one Ash detests. There is no time or inclination to continue, to bleed and skin this and consume more blood which will end this particular meat's control.

We control, Father had said, *not the meat. Remember that!*

A last look at the corpse leaves Ash marvelling, as always, at how quickly the spirit leaves for...somewhere else. All the spiritless shells, all the animals, are all the same. There is no remorse, no grief, nothing. Ash is as empty as the shells, but it is a painless state, as painless as the state of the Christ-corpse hogging the bed. And, at last, Ash's tension drains away.

There is a mess to clean up but instead Ash showers, dressing in a genderless outfit that hangs perfectly on a near-skeletal clothes-horse frame. Fashionable leather runners, short blond hair gelled to small spikes, just so. The bathroom mirror reflects back a pale, androgynous face, arresting, high cheekbones prominent, a youthful visage neither male nor female, and that's the way Ash likes it. He. She. Words that describe what, exactly? Sculpted features, large eyes a brilliant brown, soulful. With a touch of pencil they are outlined for effect, now more oval, less round, more luminous, Oriental by design, the current vogue.

It is Sunday. The coming night holds little promise, since the bars and clubs won't be teeming with the hungry tubbies who have to get up for work on Monday. Still, there will be something. There's always something to look forward to.

Without a glance at the bed and barely an intake of the strong odor of blood, this meat is relegated to a *déjà vu*, an almost-memory, somewhat pleasant as memories of the dead can be, all the bad bits forgotten, quickly fading and melding with the other slabs of fat and muscle from the past. Father always said it isn't good to speak ill of the dead and Ash figures thinking negatively is just as wrong.

Stylish boot heels clack smartly on the hardwood towards the door, thoughts turning to brunch. Brunch. Yes, brunch. In some fancy bistro. A place to see and be seen!

On a hook beside the door is the battered suede jacket and in the right front pocket the meat's wallet, kept there "So I won't forget it," as it was fond of saying. Every day. Five times a day. As if that remark is clever. Ash will not miss hearing it.

The wallet is crammed with large bills, taken from an automated teller machine just yesterday so that the meat could pay for its ticket home with cash, because it always liked to pay cash for everything, not trusting credit cards. The ticket would have required Ash to vacate the apartment at the end of the month. In two days. No need for that now, but maybe a better apartment is in order, someplace grander. Yes, move on, leave the fat mess behind.

Ash abandons the flat, leaving the door unlocked but closed, and walks to the taxi stand on the main road, catching a cab heading downtown to a trendy restaurant for Eggs Florentine and a latte. No flesh. Ash is no carnivore.

The day suddenly becomes brilliant, blazing sunlight, clear blue summer sky with the odd fluffy white cloud, the air not as polluted as usual. Surely these are positive signs. Signs are always welcome; they indicate new beginnings.

The terrace of the trendy cafe overlooks the rectangular park and Ash sits outdoors under a Cinzano umbrella, facing the park, assessing over eggs drenched in béchamel sauce the half-naked bodies parading through the greenery. Most are toned, fit, mesomorphs. Not of interest.

The fat ones are the best, Father always said, *the endomorphs. Not like us. We're Ecdomorphs. They have more meat. Juicer cuts. Bigger profits.*

At the age of nine, Ash did not care about profits, but learned to. That is the way of the farm, focus.

The kills are as imprinted as the techniques—fat equals better, learned slowly through Father's patient tutoring, resulting in the ability to automatically assess livestock on sight.

The park is crowded with walkers, runners, the ones sitting on the grass or at picnic tables reading or eating, standing by the fountain, lurking in the bushes, flirting with one another as a prelude to their senseless rutting. Some push buggies with offspring—Ash isn't interested in those. The ones on bikes are annoyingly confident and it would be fun to hide in the shrubs and ram a stick between the spokes and watch the meat propel headfirst over the handlebars, the way Father wacked the livestock on the knees with prods to make them fall forward before he took the enormous butcher's knife and slit their throats.

It is the screaming that Ash dislikes, then, now. Those sounds, deep and guttural, coming from low in the throat, a distorted tone like a low note on the piano when Father plays Malher, a cry that for a long time Ash identified as pain but now knows is really some nihilistic hopelessness, noise reeking of doom. The noise of the loneliness of death, caught while there is still life. Fascinating...

"Are you alone?" comes a husky voice from behind and Ash's thin neck twists left. "Is this seat taken?" Larger than the last meat, fatter, taller, fleshier. The dumb features the same, as they are the same on all meat, the imitation of intelligence. Bovines who can only eat and fuck and produce replicas of themselves. Whose existence culminates in an oral expression of fear as the life drips from their arteries and veins into a pail.

Ash doesn't bother with either a smile or a scowl. Or a reply. They do not care, these bovines, so preoccupied with their own needs. They want food and sex and while they often manage to forage for themselves for the former, the latter is something Ash can provide. For a profit, of course.

Like always, this one takes this non-reply, this existential nothingness as an invitation, intrigued by the empty space left in the air, as if it needs to be filled and all meat desperately long to fill space with their base desires.

The fat livestock grabs a plastic patio chair and pulls it out noisily then takes a seat uninvited and is soon talking about itself. Ash has noticed that they like to talk about themselves, reviewing the present that always leads into the past, to better days, when everything was fun and easy and "awesome," a word they like to toss around because they imagine that Ash will relate to it and they will get what they want sooner.

Never trust livestock, Father always said. *They can turn on you any moment. That's why the fat ones are good. They're slow and old and stupid and don't anticipate. The fit ones, the thin, the young, they're trouble.*

That concept was only tested once, on the farm, and stupidity resulted in a broken toe bone when the young, thin animal saw the knife. Ash remembers the pain, the embarrassment, and those words, and now lives by them.

The one seated on the cafe chair across from Ash is not thin, not athletic, just the usual endomorph, arms and legs and chest and stomach full of the juicy fat that makes the muscle tasty. And the blood.

"You from around here?" it asks, and Ash usually tells the truth, knowing that meat hears what it wants to hear anyway.

"I'm from a small town about two hours north of here."

"Farm country?"

"Yes."

"Miss the farm?"

Ash knows this creature doesn't care about the reply and again, honesty is the easiest policy, especially because this endomorph won't live to check out the details. "Sometimes."

"I lived on a farm for a little while. Hated it," it says. "All that slaughter. The suffering of the animals. Why?"

It is a rhetorical question but Ash feels compelled to answer, somehow defending Father, although that makes no sense. "It's painless. The animals are stunned first, and the killing is quick. They don't suffer."

"How would you know?" the meat asks, and Ash wonders about this, a twig of memory from long ago sprouting through the synapses to become recognizable, as if this question has come up before.

Suddenly Ash feels tired. A strong, sweeping urge rises like a tidal wave—get away, from this meat, from this city, from this country, find somewhere new, where there is no past, no history, no men who also lived on farms to ask questions, a place where a new identity can be forged, a life recreated. Resuscitated.

"Yeah, it was the slaughter," the meat continues. "Turned me off beef and pork for a while, know what I mean?"

Ash does not reply.

"You know, the blood and gore. All that mess. Guess I like my meat wrapped in cellophane at the supermarket where I can't tell what it used to look like!" A big guffaw.

Ash feels determination rise. This one. Just this one. Quick. Then, somewhere else. Away from here.

The conversation goes the usual route and as afternoon fades towards evening, the man suggests going to his place for supper and Ash automatically hesitates, knowing this tactic works wonders. The meat pulls out a wallet thick with bills, with promise, to pay for the consumed food and drink and "treats" Ash, and that's when suddenly Ash says, "Yes, let's go to your place." If there was no cash, it would have been disappointing. But the fat one has a fat wallet and the lure of a new and better world becomes overwhelming for Ash who is tired of this pre-destined one.

And so it begins. The offensive seduction. The predictable come-ons. The feeble attempts to disguise who will be dominant and who submissive, though it always ends up the same—they want to dominate, but they want the puniest meat on their bodies taken care of and Ash is only too happy to taste this appetizer.

Post-eroticism, the meat is relaxed, breathing steady, the muscles of the face smooth, eyelids closed, lingering in the after-pleasure of what it anticipates to be a night of recurring pleasures.

As the meat lies supine, resting between envisioned bouts, Ash makes an excuse to use the bathroom, picking up the shoulder bag en route. Inside is the mallet, the 6" hand hook, the clever, the 12" butcher's knife—most tools Ash no longer uses—and the Taser—a modern stun-gun. This will be a short night—Ash is eager to get going, away from this city, away from these demanding endomorphs. Food should never be demanding. Father would be appalled.

When Ash returns, carrying the bag, open now, ready, the tools of the trade disguised, the meat, eyes closed, says, "You're so thin. A waif. Maybe you should eat more."

Ash says nothing, just moves to the side of the bed slowly. When it's time for action, that action will be swift. This one is large, plenty of flesh on the bone to get through, not so much fat, almost a mesomorph, so Ash needs to be careful or this slightly athletic animal might retaliate.

The kill should be quick, Father always said. *Disable them, then go for the carotid. It's humane.*

Quietly, Ash reaches into the bag and feels for the Taser, fingers gripping the gun-like weapon and releasing the safety, which makes a loud click in the silent room, but the meat does not react. The meat is within the seven to ten foot range of the probes that will attach to its flesh so the electrical charges can ride through and override the meat's neuro-muscular system's impulses. The perfect stun range. And being naked there are a lot of places to aim for. Ash likes the Taser so much better than the old stun-guns of the past that needed to be pressed right up against the body.

Slowly Ash pulls the Taser from the bag.

Eyes still closed, the meat says softly, "I remember watching my uncle slaughter a cow," and Ash stops moving. "I was just a kid, nine, visiting my uncle's farm—well, I thought I was visiting for a couple of weeks one summer, but it ended up my parents left me there for the whole summer while they went off to Europe for a vacation." A small laugh, childish, full of worry and fear.

The Taser is in full view, and if the meat opens its eyes it will see the weapon, so Ash lowers it back into the bag but still grips the handle tightly, finger near the trigger.

"I liked the farm at first," the meat is saying. "It was all new to me and I had the freedom to roam around and investigate everything, the barn so full of cool stuff, the tall grassy fields, and the animals. My favorites were the cows. My dad taught me to play guitar and I had it with me and used to sit on the fence and play and sing to the cows at sunset. They became so quiet and moved up close, nudging my legs, looking at me with their soulful eyes... My aunt made these delicious dinners every night but it never occurred to me we were eating chickens from the coop or pork from the pig sty, pigs I'd just petted that afternoon." It paused, and Ash felt disturbed.

"They had no kids at that time so they were happy to have me, I guess. It was all good, until the day my uncle had me help him kill the cow."

The silence lingers and Ash feels curiously unnerved, waiting to hear more, terrified to hear more. Finally, the meat says softly, "And that's when I saw this poor creature with huge brown eyes, so human-looking, so full of something, life maybe, those eyes trusting and then frightened and then the bellow as the stun-gun hit her and she fell to her front knees and he zapped her again and I could only stand there staring, horrified, tears running down my face. I was just a kid. I couldn't help her. And then the knife..."

Ash sees these images. They are real, lived images that connect with feelings of powerlessness in the face of brutal horror. The pain in the cow's eyes, the betrayal. The sound, so loud, so real, even now, like a haunting moan from the other side of life, echoing through a long tube—Death is coming. Cruel and pointless death. And the creature's knowledge of this.

Suddenly Ash yanks the Taser from the bag and shoots the meat in the chest with 50,000 volts. The meat's back arches as it screams, eyes wide open, a look on its face of horror and betrayal.

Ash pulls out the big knife, avoids looking into the large brown eyes, and tunes out the noise—all of the bleating but for the gasps that sound like "Why?" over and over. Ash hesitates a moment, thinking: *Why do this? Why continue? Blood can be gotten in other ways and I don't need much.* The memories of this meat are mutual memories, the horror shared by both predator and prey.

Ash is not cruel by nature and there is no hesitation in slicing the artery with the blade still honed sharp from the night before.

The life's blood spurts high into the air, a testament to this mesomorph's fitness. It is like a colored fountain that delights a child.

The meat trembles and jolts and gasps and clutches its throat but soon everything stops, as it always does.

Blood is drunk, a shower taken, clothes changed, money removed, and Ash is out the door within the hour. Somewhere new, where the past and the present do not collide. Ash walks briskly to the train station, heading into the future, smiling with the happy memory of the brilliance of the red fountain of life, mulling over what this meat said and concluding this: Yes, the meat had a point. But, so what?

🐄🐄🐄

TINTYPE

By Elizabeth Massie

Oliver sweated heavily at night, even in the colder months, because evening was too silent, too dark, and that was the time that memories – the worst of them all, the most foul and intimate and dreadful – jeered and paraded across the bare walls of his tiny room or across the backs of his closed eyelids.

War was hell. General Sherman had made that clear. He'd written, "Some of you young men think that war is all glamour and glory but let me tell you boys, it is all hell!"

But for Oliver, still a young man at twenty, it wasn't war that was the greatest of all hells, for war had an end to it. Rather, it was the weeks that followed the war. The months after the last cannon was fired, the last bloodied soldier hit the ground, the last man stumbled free from a prisoner of war camp. Yes, that was hell. The time after. When one could think. Was forced to remember over and over again. To marvel in horror at what he had seen, what he had done.

The late November wind was fierce. It howled through the street below like a banshee seeking the next to die. It shook the shutters and window glass of Oliver's grimy fourth floor Philadelphia boarding house room.

Oliver lay on his cot, hands clasped to his chin, his heart pounding, staring at the ceiling. There, too, the dreaded memories danced. Danced and taunted, leered with dust-bleached eyes and threatened with skeletal fingers that clicked like bits of tin. Oliver shook his head and dug at his eyes, but the visions remained.

Accusatory grins filled with blood-stained teeth.

Oliver rolled off his cot, kicking the blanket away, and walked to the window. There he leaned, panting, his forehead against the glass. He watched as dead leaves spun about in macabre, air-borne pirouettes and stars winked accusingly in the distant blackness. Two blocks away, beyond the roofs of shorter buildings, he could see the moon's reflection on the Delaware River. Ripping, undulating, damning.

"It will never leave me," he whispered, his breath fogging the pane. "My sins will never be forgiven."

Turning back, Oliver shuffled to the caned chair by the bed. He sat and looked at his shoes, overturned on the floor. They still bore the mud of Georgia. No matter how many times he'd scrubbed them, it remained.

The memories remained.

⚬⚬⚬⚬⚬

He was captured at the Battle of Mansfield and transported with thirty-seven of his fellows to the Camp Sumter prison in Andersonville in April of 1864. What he saw as he entered the gates of the stockade with his fellow Union soldiers froze the blood in his veins.

The prison was little more than a huge outdoor corral for human beings, surrounded by a tall and solid wooden enclosure. Mud. Flies and gnats as heavy as fog. A central, rancid swamp in which human feces floated and rats swam. Moldy tents, both issued and makeshift. Mounds of debris. And most horrific of any sight possible – men who were no more than skin stretched over bone, men shuffling about with eyes sunken back and away from reality, some nearly naked and others completely so, dotted with welts and sores and streaks of diarrhea down their pitiable legs.

"Heaven have mercy!" said Robert, a freckle-faced redhead from the 48th Ohio regiment, and Oliver's best friend since joining up in January. "We're going to die here. Would that I have been hit by a ball in the forehead and died on the spot!"

"Don't say that," said Oliver, though he was thinking the same. "We'll get out of here soon. We aren't going to end up like…" he cocked his head in the direction of one man, naked, lying in the mud like a corpse dug up from a grave, yet still breathing. "…like him."

"Oh, yes, we will," said Robert. "Ain't nobody gonna get out of here alive!"

"Shut your mouth, Robert. We will. We will."

Robert grabbed Oliver's sleeve. His eyes were wide, red. "How, tell me! How, when this is Hell itself?"

Oliver didn't know. His gut was so knotted, his mouth so dry, and his mind so twisted that he could only utter what he wanted to be true but knew could not be true. "We will. We will."

He and his compatriots were given eight tents and a tiny spot of ground near the swamp on which they would live until the war's end. If they lived.

The first days were excruciating, thirty-seven men trying to make a camp for themselves amid the stench and squalor without losing the little they'd been allowed to keep by the guards – canteens, boots, tin cups, belts, caps. One particular horde of inmate marauders, nicknamed the "Raiders," had survived by perfecting their thieving. Wielding clubs, they attacked anyone who had something they wanted, and either scared it out of them or beat it out of them.

Oliver earned a brutal scar on his left leg when the Raiders attacked their pathetic little campsite by the swamp on the third day. He had given up a small tintype of his mother (why the Raider had wanted it, Oliver couldn't fathom, except perhaps the grizzled man had merely enjoyed the pain he saw in Oliver's eyes when he snatched it and stuffed it into his trousers), two cans of tinned salmon, a dented pot he'd been given when assigned the job of master cook for his company, and the extra pair of socks he'd darned just before the Mansfield battle.

⚬⚬⚬⚬⚬

In the room below Oliver's, old man Johnson and his wife were snoring. The sounds were nearly as loud as the wind outside. It was curious that they were able to sleep through each other's snorts and rumbles. Oliver wanted to stomp on the floor to make them shut up, but he knew the effort would be wasted and only make him more tired, more angry.

Licking his dried lips, he stared at his socked feet. The socks had holes in them, but he didn't have the energy to darn them. They were threadbare, ready for the dust bin, yet they were the pair he'd been able to keep in Andersonville prison. The ones the Raiders hadn't stolen. They were the ones he'd worn the day of his release seven months earlier, the ones he'd worn on his long trip North.

Not a journey home to his mother and father in Ohio, oh, no, but one to Philadelphia, following the butcher Doctor Marcus Calhoun. Calhoun, who had served in the Army of the Confederacy on behalf of his Georgian family but when the war ended, had relocated to Philadelphia.

"Maybe you left Andersonville, Doctor Calhoun," Oliver swore each night before he fell asleep in his little boarding house room, "but you cannot leave behind what you've done. What I've done. I will seek you and we will both pay."

Oliver put his face in his hands but didn't weep. Weeping was worthless, and his tears had dried up many months ago.

The first week in the prison had ground down into the second and a third, then April into May and May into June, more hot, humid, and foul with the passage of time. On the battlefield, Oliver had seen men bleed out in minutes and succumb to infection or disease in a matter of days. He'd seen men spent and suffering from not enough rations. But he had no idea how quickly a man could become an unrecognizable creature from intentional starvation and dehydration. He watched as Richard began to fade away from fear, limited rations, and fouled water. And Oliver himself, who had been a stouter young man at the beginning, was soon able to wrap his fingers around his wrist, and he wore his belt at the tightest notch so as not to lose his pants around his ankles.

The armed Confederate guards, high in their pigeon roosts, took sport in watching some of their imprisoned enemies devolve from robust, honorable men to thieving gangs who threatened and beat one another to steal clots of molded corn pone and tattered scraps of blankets while others become shambling, disoriented, stinking ghouls whose ribs and hipbones pressed against paper-thin flesh. Sometimes Oliver could hear the guards laughing high up along the wall, and the sound was that of crows waiting to pick away at carrion. Sometimes Oliver dreamed he had a fine hunting rifle, like the one he'd owned as a boy back home, and one by one picked the guards out of their roosts to the cheers of the other prisoners. When he awoke from these dreams he cursed and spit that they were not real.

Twice a week two guards and a prison doctor condescended to walk out among the prisoners, collecting those they would put into their ox-drawn wagon and take to the prison hospital outside the stockade. How they made their selections was a mystery. They might scoop up a few living skeletons and several men with severe stomach pains or festering sores, yet not come back for others as bad or worse. Ambulatory prisoners, some with shoes and some barefooted in the muck, upon seeing guards and the physician in their midst, would swarm the wagon with demands. Hands would reach up and out, clutching, begging.

"The Raiders stole three days of my corn pone ration, sir! I'm going to perish like the others!"

"We got to get some fresh water, sir! My tongue's swelling up like a fat catfish and I can hardly swallow!"

"Please, doctor!"

"Listen sir!"

"Have pity!"

"Shoot me, sir!"

"Put m' buddy out of his misery, sir! He's in so much agony!"

And thus life in the prison dragged on.

It was a fateful day when Oliver bargained for help for Richard. It was mid-June. Richard was lethargic and only able to hold down a few bites of the corn pone that Oliver tried to feed him. He could only lie silently in the stinking tent by the swamp, waiting to die, his chest heaving, flies rimming his eyes.

Oliver pulled himself to his feet and went after the wagon. He grabbed the ox's harness and pulled the animal to a halt.

"Sirs!" he called. "My friend needs the hospital

real bad."

One guard shoved Oliver back. "Move on!" he snarled. "Can't help all you damn Yankees, now get out of our way."

"My friend is quite sick!"

"Pfft, aren't you all?" asked the doctor.

"Please."

"Move away or I'll knock you away," said the first guard.

⌒⌒⌒⌒⌒

"Or shoot you down," said the second guard.

"I…" began Oliver. The lie then tumbled out of his mouth with ease. "I'm trained in medicine. Take Richard to the hospital and I'll come, too. I'm quite skilled. I can help there, when I'm of no help here in the compound."

The doctor, a tall and imposing man with black eyes and a white beard, took a step toward Oliver. "You're a doctor, you say?"

"I know a great deal about treating the sick and injured."

"Push him back," said the first guard. "He's wasting our time."

But the doctor rubbed his beard and said, "We could use another pair of trained hands."

"Doctor Calhoun…"

The doctor considered Oliver. "What's your name, son?"

"Oliver O'Donnell."

"From New York?"

"Ohio."

"Got an aunt and uncle in Ohio."

"It's pretty land, Ohio," said Oliver.

The doctor tapped his front teeth with a finger, and then looked at the guards. "We'll take him with us. Never hurts to have an extra pair of hands that know what they're doing."

"But you must take my friend, Richard, too. That's the bargain."

One guard stepped up and slapped Richard so hard he fell back into the mud. "You don't dare bargain with us!"

"Let him be," said Doctor Calhoun. "Get up, boy. Where's your friend? We'll put him in the

wagon with the others."

And so it was that Richard and Oliver left the main stockade and went to the hospital. Where Richard died. Where the nightmare to Oliver's nightmares began.

⌒⌒⌒⌒⌒

It wasn't long before Doctor Calhoun realized that Oliver had no medical training. He watched Oliver carefully with pursed lips and an arched brow, though he said nothing. Oliver had little choice but to continue the ruse, observing and imitating the actions of the doctors and assistants as best he could.

The hospital sat in a small field just south of the stockade, and consisted of numerous tents, three or four tents together creating "wards" in which men of various conditions were tended. Oliver had been assigned to the ward of the dying. No hope for these men, who had been transferred from other wards to get them out of the way and clear spaces for more patients. The staff in the dying ward was limited, and they feigned at care, cleaning up the fluids that leaked from boils and festering wounds, patting down foreheads with damp rags, though offering no food and very little water to drink. There were no bandages for these men, in fact, few bandages for anyone in the hospital, but to cover wounds of those who had no chance of recovery was considered folly. The dying men's grave injuries, rather, were covered with frantic flies and swarming with maggots. The men moaned and writhed on their blankets on the ground, begging for someone to help them. When no one was watching, Oliver poured turpentine into these men's wounds, which caused them to hiss and clench their teeth, but which killed the wriggling worms for the time being.

Doctor Calhoun, one of the hospital's five surgeons, always visited the death ward as the last stop before he retired for the day. The old physician seemed to be intrigued by the dyings' mental states as much as their physical conditions. He would hold a man's hand and ask, "How's the pain?" And then, looking more closely into the man's eyes, he'd whisper, "Are you afraid to die? Do you imagine you're heading to Hell as reward for those you killed in battle?"

Oliver felt his stomach twist whenever he saw the doctor coming, but kept on dabbing, wiping, patting.

Richard was placed in the ward for those with dysentery. Oliver hoped his placement meant there was hope, but Richard was dead in eight days. He never made it as far as the dying ward. Oliver grieved mightily, weeping into his blanket in the hospital assistants' tent at night, and thought in moments of dark weakness that he would prefer to up and die, himself. War was hell. Andersonville was Hell's hell.

One afternoon, as Oliver helped another assistant drag one of the dead away from the tent and out toward the road to pile up with the other corpses to be collected by mule-team wagons, hauled off, and buried in mass graves, Doctor Calhoun grabbed him by the elbow.

"Let's talk, boy," the doctor said.

Oliver cringed and dropped the dead man's legs. Surely it was time now that Calhoun would tell him he knew about his lie and would send him back to the stockade to face a dire punishment. Whipping perhaps. Maybe even hanging.

"Go on," Calhoun said to the other assistant. "This dead man doesn't weigh what a baby weighs. You can get him to the road on your own."

The assistant nodded glumly and dragged the body off.

Oliver looked at the doctor, at the deep-set, unreadable eyes. "What do you want?"

The doctor smiled a dark smile. "In my tent, then we'll talk."

The doctor shared a large tent with the other physicians, who were currently out and about in the wards. Calhoun ushered Oliver into the mildewed and damp shadows.

Calhoun packed and lit a pipe. "So you lied to me, didn't you, boy?" he asked. He was smiling a most bizarre, raptor-like smile.

"You know that. Why ask me?"

"How did you feel when you lied? Did you feel brave and compassionate, trading the truth for your friend, Richard?"

"I..." Oliver frowned. He could think of no man he hated more than Doctor Calhoun, but the man held all the power here. "Yes, I did. Of course I did."

"I see." Calhoun nodded, frowned, crossed his arms. "And then Richard died. Did you feel betrayed?"

"I felt he was gone."

"Answer my question."

"No. I didn't feel betrayed by Richard."

"Did you feel betrayed by God?"

"I am too tired to feel betrayed by anything or anyone."

"Yes, all right, that makes sense." The doctor nodded again, then said, "I could kill you for lying, you know."

"I know."

"I asked about you over in the stockade. I talked to some of your fellows in their site by the swamp."

Oliver waited.

"They told me you were a cook for their company."

"Yes."

"And that you were a cook back in Ohio."

"A cook of sorts."

"You worked in a canning factory?"

"In Cleveland. For a year or so."

"Indeed." Calhoun's lip twitched. He scratched at his beard thoughtfully. "What did the factory can?"

"Beef, mostly."

"And you cooked the beef?"

Oliver stared out through the open tent flap. It had begun to rain, a steaming, foggy rain. The ox-drawn guard wagon pulled up to one of the main hospital tent with its load of the sick. He wondered if any of them were from his company. Samuel. Winston. George. He looked away, not wanting to know.

"You cooked the beef?"

"Yes," said Oliver. "Why?"

Doctor Calhoun said, "Come with me."

～～～～～

He woke with a start in his little cane chair near the window. The wind was still howling but the night was giving way to dawn, with faint sunlight bleeding in and onto the floor. Oliver wiped the crust from his eyes and pushed upward. His back ached, and his legs. They had ever since the war, ever since Andersonville, in spite of his young age. Torment and bad food and guilt will do that to a man.

Tugging on his trousers, shirt, suspenders, and shoes, and grabbing his jacket from the doorknob, Oliver made his way down the stairs to the first floor where Mrs. Warren was setting out the dishes for breakfast in the dining room.

"G'mornin', Mr. O'Connell," she said. "Up early, I see."

Oliver nodded and slipped into his jacket.

"Joining us for breakfast, I trust?"

"No, ma'am, I'm not hungry."

Mrs. Warren put her hands on her ample hips. "Now, I'm not your mother but you must eat. You're little more than skin and bones."

Oliver buttoned his jacket.

"Molly and I are cooking eggs and potatoes, some bacon and some fine tinned meats."

Oliver knew she hadn't said tinned meats but she might have. She could have. His jaw tightened. "I'm going out, Mrs. Warren."

"Are you quite sure?"

"I'm sure."

He left the boarding house, heading west toward Locust Street.

Doctor Calhoun gave Oliver his own small cook tent, back and away from all the other tents of the hospital, deep in the pine trees. The doctor used his authority to tell the other staff member that it was his own private tent and no one was to bother it under any circumstances. The doctors and assistants assumed Calhoun would use it for trysts with local and willing ladies, so left well enough alone. Oliver was also given a large cauldron, salts and spices, and implements for preparing meats for canning.

"My brother has a canning factory in Macon," Calhoun told Oliver. "Meat's scarce in the Confederacy, you probably know. And tinned meats can last more than a year."

Oliver gazed at the little tent, the cauldron in the newly dug pit, and the tools placed out on a crude wooden bench.

"You will live here, work here," said Calhoun. "I'll get the unprepared meat to you, and you will prepare it. Then I will package it and send it to my brother."

God, no.

"Not the truly diseased," said Calhoun. "But the best bits and cuts that can be salvaged."

I can't do this.

Calhoun smiled and patted Oliver's shoulder. "You refuse and you'll hang."

Oliver stared at the cauldron, then stared at Doctor Calhoun.

"How does it make you feel?" asked the doctor. "Are you conflicted? Are you shaking, trembling at the thought?"

Oliver said nothing.

"You'll do it."

Oliver bit the inside of his cheek until it bled. "I'll do it."

Doctor Marcus Calhoun had moved to Philadelphia easily. Though a Southerner, he had connections in the big city and had told Oliver that his loyalties lay mainly with himself. The man had found a house and opened a practice, which appeared to be doing fairly well.

Andersonville prison was liberated by the victorious Union and closed in May, a month following Lee's surrender to Grant. Some of the prisoners who were still alive were eager to testify against prison commandant Henry Wirz at a military tribunal. Wirz was found guilty and hanged November 10th. Oliver had no desire to testify against the commandant, though. His focus was Calhoun.

It took Oliver five months to make his way

from Georgia to Pennsylvania, stealing, lying, and cheating to gain the money and clothing he needed. In Philadelphia, he secured a room in Mrs. Warren's boarding house and a job on the docks then went about searching for the doctor.

At last he located Calhoun's tidy brick house at the corner of Locust and Seventh Streets, and in the early mornings he watched it from the shadows, noting the man's comings and goings. Calhoun lived with another man, a cousin, perhaps, and spent a lot of time in the house. Patients came to him, though on occasion Oliver saw him leave by carriage with his black bag in hand.

He needed a firearm. A pistol, something to hide in his coat, something Calhoun wouldn't see until the last moment. And so he put as much of his earnings away, hiding the money in a dresser drawer, counting it each night.

And then he had enough for a Colt revolver. A weapon he knew well.

"At least take a biscuit with you!" Mrs. Warren called from the boarding house door as Oliver strolled off down the street. "Mr. O'Donnell?"

He pretended not to hear her. He had no appetite for breakfast nor for what he was doing to do.

Though it had to be done.

❧❧❧❧❧

Arms. Legs. Slices of thighs and buttocks.

He cooked them all in the cauldron over pine wood fires, boiling them down, seasoning them as best he remembered how to, letting them cool then wrapping the meat in bundles. He slept little and thought even less.

Feet, shoulders, bellies.

Once Doctor Calhoun brought over a head with the rest of the parts. When the man was gone, Oliver flung it far into the trees. That night he dreamed the head was making its way back to his little tent with its accusatory grin and blood-stained teeth.

The day after the head was sent, Calhoun stopped by to watch Oliver work, stirring, straining the meats.

"What did you think when you saw the head?"

"Nothing."

"No, how did it make you feel? Was it someone you knew?"

"No."

"Were you upset? Did you think you'd become an animal?"

"I am what I am."

"Are you an animal, Oliver?"

Oliver scraped a layer of grease from the top of the cauldron. In the corners of his vision, in the shadows of the pines, skeletons jeered and pointed at him. "I am what I am. Go away, let me work."

❧❧❧❧❧

He hid across the street from Doctor Calhoun's house until twilight, crouching among the hedges of a well-tended garden. He had not seen the doctor leave, only his companion, but Oliver would not go up to the house and knock. The confrontation had to be in the open; Calhoun could not have an escape into his home.

Late-season flies hovered around him, knocking into his face, crawling on his sleeves. He thought of the faces of the men in the stockade, trying feebly to brush the flies away, and of the men in the dying ward, no longer able to move a hand against the insects. He shut his eyes for a moment, and saw flies dancing greedily in the oily air above the cauldron in the pines as the meat bubbled and turned.

Damn you to the worst of Hell, Doctor Calhoun!

He opened his eyes as a wagon rumbled past, and though it was filled with pumpkins, Oliver saw heads with eyes wide, gazing at him, glaring at him, as their brittle lips attempted to speak.

Then – there. The door to the house opened and Doctor Calhoun stepped out onto the stoop, dressed in a nice overcoat and top hat. Oliver clambered from the hedges and darted across the street, one hand inside his jacket, fingers around the revolver.

"Doctor Calhoun, sir!" he called.

Calhoun looked over his shoulder at Oliver. There was no recognition in his expression.

"Go away, boy, I don't give to beggars."

Oliver stopped two feet from the man. He stared, struggling to breathe, his hands slick with sweat as the memories of Andersonville, one upon another upon another, slammed into his mind.

"You," he managed, "you don't remember me."

The doctor sneered. "Should I remember you?"

"You must remember."

The doctor tipped his head, tugged at his chin, and then said cheerfully, "Ah, wait! Yes! Fate has reunited us! Prisoner O'Donnell, if I live and breathe!"

"I found you."

"Was I lost?"

"We have business."

"Do we? I don't think so."

"Unfinished business."

"War is over, son. War is in the past."

"It's not in the past. It's never in the past. The war is over but the torment isn't! It never leaves me. I'm never free of it." Oliver pulled the revolver from his coat and pointed it at Calhoun. It shook wildly in his hand. "Never free of what you made me do."

Calhoun grinned. "I didn't make you do anything. You did it of your own free will."

"You would have had me hanged!"

"No, I would not have."

"What…no?"

"I'm not a killer, boy. I'm a healer."

"Healer! You've destroyed me!"

Calhoun crossed his arms and stepped closer to Oliver. He leaned in. "Tell me, then. You are still in agony over what you did for me? You have nightmares?"

"Of course!"

"They've not abated over all these months?"

"They've grown worse! Ghosts! Phantoms! I dream of tins of foods splitting open, and of hands grabbing me and pulling me into inescapable maws! I dream of the screams of the men who have been consumed! I dream of those hapless souls we reduced to meals for unknowing hundreds, maybe thousands! The terror does not end, Doctor!"

"Ah!" The doctor clapped his hands. "Yes! I shall write this in my study! What a twist of fate we've found each other."

"No twist of fate." Oliver panted, swallowed hard. "I've hunted you. I will kill you for what you've done, and then myself. You and your brother have tinned the flesh of helpless prisoners for profit. You have spread cannibalism throughout this country, and made me part of your hideous scheme!"

"So, young friend, do you fear eternal fires of Hell for what you've done?"

"What? Yes, of course!"

"Are you able to work? Do you have appetite or is it hard to eat chicken or pork? Beef? What is it like to be so troubled?"

"Shut up!" screamed Oliver. "Why are you asking me such questions? What difference does it make in light of our mortal sin?"

Calhoun made a tsking sound, then said, "We've done nothing, boy. There is no canning factory. I haven't even got a brother."

Oliver stared.

"The raw meats I sent you to cook were just parts of bodies bound for burial. I wanted to know what would become of the mind of a man if he thought he was committing an atrocious act, something unforgiveable in the sight of God. Ah, and you were so dutiful. What a fine job you did with the meat. It smelled almost good enough to eat, but heavens! That would be ghastly, indeed. I learned that a man might become numbed to such an act, as you seemed to have. But now, now I see that the numbness was only temporary, and the anguish lingers in the mind. It bores in and remains much like a beetle in the soft wood of a pine tree."

Oliver stared. "You did that to me? I was an experiment?"

Calhoun said, "I will add this to my journals. Thank you, Mr. O'Connell. And let your worries go, now that you know the truth." He turned and strode off through the darkness of approaching night.

Oliver stared. The revolver slipped from his hand to the walk.

Oliver followed it, down to his knees.

All was Hell.

༺༻༺

Photo Courtesy of Lynn Lowry

LYNN LOWRY: GRINDHOUSE GODDESS

By James R. Beach

Southern Belle Lynn Lowry made her leap into acting in the early 1970s after having moved to New York. Forging a path on the drive-in circuit, Lynn made her career with directors as diverse as: George Romero, David Cronenberg, Jonathan Demme, Radley Metzger, Paul Schrader and even the notorious Troma man himself, Lloyd Kaufman. She recently took the time to chat with me a bit about her continued popularity from her early days, as well as her newer work in the world of horror films.

James Beach: Let's go back to the beginning, if we could. How did you get started in acting?

Lynn Lowry: I started when I was about five years old. I played a sheep in the church play (laughs). My dad was also a trumpet player and had a very "entertainer" quality about him that I'm sure I picked up over the years. At age five I started playing the trumpet as well and was in a band and won all kinds of contests and awards. I went through grade school doing skits and any time I could get up in front of people, I would. I was shy but when I got up in front of an audience, I could become somebody else.

JRB: I've heard of other people who were shy growing up, but then broke out of it by performing on stage.

LL: It's quite amazing actually. You are who you are, but when you go on stage or in front of people, you can feel the change come on and you start to become someone else, whatever persona of the character. It's a great thing to get to be different people.

JRB: I heard that you've gotten involved with doing plays and even writing some yourself, is that true?

LL: Yeah. I was pretty much involved in it all through high school, and then I got a scholarship to the University of Georgia. Took drama in college and then went to New York. I also did Summer Stock during my first year—I think I was 18 then. My second year in Summer Stock I actually worked with John Belushi.

JRB: Wow!

LL: It was at Shawnee Summer Theater in Bloomington, Indiana. John was in three different plays with me so I got to meet him and work with him. He was pretty interesting, to say the least, even back then (laughs).

Photo Courtesy of Lynn Lowry

JRB: Did you ever see Belushi later on when you were acting in films or in New York?

LL: No, I never ran into him again. He just went into a different area with Saturday Night Live and all that.

JRB: How did you get into the movie business?

LL: When I was twenty-one I worked at the Playboy club in Atlanta and was married with a baby. I decided that wasn't what I wanted to do with my life and moved to New York. I had about $50 and my one-and-a-half-year-old son on my hip and got on a plane. My husband joined me there later so it wasn't actually as bad as it sounds.

I got there and started going backstage and looking around for parts. The first one I went on was John Avildsen's film, *Cannon Joe*, and in the waiting room I met Lloyd Kauffman. And he said, "Oh my God, I'm doing this short film called *The Battle of Love's Return*. We just lost the actress playing my dream girl and you'd be perfect for it. Would you like to do it? It's free. Not paying you anything but…" The usual for Lloyd, but it was a start. And Lloyd was working with Appleton. He was like his production manager or assistant or something. So that was how I met Lloyd and that was the very first thing I did on camera: *The Battle of Love's Return*. At that point it was a short. A lot of people think that was my first feature, but my first feature film was *I Drink Your Blood* . After I did *I Drink Your Blood*, Lloyd expanded *Battle* into a feature film.

JRB: I see.

LL: The way I got *I Drink Your Blood* was there was this little paper called Backstage, and they were looking for people. So I went to the audition but got there late. David Durston, the director, was packing everything up. I came in and David was very wonderful, extremely flamboyant. And he just said, "You're gorgeous! I must have you. I'm going to call you tomorrow and put you in my movie." And I went yeah, yeah, this is bullshit. Never gonna happen. After six months in New York I was already pretty jaded. But he did it! He called me like the next day or the day after and said, "We're doing this

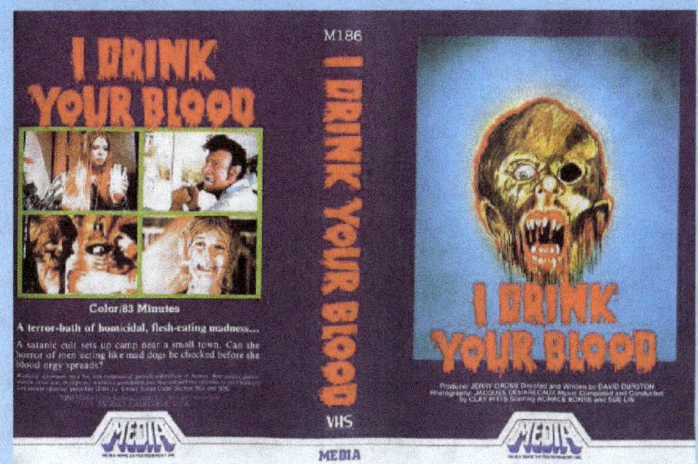

movie called *Phobia* (later to be retitled *I Drink Your Blood* by producer Jerry Gross) and I want you in it. I don't want to write anymore lines, so I'm going to make you a mute. We're leaving for Sharon Springs next week." And that was that.

JRB: What came next for you, Lynn? Was it George Romero's *The Crazies*?

LL: The next movie I did was *Sugar Cookies*, I believe.

JRB: Mary Woronov was in that, wasn't she?

LL: Yeah, and Lloyd Kauffman was the producer of it. That's how I got the part. For *The Crazies* I believe I went on a casting call again for it. Lane Carroll, who was one of the leads in the film, was also the casting director. She was actually Lee Hessel's girlfriend and Lee was the producer of *The Crazies*. She was casting and I think I went in a couple of times and read. I guess I had the right look for the part.

At that point, George had done his first zombie film, which is my favorite, *Night of the Living Dead*. But he wasn't famous yet. So I was cast and we took off to Pittsburgh. It's funny but in retrospect you look back and say, "That was an amazing experience to be a part of." But at the time you don't think like that. You think it was muddy and dirty and dreary in Pittsburgh. You have no idea that there's a possibility this movie is going to be seen and remembered for forty years, or that there'd be a twenty-one million dollar remake, as well. It never enters your mind.

LOOK OUT! THE CRAZIES — LANE CARROLL · W.G. McMILLAN · HAROLD W. JONES — DIRECTED BY GEORGE A. ROMERO · COLOR

JRB: It's interesting that a lot of the low-budget movies from the early 1970s like *The Crazies* and *I Drink Your Blood* didn't do that well at the time, but forty-some odd years later they're still cult classics with a following and are being reissued on DVD, Blu-ray, and so on. A lot of the remakes with a big budget and the big-name stars will probably fade away.

LL: I know. There's a reality about them. A grittiness. When they talked about twenty-one million dollars I said I wouldn't do that. If you want to make a 70's movie then do something that looks like a 70's movie, not the other way around.

JRB: I think a lot of the low budget films with a lack of name actors—especially some of the 70's ones and also *Night of the Living Dead*—almost have a documentary-type feel to them because of that—which makes them more realistic, in my opinion.

LL: Exactly.

JRB: You've worked with some other interesting directors over time. Radley Metzger for *Score*. David Cronenberg for *Shivers*. Paul Schrader for *Cat People*. Jonathan Demme. What were those experiences like?

LL: My experience with *Score* was pretty interesting. Radley is a very, very good director. I love the way his films look. I've seen many of them. *Score* was an off-Broadway comedy first. Sylvester Stallone was actually in it before it was a movie. Radley didn't cast him in the film though because he didn't think he was handsome enough. Sylvester lost out on that, which I always found very funny.

JRB: (laughs)

LL: So we flew to Yugoslavia to do that one (*Score*). I had already done nudity in *Sugar Cookies* so that wasn't a new thing for me, but it *was* a new thing for me to do nudity with a woman who hated me. That was different. Claire Wilbur, who is no longer with us, was the star of the off-Broadway show, and the woman who played my part in the show was not very attractive. Claire was the beauty and she got all of the attention. So when Radley cast me, she was extremely jealous. She thought I was getting all of the close-ups and that Radley liked me better and I was making more money and on and on and on. We hardly spoke to each other the whole shoot.

The other interesting thing (and I avoided it throughout my career up to that point and never wanted to be in one) is that I was now in a porno—because *Score* is X-rated and the men have hardcore sex. Although I was never told that. I agreed to do the film because it was going to be R rated. But Radley shot the men on a closed set. I never saw what they did until it came out. If you've seen the film, what they do is quite different from what the women do. But it's a beautiful film, quite funny and delightful, and my character is great. She goes through all these changes and becomes an independent woman in the end and is willing to have sex with two men. I don't know if that's a big accomplishment (laughs), but in the movie and based on her character, it is.

JRB: Sure. Metzger shot two different versions of the film, if I'm not mistaken—an R-Rated version and the X-Rated version—something common in those days. He is an interesting director stylistically and did

"STYLISH, WICKED

"GOOD ACTION, VERY GOOD DIRE AND UNUSUALLY INTERESTING LOCA

Sugar Cookies

STARRING
GEORGE SHANNON
MARY WORONOV
LYNN LOWRY
MONIQUE VAN VOOREN

DIRECTED BY
THEODORE GERSHUNT

Photo Courtesy of Lynn Lowry

straddle both the soft and hardcore markets. Certainly sounds like a bit of a surprise for you though!

LL: It was definitely a surprise for me. They just brought it out again last year. I did an interview for it at the time, but again it's just kind of weird to be in a porno at this point. But I don't care. I'm proud of the film and proud of my acting in it, and I think everybody looks gorgeous.

JRB: So next came *Shivers* (aka: *They Came From Within*)?

LL: That was another interesting film to do. I got that part—I don't know if they had seen me in something—but I got a call from Ivan Reitman in New York and they cast me. So I flew to Montreal to do this film with a completely unknown director named David Cronenberg and it was his first movie. That was an amazing experience. Looking back, working with David, being in Montreal, I wish I could do that now (laughs). I would appreciate it a lot more if I could do it again. What an incredible film. First movie ever to show "body horror."

The story about that film is that I was not supposed to be in the "swimming pool" scene—which is considered one of the iconic moments in my career. They had actually wrapped me and flown me back to New York and I guess somebody thought, "Wow! It might be really cool for Nurse Forsythe to give the Doctor the parasite." So they flew me back to Montreal and put me in the pool and I love that scene. It's one of my absolute favorites. When I come up out of the water and I turn and I'm coming towards him… I just love that.

JRB: Very memorable, definitely.

LL: And then working with Jonathan Demme. Although a lot of the "horror" people might not have seen *Fighting Mad*, it was incredible. Working with Peter Fonda, John Doucette, Scott Glenn—all those people. It was fun.

JRB: It's one of those that is often forgotten nowadays. One of Roger Corman's productions and directed by one of his protégés, Demme.

LL: Yeah. I got the part because Jonathan saw me in *Score* and loved my performance in it. I was in New York and they were casting in L.A. and nobody had the money to fly me out. So I bought my own ticket and flew there on my own dime. And it worked out! He loved me and he cast me in the part. I was so nervous when I met Roger and wanted to do the part so badly and wanted to work with Jonathan and Peter and everything, that I just did my interview and left. And this is lame, but I thought I just needed to say one more thing to him. I thought, If I don't get the part I will always think that if I had just said that one last thing, I would've gotten it.

So I went back and told the secretary that I had to go back in and see Roger for one more minute. They let me back in and I explained the whole thing to Roger, what I just told you, about how if I didn't come back and so on. I'm sure he thought I was nuts, but I told him, "I just wanted to tell you that if you cast me in this part, I'll work my ass off for you." And that was it. That was all I wanted to say and then I left. And I got the part! I don't know if it was that one last thing I did that made him remember me or what, but it was pretty funny.

JRB: I've heard that things like that are what make you stand out to a director or a casting person.

LL: You never know how far to go or what to do, really. But there are no rules. That's something for people in this business to remember. There really are no rules. You might not get the part if you don't do it, or it might not cost you the part if you do, but you never know unless you try. You might get the part. That's how I like to think about it.

JRB: You also worked with Paul Schrader on the remake

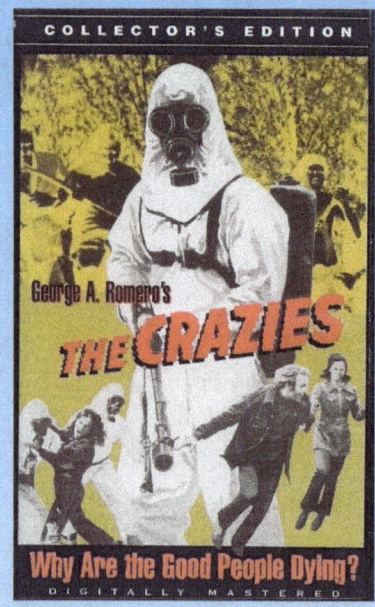

of *Cat People*. What was that like?

LL: That's not one of my favorite experiences. I don't regret doing the film, and I've gotten a lot of attention from that one scene. But at the time, I found that Paul was pretty insensitive to me. The cat grabs my leg from under the bed, so I had to keep falling on my knee. The mechanical claw they had that was supposed to grab my leg didn't work, and they kept trying to make it work, and of course every time they tried to make it work, I had to fall on my knee. So my knee was all black and blue and bruised and swollen by the end of it. Then I had to go outside and fall down the stairs. And the stuntman didn't work with me. I was told later that the stuntman didn't like to work with small-busted women. I don't know if that's true, but he didn't work with me so I don't know. They also didn't take the tacks out of the stairs. When I went down for the first time, my hands got all cut up from the sharp stuff. Then they had to take me to get a tetanus shot. And then they couldn't get the shot and I had to keep falling down the stairs and coming up the stairs. And I was rug-burned and bleeding. And they couldn't get the turnover at the bottom of the stairs when my bra pops open—they couldn't get the bra to open! They wanted to get the whole shot in one take, too, and so I had to keep going up the stairs and crawling out the door, tumbling down the stairs again, rolling over and my bra pops open and then I had to scream. But they couldn't get it. I had to do it again and again and again. Finally they said they got it and literally two days later I could hardly walk.

JRB: Ouch!

LL: Then they called me again and said they needed me back. And I said, "Look, I really can't fall down the stairs again." And they said, "Oh no. We just need you to roll over and scream." So I said okay. But I came back and then they said, "We're really sorry about this, Lynn, but we lied to you. We really do need you to fall down the stairs again."

JRB: Oh God. (laughs)

LL: I said oh no. I'm not going to do it unless you pad me and get somebody to work with me. I mean I was black and blue, literally. I said, "If the padding doesn't work and we can't get the shot, then you're going to have to pay me more money." And they actually tried to *not* pay me for the stunt work, until somebody told me they were supposed to pay me money for the stunt work *and* the acting. I had to get that all straightened out. The padding didn't work anyway and of course it's always the last shot and the end of the day and they're losing the light and here's little ol' me saying, "We need to renegotiate. I'm not going to fall down the stairs again unless you pay me more money." Paul wasn't happy of course and he never used me again—which, you know, might have been my fault (laughs). I just felt, at that point, "This is not right. You've taken advantage of me and you've hurt me and were insensitive to me and I'm not going to do it."

But we renegotiated and did it one last time. They wired my bra so it would pop and it did and we got it. I always tell people when they see that movie and it looks like I'm really crying and in pain, it's because I am!

JRB: Crazy. So a lot of attention for *Cat People*, but maybe not worth the trouble, eh?

LL: The funny thing about it is that I've made more on that movie from residuals than anything else. So it turned out to be worth it.

JRB: Other than doing a little television in the 80s, you pretty much got out of acting, at least films. What happened?

LL: I was out in L.A. at the time. I had no idea I had a horror/cult legacy. I didn't tell anyone in L.A. I did those movies. I didn't think that when they were casting for *Happy Days* and so on, they would want to know I

Lynn Lowry in "Cat People"

Photo Courtesy of Lynn Lowry

did *I Drink Your Blood*. So I kept all of that in my past. I figured no one would ever see them and no one would ever know me from those movies. I basically kind of gave up in 1995. I did theater. I had a jazz band and I sang. I kept acting, but I stopped pursuing my career.

About ten years after that I got a call from Blue Underground to do the interview for *The Crazies* DVD. I got calls from Bob Murawski (Grindhouse Releasing) for *I Drink Your Blood* to do that DVD. I kept getting calls. I was literally sitting in my office at one point and said, "You know, I'm getting all these calls, I'm going to look it up and see if there is anything about me on the Internet." And I typed in my name and I was just stunned that, like, thirty pages came up on me. I was like, "Holy shit!" That's when I first started to realize I had this huge cult horror following. And then those DVDs came out and I started getting calls from people to come to conventions and then I started getting calls from people to do films. Since 2005, I've been working constantly.

JRB: That's incredible! What other new movies do you have coming out?

LL: The most memorable thing coming out, and it's going to be pretty shocking, is *Model Hunger*. That's directed by Debbie Rochon and it's her first film being behind the camera. I play a southern belle serial killer. I have played southern belles since I was sixteen, but this is the first time I created one on film. I don't know how to tell you what she is, only that she isn't very nice. She's a sweet southern belle, but the things she does are really horrific. I doubt I'll ever be cast as a victim again after they see this, but I'm very excited about it.

Dante Tomaselli's *Torture Chamber*, which we shot

like three years ago, is finally coming out this year, and I have a really good part in that. And I'm doing a film called *Cannibals* that Joe Hollow is directing. I'm actually starring in that. Michael Berryman is in it. Kane Hodder is in it. Bill Moseley is in it. We're supposed to be shooting in November. I also just did a picture called *Grim Becomings* that Death Pictures in Buffalo is putting out. Some of the older ones I did in the last few years are: *The Super, George's Intervention, Basement Jack*. Those are all great. I'm proud of all of them.

Oh and I'm in the remake of *The Crazies* too. It's a small part but it's nice they paid homage to the original and put me.

JRB: You're the lady on the bike, right?

LL: That's right.

JRB: It sounds like you have a lot going on.

LL: I want to say too that if anybody wants to email me or contact me you can always go to my website or reach me on Facebook. It seems like it's always under construction (laughs) but my email address is on my website, www.lynnlowry.com, and you can reach me directly.

JRB: Thanks Lynn. Any last words?

LL: It's been great to have had so many good parts and it's been a lot of fun. I'm happy to have done it and I'm still having a ball. I'm also very appreciative to the fans and I hope they keep watching!

Photo Courtesy of Lynn Lowry

CHARLAINE HARRIS: TRUE BLOOD OF LIFE

Photography by D. Woldan

By Joel B. Kirkpatrick

Create a strong character that can carry your entire novel and you will have taken one of the final steps in your journey to become a respected author. Create a strong character, who can assume their own life, while you write as many books around them as you might care to—and your journey will have entered a country that few other authors ever find. Series authors will unanimously admit to you, it is no easier to write the same character even when they seem to have creative control and do a lot of the author's work.

Is there a quality of writing rarer than even this? Charlaine Harris will admit there is. Her characters have found life outside her books, to live on the screen. Now her characters have fans who may have never read a single Charlaine Harris book.

Writing Mysteries around her characters for more than thirty years, Ms. Harris covers a tremendous amount of territory under that single word. Her four series creations: Aurora Teagarden, Lily Bard, Harper Connelly, and (most famously), Sookie Stackhouse, have solved crimes but also battled monsters. These women can be ordinary, familiar even, and at the same time possess unique talents and supernatural powers of their own.

Such a delightfully rich career has earned her acclaim as a *New York Times* best-selling author; an Anthony Award for Best Paperback Mystery in 2001; a nomination for Best Novel Agatha Award in 1990; and the wildly popular HBO series *True Blood* in 2008. After penning thirty-one books, Ms. Harris may admit one more thing to you; that she has more control over her characters than you may imagine.

JBK: Who ever utters the phrase, "Well, that seems to be enough of that.?" Do your characters reach the end of their story, or do you?

CH: I do. I think it's a bit cutesy to imagine that your characters write the books. The writer is in control.

JBK: You have said you felt the book *Dead Until Dark* was hilarious. Sookie Stackhouse has survived every peril you designed for her, through a stunning thirteen books. With the last installment just released, *Dead Ever After*, is this number 13 a bit of a wink to that humor you have always felt was there?

CH: I thought the number 13 book was a good ending for several reasons: it was the last book I had a contract for (though I'm sure my publisher would have extended another one to me), I felt I'd reached the natural end of the story, and I kind of like the number anyway. I did think it was at least a little funny.

JBK: Here is a clue to a mostly unknown fact-of-a-best-selling-author's-life: You wrote *The Southern Vampire Mysteries*, which is also known as *The Sookie Stackhouse Novels*, which is also known as *True Blood*. That indicates a lot of meddling by other people with your creation. How does that make you feel, to see the public take such tangible ownership of your work?

CH: At first I got pretty irritated when people referred to the novels as "the True Blood books." But I came to see that was just false pride. Whatever name you call them, they're my books. On the practical side, the money rings up on my cash register, and on the creative side, I can only be glad I've been associated with Alan Ball, who is a class act.

JBK: Who first told you that Alan Ball was interested in creating a series for HBO from your books? Had you ever discussed film or television projects from you work, before *True Blood* became a reality?

CH: Yes, I'd had an option on the books before, but it came to nothing, as most such options do. When that option lapsed, I had a choice of three offers on the books. With respect for all the other people who were interested, Alan Ball's offer was the most interesting creatively.

JBK: What was your reaction to seeing the first episode? Have you become a fan?

CH: I have to admit, I was totally shocked. I thought we'd have to move! I thought it was brave, vivid, and beautifully written …but that didn't mean it would be successful. I've always been a fan.

JBK: More recently, in 2012 you began discussions with the SyFy channel to work something up for your Harper Connelly Mysteries. Have there been any strong developments to make that a reality?

CH: Sadly, no. I've had two options on the Harper books, and they both came to nothing. I'm waiting to hear on another interested approach, but I'm not holding my breath.

JBK: The supernatural has always been a favorite topic of yours; your earliest writings were primarily ghostly poems. When did you begin to write?...and when did you feel the urges to write an entire book?

CH: I began to write when I could hold a pencil. When I realized that real people wrote books, I wondered if I could be that special. My family were all great readers, and becoming a writer seemed the most amazing ambition I could hold.

JBK: You've been called an author who …*put(s) the bite on cozy mysteries*...but your writing, (and publishing overall) is more fluid than that. You are really writing in a broad group of genres. Is that a freedom that you have earned?...to write as you wish to write?...or is it a hard-won reward? Have you ever felt constrained to fit a theme?

CH: Hmmm. Well, when I wrote conventional mysteries for many years, I began to feel the conventions governing them a little constricting. At the same time, I still love to read them, and the mystery is the basis of all my books. I began crossing genres because my readership was so small! I wondered if I threw in some supernatural if I'd attract science fiction readers, and if I threw in a more explicit sexual element, maybe some romance readers would find that interesting. At the time, the only person writing anything like that was Laurell K. Hamilton. It was a combination I thought might work for me.

JBK: Sookie is a telepathic waitress, while Lily is an amateur sleuth who cleans houses, and Aurora is a librarian. Harper has the distinction of being nearly as ordinary—until she was struck by lightning. What fictional characters were some of your inspirations for creating your own stories with young women who can blend-in yet stand-out at the same time?

CH: If there's any specific antecedent, I'd have to say Jane Eyre, the plain and prim little governess with the backbone of steel. Jane looks mild but she is a ferocious character.

JBK: Science fiction has been a favorite subject of yours to read, and you even admitted to *Dead Until Dark* being your Sci-Fi/Mystery combination. Do you have any story ideas strong enough to ever turn you in a purely science fiction direction for a book or two? Where might your interests lie?...a space-bound adventure, or an earth-bound dystopian?

CH: I did write a novella, "The Britlingens go to Hell," for the anthology *Must Love Hellhounds*. It was pure science fiction, or at least as pure as I've gotten, and it was lot of fun. I don't know if I could sustain those characters for a whole book, but I enjoyed the experience.

JBK: What is the difference between a series on hiatus, and a series that has ended? Do the characters/you/fans require a final story? Is Aurora currently in a creative hiatus, or a schedule hiatus?

CH: Hard to say which, but the result is the same. I haven't writte a new Aurora in years, because my time has been totally taken up with other projects. I'd really like to write another one. The Lily series has ended. The Harper series, well, only if I have a great idea.Sookie has ended for sure.

JBK: Has your career been filled with near-endless book tours and public appearances? Or, have you led a sweet, quiet life of only writing and raising your family?

CH: The first fifteen years of my career were fairly quiet. I wrote and raised a family, and I did a signing every now and then. I didn't tour. That's all changed. My kids are grown now, and I have done a lot of interviews, a lot of signings, and I work the rest of the time. Of course, this is what most writers want more than anything, which I must keep reminding myself when the world is too much with me.

JBK: You have rarely stopped working in your thirty year career, sometimes putting a series on hold to work on another. No one could possibly believe that *Dead Ever After* is going to be your last book.Can you tell us anything about your current project? We hear it might be a graphic novel called *Cemetery Girl*.

CH: Okay, here's my Charlaine Service Announcement. This October, a sort of coda to the Sookie series, *After Dead*, will be published. It's not a novel, but a fun collection in alphabetical order of the characters in the novels and what happens to them after *Dead Ever After*. In January, the first volume of *Cemetery Girl*, a graphic novel by Christopher Golden and myself, will come out. The artist is Don Kramer, and it's very cool. Also in January, the next anthology edited by Toni L.P. Kelner and me (*Games Creatures Play*) will be available, and the lineup is dynamite. These are all supernatural sports stories. In May, provided I finish the book in time, I'll launch my new series, the first of which is titled *Midnight Crossroad*.

JBK: Thirty years is a wonderfully long career, and you have surely met many thousands of your readers. We know you love to hear from them. How has your relationship with your fans changed over the years, and, has the explosion of technology also brought you a similar explosion in reader contact? Is that increased contact ever a strain on your creative direction?

CH: Yes, it's a greatly increased strain. When reader reaction is overwhelmingly negative, it is really hard on me, and I have a hard time writing for a while. Though I know there are so many factors to this, and I am fully aware that some readers are simply not reading the same book I wrote because they've become fixated on their own plans for the characters, it's still very upsetting. And now that writers are far more accessible, disappointed readers seem determined I MUST listen to how disappointed they are. Would they rail at a concert violinist or a painter the same way? I don't know. Maybe. For thousands of years writers were able to stagger along without knowing the opinion of every person who sampled their work, but no longer. It's a different relationship. I haven't adjusted well, I guess.

JBK: Did you ever receive any complaints about closing Lily's, or Harper's series of stories, the way you have received them about ending Sookie's own books?

CH: Oh, gosh, yes. Not in as much volume, and not as vehemently, but I hear from fans of all the series.

JBK: Readers have found their voice in recent years; of that, there can be no doubt. In fact, readers have never been able to express themselves directly to an author as they can now. Without trying to make that mean it adds to your responsibility as a writer, it must certainly be something that you take to heart as never before. Have you *ever* only written for yourself? Have you become *responsible* to your readers?

CH: My responsibility to my readers is to write the best book I can. No more, no less. I can't write according to someone else's expectations and be true to myself as a writer. I don't think I'm pretentious for saying that the book is my world, which I created.

JBK: At about the time you began seriously writing, there was also a rich growth in fiction, both Science Fiction and Horror. New authors found fame, and many now are icons on bookstore shelves worldwide. Stories abound from many of them how difficult it is to be published, yet you have apologized that your own success story was not one of terrible rejection. You credit Shannon Ravenel with recommending your first book to a publisher (*Sweet and Deadly*), and it being accepted. Since that first book, you have endured the reality of every other author's trials, haven't you? Publishing is a harsh industry, isn't it?

CH: Golly, yes. It's very tough. I'm not sure I would be as successful now if I was trying to break in. But during the course of my career, I've earned as little as 4K for a book, my series has been cut, my editors have left, you name it. Somehow I've always managed to stay afloat.

JBK: Readers surely love to tell you why they enjoy your books, and it is certain that you also attract a good number of struggling authors in your fan base. What is the most common question they might ask?

CH: "What do I do with my book after I write it?" There are two parts to my answer. First, *write the book.*

Photography by D. Woldan

Don't worry about what will happen to it afterward. Nothing will, if you don't write the best book possible. Second, *do your research.* There's no excuse for being ignorant of the publishing options in this day and age with information literally at your fingertips. Don't approach a writer and say, "Now what do I do?" *Find out.* Know what your options are. Go to conventions. Talk to other newbies. Go to panels led by editors and agents. Research the industry as you would any industry where you wanted a job.

JBK: Try as we might, we cannot find you described as a Horror writer. You don't even think of yourself that way. With vampires, werewolves, maenads, ghosts and murders everywhere in your books…how can that be? Why is Horror such an unused tag for such a delightfully wicked author?

CH: Sometimes I find myself shelved in Horror and I'm always surprised and secretly thrilled that someone finds me scary. I'm really benign on the inside, but maybe that's because I write such violent stuff!

JBK: Your readers may already know that you dabbled as a playwright in your college years. It is harder to learn that you produced one-act plays while at Rhodes College, and saw them performed there. You had the pleasure of seeing actors bring your characters to life more than thirty years ago. How did that come about?

CH: That was a very long time ago, and I'm trying to remember. I think the theater department decided to perform three one-act plays I'd written the year after I graduated, and they kindly invited me to come see them. It was really exciting, and I've never forgotten it, though I don't think about it too often.

JBK: As a playwright, we assume you have tight control over an actor's presentation of your work, but television and film is a vastly different relationship for you, the author, isn't it?

CH: Okay, I'm laughing. Vastly different is a good way to put it. Very few writers get any kind of say-so in casting or scripting. And that's certainly not the kind of deal I had with Alan Ball. In a sense, I felt a bit bad about letting go of my babies, so to speak. At the same time, geez, it's ALAN BALL. A little trust was involved.

JBK: Have any of your plays, or your earlier poems survived into print? Can anyone find your writing from, say, your teenage years?

CH: No. And it'll be burned when I pass away.

JBK: Do you feel you were predisposed to be a writer?... your father having been an educator and your mother a librarian, them rearing you in the South? Couldn't you have been a policewoman, or a detective? Why not a schoolteacher?

CH: You wouldn't suggest that if you'd ever seen me trying to teach my children how to tie their shoes. They still do it in a way that attracts startled looks. I am an abysmal teacher. I'm not confrontive enough to be a good policewoman or detective. I could possibly be a librarian. But I think I'm best, and happiest, as a writer.

JBK: Though you claim, with perhaps a giggle, that you made up most of the vampire lore you have written into your stories, not everything can just be written without much research. Fans are so savvy nowadays, what with over-the-top graphic movies and TV shows;

they require a good bit of realism, don't they? Have you become a researcher, or at least, a better one?

CH: Yes, a better one, though I don't revel in research as some other writers do. When I'm talking about something factual, I try to get my facts right. When it's the supernatural, I feel free to adapt the "rules" to suit my purposes.

JBK: In one interview you said that you do not like graphic movies, but that you don't mind a graphic novel. How are those two types of entertainment different, for your tastes, and do you entertain your own readers the same way you allow yourself to be entertained?

CH: I don't like movies that exploit violence for the sheer pleasure of showing blood and dismemberment. That's not entertainment, to me. A graphic novel has another step of removal from the explicit depiction of gore or sex or whatever is being depicted. I don't include some details in my work because I think an extreme level of violence or sexuality will yank the reader out of the narrative, which is the most important thing.

JBK: You have also described yourself as a somewhat free-thought writer, letting your work invade your daily life and activities rather than writing to an outline in a structured setting. Is your writing style something you have settled into over the years, or have you always just let the work flow at its own pace in your mind, wherever that might happen?

CH: I've tried to write an outline, but it seldom seems to work. I wish I could, because then I'd know what to do every day instead of constantly inventing. I do work every day, very regularly.

JBK: Though it is doubtful that you have ever met a vampire, or had a vision of how someone else might have died, you do share some kinship with one of your characters: Lily Bard. In fact, you tend to disbelieve that characters can have a personality completely their own, but their authors must be in there somewhere...

all little pieces of you…. When you knew that you were going to purposefully write your own experiences into your character's story, was it a struggle to do? Do you ever try to censor yourself *out* of a character?

CH: Writing is always a struggle. It can be both liberating and terrifying to reveal yourself to the reader, but the writer has to be careful to make the character's experience unique to the character, though the emotions raised by the experience may be the same as the writer's own. Being sure to keep the experiences true to the character, and keeping the reaction to them true to the character, well . . . writing is always a struggle.

JBK: On your website you list a few organizations you feel are worthy of public attention. Yet, surprisingly you mention the Crime Lab Project (www.crimelabproject. com); the surprise being the reason you mention it. Please share with us how you came to be aware of this organization's need, and some of the startling facts you would like your readers to know.

CH: Why is that surprising? I'm constantly aware that justice is not always served, no matter how many episodes of CSI we enjoy on television. Crime Labs are always backed up, have their funding cut, lack the most up-to-date equipment. When DNA testing is backed up for a year because there aren't funds to hire the staff to process them, who suffers? The public, waiting for justice. My friend Jan Burke raised my awareness of this. Just Google Crime Lab Project and learn more about it.

JBK: Your husband encouraged you to stay home and write full time, all those years ago. Have you rewarded his brilliance by letting him read all your books first, or is that privilege reserved for your agent?

CH: Okay, I'm laughing in a major way. Actually, my first readers are my good friends Dana Cameron and Toni L.P. Kelner, both award-winning writers and both great human beings. They're honest and frank in a tactful way. After I absorb their comments and implement them, I send it to my agent, and then my editor, Ginjer Buchanan. My husband reads them when they've been smoothed a little and decorated a lot.

JBK: Are Charlaine Harris books a family project in any way, with pages flying between family members as you work? Who in your family is your best reader?

CH: Okay, again laughing. I'm pretty sure one of my kids has never read any of my books, and one has read all of them, though if he's reading something else when I send him a copy, he won't put his current reading project aside to pick up mine! My other son has read some of my books. My family doesn't really comment too much on the books. That's probably wise.

JBK: Writers absorb nearly everything they read, watch or hear—always gleaning life for little threads of ideas to weave into their books. Are you that way at all?….absorbed in reality to enhance your fictions? Have you ever imagined that you might write a non-fiction, or have a unique voice for putting true life into a crime novel?

CH: I don't think of myself as a non-fiction writer, though I've really enjoyed a lot of non-fiction, especially Jon Krakauer and Bill Bryson. I've also read a lot of true crime, but not for a while. But I think everything I read and see, and the people I talk to, and the conversations I overhear, keep feeding my inner grist mill.

※ ※ ※

Photography by D. Woldan

DEAD LITTLE PIECES

by Yvonne Navarro

Rob stared at Andrea in dismay as she recounted the story of how his mother had once mistaken a microwave oven for a television in his uncle's furniture store. It was a wonderful little tale and he could tell by the laughter and tolerant grins that were coming his way from her friends (*"Bet your old lady's a real prize, huh, Rob?"*) that everybody loved hearing about the incident.

He didn't remember it.

Take that back. He remembered *telling* Andrea about it Tuesday—or maybe it had been Wednesday, yet no matter how he tried Rob could no longer bring to mind a picture of his mother, presumably standing in the showroom of Nelson Brothers on Lincoln Avenue, pointing at a microwave oven and saying (according to Andrea), "That's the strangest looking television set I've ever seen."

"Too much booze," he mumbled into his glass. He peered at the last half inch of watery Chivas surrounding the melting cubes, then drank it anyway.

"You say something, honey?" Andrea was smiling at him, her olive-colored skin flushed with a mixture of wine and excitement. He'd read in books about 'sparkling eyes' but had never realized it could be true until now.

"I said I need a refill." Rob held up his glass to show her and she nodded and smiled again. A second later she'd plucked the glass from his hand and disappeared through a doorway toward the kitchen of Bill and Candy's apartment, slipping easily through the people jammed in the opening. The music, volume roaring, moved in to fill the space she'd vacated, Jethro Tull fighting the incoherent clamor of voices to scream about a homeless old man on a park bench.

Rob let his attention drift, glancing around the room at different people but trying not to look too obviously awkward. Bill and Candy were Andrea's friends, not his, and Bill worked with Andrea at the hospital as a radiologist or something. Since Rob and Andrea had been dating less than a month, he didn't know many people here. Andrea had driven tonight and he hadn't bothered to pay attention to the address—Christ, he didn't even know where he was. To say he was shy was an understatement, and the party brought to mind uncomfortable memories of sitting along the wall during Friday night socials in eighth grade, too nervous to ask a girl to dance, terrified that a girl would ask *him*. The scotch helped somewhat, as did the music— the *Aqualung* album had been a favorite at the college frat parties where he'd finally learned to loosen up. He wished he had some more Chivas now.

Moist coolness filled his fingers like a wish granted as Andrea pressed a full highball glass into his hand, then slipped her arm across his shoulders to give him a brief hug. For a moment they just stood there, Rob sipping his drink and humming along with the music, Andrea gazing around the room with an almost predatory concentration. It was only when the ache in his legs wormed into his back that he realized they'd been standing without speaking long enough for him to drain his glass once again; he was beginning to feel giddy. Before he could protest, Andrea had taken his empty glass and disappeared again. Sometimes she seemed to move so fast his sight couldn't keep up with her, like the chunky action of the human eye as it tried to follow the deftness of a magician's hand.

This time Andrea returned much quicker and handed him a glass only a quarter full with an apologetic look. The movement of her full lips told him she was saying something, but he couldn't catch the words above the music; someone had left the CD player set on REPEAT and Jethro hammered on.

"What?" he asked, straining to hear.

"I said somebody else found your bottle," she shouted. "This is all that's left."

Rob nodded a little numbly; the scotch had dulled the nerves in his neck and fingertips, though he could feel the effort it was taking to make sure his fingers were closed securely around his drink. Andrea stretched on her toes to bring her mouth close to his and he bent his knees rather than move his head again, vaguely concerned that the room had tipped slightly a moment earlier.

"Let's go home," she said in his ear. "I'm tapped out—how about you?" She pulled on Rob's hand and pointed toward the door and he nodded in relief. As he went to set the glass on a coaster, it seemed a shame to waste the last of a good bottle of Chivas Regal, though he really *was* blasted...

What the hell, Rob thought. He downed the last two fingers of liquor in one swallow.

***

"Shit," Rob said miserably. He'd had other things in mind when Andrea had helped him stagger through the front door, and hugging the dripping sides of a toilet bowl in the humidity of his bathroom hadn't been one of them.

Andrea poked her head through the doorway and clucked. "You okay?"

Rob waved her away, embarrassed at being seen like this; they'd only been at the party a couple of hours— what had he been thinking to consume that much booze in so short a time? He felt a twinge of self-pity. He didn't want to be sitting here on a damp tile floor, yarking his guts out while the world rocked and rolled around him. He wanted to be in the bedroom, with Andrea in his arms, rockin' and rollin' to a different song, indeed. Yet the idea that he could actually do this was like a mountain too high to climb—it had become physically impossible to command his muscles to stand, much less make love to a woman. The thought of the waterbed and its motion made him gag and he threw his face below the porcelain rim once more.

Finished at last, he managed to find his footing and direct himself out of the bathroom, but before he could decide whether he should brave the waterbed or opt for the couch, Andrea was calling for him to come into the kitchen. Rob turned toward the sound automatically, trying to ignore the short hallway with its crazily lurching floor, then found he could move through it only by squeezing his eyes into slits and groping along the wall. He turned the corner into the kitchen and its glaring yellow walls made him groan as he slid onto a chair. The laminated tabletop beckoned and he folded his hands on his lap and lowered his face to its cool surface.

"—fix you something to eat in a jiffy."

Rob was able to pick his head up but the effort was exhausting. "No," he choked, "don't want to." He face found the tabletop again of its own accord; boy, he thought hazily, what an exciting date I am tonight.

"You *have* to eat," Andrea insisted. She was already pulling out pans and searching through his refrigerator. "Otherwise you'll have a hangover three times worse than the one you're going to have anyway. Is that what you want?"

Thinking of a quick response would take far too much energy, Rob decided. And the woman was just too damned logical anyway.

More of Andrea's amazing speed—or perhaps he'd simply passed out for a time. In any event, it seemed like only seconds before she was shaking his shoulder and making him sit up to a plate of bacon and eggs, to which she quickly added two pieces of lightly buttered toast. His mind wanted to say 'Forget it" as his eyes focused unwillingly on the food, yet his stomach rumbled. Maybe just a few bites, Rob thought; he was still drunker than hell but he was also hungry.

Each bite of food tasted better than the last and with each one Rob was surprised anew that he didn't have to sprint for the bathroom. Andrea sat across from him with her own small plate of breakfast, nibbling and watching him as he shoveled it away, an amused smile turning up the left corner of her mouth. As his mind cleared a little, the notes of *Aqualung* drifted back into his mind and he couldn't help humming a few bars in between bites.

Andrea's smile grew wider. "What's that you're singing?"

"*Aqualung*," Rob answered around a mouthful of scrambled eggs. "They were playing it at the party earlier. It brings back memories of college—we used to have these terrific parties." He shook his head and tore off a piece of toast.

"Really?" Andrea pushed her plate away and fidgeted with her napkin. There was a vaguely yearning expression of her face as her fingers reached up and toyed with a strand of her waist-length black hair; even in his present sad state, Rob thought she was a knockout. "I never went to college—only night secretarial school. What was it like?"

"Oh, jeez," he said. Part of him was saying *Go to sleep, you idiot*, while another still thought he could salvage the evening and end it the way he had originally planned. What the hell, he'd at least give it the old college try. "Well," he began, trying diligently to keep the slur in his words to a minimum, "I hung out with about five guys. We all stayed in the same dorm until we got in this frat, see..."

Rob babbled for about three-quarters of an hour, until he simply couldn't hold his red-rimmed eyes open any longer. One moment he was muttering about a practical joke he and his pals had played on a chemistry professor, the next his forehead was hitting the table with a firm thump in the same spot from which Andrea had so thoughtfully yanked his plate an instant earlier. He was never aware that she not only helped him to stand but maneuvered him down that same treacherous hall and into his bedroom before quietly leaving the apartment.

***

Sunday sunlight.

Bright, beautiful, and perfectly vicious as it slipped through the mini-blinds and striped his face and the bed. Feeling like a ball that had been flattened into four uneven sides, Rob rolled over and shoved his face between the two pillows—one of which was obviously lacking Andrea. So much for my grand plan, he thought as he tried to push himself toward the edge of the bed. His bladder ached and he thought of the bathroom but decided to wait when the back of his eyelids began a bass-beat headache; instead, he kept his eyes tightly shut and eased himself back against the headboard.

Andrea. In spite of his hangover, Rob smiled. From what he could remember of the previous night she hadn't seemed upset with him, only slightly amused at his antics—that is, if you could call getting sloshed an "antic." He just hadn't realized the Chivas would hit him so hard, and even the best plans sometimes got sidetracked. As soon as he felt well enough to get out of bed, he'd down three Excedrins and give her a call—God, it'd been years since he'd found a woman who was willing to listen to him ramble like that. What was it they'd been talking about when he'd fallen asleep at the table?

Collage—that was it. He remembered talking about college, telling her about... The thudding in his head suddenly increased to sickening proportions.

Rob couldn't remember ever *going* to college.

***

Yes! Rob thought triumphantly. Here it is—proof! I *did* go to college, I *did*. The eleven by fourteen framed diploma he had dug out from under a moldering pile of old term papers and now held in his unsteady hands should have felt reassuring, yet it managed only to confirm his worst fears. *Southern Illinois University*. He, Robert A. Wensson, had earned his degree in mathematics, which logically explained why—outside of being an openly masochistic individual—he had opted for a teaching position in one of Chicago's lovely inner-city high schools. And the technical knowledge was there, oh yes; deep in his brain, hangover or not, he could feel the wheels burning in calculus and geometry, cotangents and integrals. What was missing—*gone*—was the memory of *how* that information had actually come to find its home in his intellect.

I'm a mathematician, he thought. The concept filled him with awe.

***

He met Andrea for dinner on Wednesday night; between the mother of all hangovers he'd had all day Sunday and part of Monday and the prospect of his insidious memory loss, as much as he wanted to see her, Rob felt he didn't dare. Would it show, this creeping thing destroying his mind? Would this lovely woman, a woman he wanted so badly to include in his life, be able to tell that her college-educated boyfriend was shedding bits and pieces of his past like dead snakeskin?

"You're certainly far away tonight," Andrea said. They were in a tiny Italian place on Taylor Street with quaint red and white checked tablecloths and tiny globe-covered candles at each table. The candle glow flickered on her dusky skin and the deep blue of the satin blouse she wore; Rob's gaze couldn't seem to take in enough of her. While the meal the waiter had placed before them was excellent, the couple had almost forgotten the food in the warmth of the wine and escalating attraction between them.

"Am I?" he asked warmly. "I was thinking about you."

She smiled and blushed a little. "I'm almost afraid to ask what."

Rob grinned and raised his glass in a toast, although he'd kept a stern eye on his intake throughout the meal. "Don't be," he said. "They were... good thoughts, I promise."

"I'm sure." He watched as she carefully folded her napkin and placed it on the table, then looked at him expectantly.

"Would you like to leave now?" he asked. "We could go to—" He hesitated.

"—your place," she finished softly.

***

Rob couldn't get over the beauty of having Andrea dozing within the circle of his arms. The feel of her skin was cool silk against his, the taste of her lips like the exotic Hawaiian flavor of passionfruit—he would never get enough. He couldn't stop his fingers before they brushed her hair, now tangled and damp with perspiration but no less lovely, away from the clear lines of her cheek. She sighed at the movement and opened her eyes.

"Hi," she said. "Why are you still awake?"

He shrugged. "I was wondering about you."

"Me?"

Rob settled himself more comfortably and pulled her closer. "I've told you all these things about myself," he said. "But you haven't shared all that much with me. I'd like to get closer to *you*."

"I've told you things about me," she protested.

"Sure," he agreed. "Basic stuff, like how old you are and where you work. But I want to know the good stuff, your feelings, fears, what your childhood was like—the real *you*." He looked at her questioningly.

"Oh," Andrea said lightly, "my childhood was an... ordeal. I spent most of the time in different foster homes. I'm afraid it doesn't make for very pleasant recollections."

She averted her eyes and Rob squeezed her shoulder in sympathy as he waited for her to continue. When it became obvious she wasn't going to, he shifted uncomfortably, afraid he'd been too prying in his questions but perplexed at her reluctance to talk about herself. He opened his mouth to say something to break the building tension, but she cut him off with a smile that was just a shade too big.

"Tell me about you instead," Andrea suggested. "I'd love to hear about how you grew up. You have no idea what it's like when you can only dream of that sense of stability. Of *family*."

"I was secure," he admitted. "But there's bad times as well. It's like you know there's pain, underneath all the love that comes from the folks in your family, just waiting to happen. You love all these people but one by one they die off, and little pieces of yourself die with them." Rob chuckled self-consciously. "Remember the mistrust in the nineteen-sixties of anyone over thirty? Well, when I was twenty-six, after my dad's funeral, I flipped out a little and tried to avoid older people as much as possible. I just didn't trust someone over say forty or forty-five not to up and die on me. I even found a doctor who was just starting his practice, figuring he wouldn't retire for years, and I came across an eye doctor in his early thirties, too." He paused for a few moments, staring at the twin mounds of their comforter-draped feet. "Then my best friend, Patrick, died in his sleep of a cerebral hemorrhage. He was one of those guys who acted like he was going to live forever, you know? But he'd been walking around for twenty-nine years with this bomb ticking away at the base of his brain." Rob made a soft snorting sound. "So much for surrounding myself with 'safe' people, huh?"

"What happened then?" Andrea asked.

"Nothing, I guess." Rob felt suddenly embarrassed at his little speech. I suppose I learned you just have to take life as it comes and hope for the best. You can't pick and choose the people around you, or the pieces that die out. You deal with it." He glanced sideways. "This is depressing—can't we talk about something else? I'm not even sure how we got on this subject."

"I've got a better idea," Andrea said. She slid a hand beneath the sheets. "Let's not *talk*."

***

Rob spent most of Thursday morning trying to conceal the grin that kept wanting to spring to his face, feeling his cheeks heat up now and then as his brain supplied instant replays of the previous night. He hadn't felt this infatuated since high school and his first lay; he was still in this state of euphoria when for some reason he opened the bottom drawer of his desk.

Nestled among the jumbled mass of paper clips, rubber bands, and half-chewed pencils was a framed black and white photo of him and Patrick that had been taken in some crowded, nameless bar on Rush Street, each hailing the other drunkenly with half-filled mugs of dark Austrian beer. Across the bottom right corner was Patrick's heavy scrawl: *"To Robbie—Strange Days, indeed!"*

After all these years, pain still ran down to his soul every time he looked at that photo. His best-ever buddy, Patrick. Buried six years now, killed by a stupid...

What?

I know this, Rob thought desperately. I do.

Then: God help me... I *don't*.

Easy enough to find out. He made up an excuse and found someone to cover his next class; in another hour he was home and digging through the old stuff again, although this set of boxes held memories of a more painful nature. It didn't take long to find the obituary that gave him the date, time, cause of death, even the name of the hospital from which Patrick's body had been taken.

That's right, Rob thought smugly as he sat back. Massive cerebral hemorrhage.

But the answer held all the familiarity of reading

the definition of a new word in the dictionary.

***

Okay, think.

Rob stared at his reflection in the mirror. His face was white beneath hair that was thick and dark like Andrea's, although his eyes were light blue and shocked. When did you start losing your memory? And what could be causing it? With the question came a spasm of panic and he fought to keep his thoughts on a rational track. "If I'm losing my memory," he asked aloud, "how can I expect to remember *when* it started happening?"

Oh, but he could.

Rob could remember lots of things, like the bike path he'd been traveling in Lincoln Park the day he'd met Andrea, when he'd tripped and almost fallen on his face trying to push off again after a stop at the stone water fountain. The near collision between the two of them, the funny little story about learning to ride a bicycle with training wheels that had caught and held her attention until he could work up the nerve to ask if he could call her sometime.

Rob felt the weight of his keys in his pocket and knew it would take less than ten minutes to pull his twelve-speed from the storage shed and climb on the seat, stand on the pedals, feel his leg muscles begin the complex but automatic functions of balance and motion. Like mathematics, the skill, the *ability*, was there.

But instead of the memory of his first bike and the childish fears of that learning experience, he could find nothing but an empty space in his mind.

***

"What are you doing to me?" he asked her.

His question halted the fork-full of veal an inch from Andrea's lips and her eyes widened in false innocence.

"What?" She smiled a little, as though confident Rob's next statement would be about how crazy she made him, or how he couldn't stop thinking about her.

"I'm losing my memories," he said. He kept his tone carefully bland, disguising the anxiety that made him want to clutch at the edge of the table. "Maybe I'm losing my mind."

Andrea lowered her fork and placed it carefully on her plate. "I don't see what that has to do with me."

Rob stared at her, letting the words and their implications flash-play over and again in his head. After a moment he said the only thing that kept bobbing to the surface of his thoughts. "That's *all*? Don't you care enough to want to know what would make me think that?"

Andrea's hands sought the napkin in her lap, brought it up in a swift dab across her lips before she folded it meticulously and placed it at the side of her wine glass. He knew the meal was over, in spite of his careful preparations of linen tablecloth and fresh flowers, the step by step instructions of the gourmet cookbook and carefully chosen scented candles. Before she even said the words, he knew the *relationship* was over, and in spite of everything he felt a flash of regret.

"No," Andrea said slowly, pushing her chair away from the table and standing. "I think it's time for me to leave now." The sway of her head as she stood caused her hair to spill over one shoulder and for a desperate second Rob wanted to bury his hands in the thick, soft waves. Instead his voice exploded from his throat.

"Give them back!" His feet finally responded and Rob levered himself from his chair and stepped toward her. He could feel the sweat squeezing from his face and neck, soaking through the collar of his suddenly too-tight shirt even as he said the insane-sounding words. She would stare at him, call him crazy, perhaps even laugh, yet he couldn't stop. "You had no right!" He tried to grab her arm but she eluded him with feline-quick reflexes. Rob snatched at her again, this time at the material of her dress, and she slapped at him.

"Stop it!" she hissed. Her eyes were dark pits in the soft glow of light in Rob's living room. "Stop it right now!"

"Or what?" Rob challenged. "Or you'll take another little piece of me? Suck up another one of my souvenirs of the past? Huh? Is that what you'll do?" He waved his arm. "I thought you were *special*—"

"I am," she interrupted.

"Not like that," Rob snapped. "Not like some freak from a carnival sideshow. I thought we could, you know, *make* something of each other, of this relationship..." He was whining and he hated himself for it.

Andrea picked up her purse. "I'm not a freak, Rob," she said. Her voice was cold but he thought he could detect a slight tremble underneath it, as though she was trying hard to put on a strong front. "I have needs, that's all. Emotional ones, like any other woman. It's just that mine are more complex and take a little more out of my partner." Her expression softened a bit as she gazed at him. "In my own way, I loved you, and I tried to be careful about which ones I took, tried to make sure they were ones that you could live without—"

"Well, you can just return them," he said loudly. "And then get out—but before you go, do me the favor of taking away my memory of *you*!"

Andrea shook her head. "That's impossible. That would be like trying to take away the fact that I exist. I can take the knowledge of almost anything, but not my actual *presence* in your life. And you can never get things back or re-learn it once they've been taken—they're gone forever."

Unreality beat at Rob from all sides, and the hurt of losing her was almost as bad as the knowledge of the whacked-out thing she'd done to him. He wanted to strike back but couldn't stand the thought of actually touching her flesh. Instead, Rob let his vindictiveness take the form of an insult.

"I understand," he said, careful to use a pitying tone. "You take but don't give. Go on and leave then." Rob swung an arm toward the door.

Andrea flinched and her fingers tightened on her leather pocketbook. "I could have *taken* more, you know." Her soft words flowed around him like cream. "I could have taken them all if I wanted—right down to your memory of how to speak. Would you like to have to learn sign language, Rob?"

He gave her an ugly glance. "You know where the door is, Andrea."

Her eyes darkened even further, until they looked like two glistening pools of oil. "I could even take away your memory of how to *breathe*—" She snapped her fingers. "That *quick*."

Rob felt his legs bend and drop his body back onto the chair as fear settled around him with an intimate caress. The whole thing—Andrea appearing in his life with her goddess-like beauty and perfect personality, his memory losses, the idea that she might have some strange supernatural ability to siphon off parts of his life—had seemed rather fanciful... until two seconds ago.

Suddenly, inexplicably, he believed it was all true, he *knew* it was: Andrea could do each and every thing she claimed she could.

Right down to killing him.

Andrea gave him a final, stunning smile, then walked out of Rob's apartment.

He didn't try to stop her.

***

Often, Rob mused, desire was one thing and ability quite the opposite; as a result, sometimes a man couldn't pick up the pieces of his life—like Humpty-Dumpty, things would not necessarily fit back together once they'd been shattered. But a person could damned well stop the other guy from stealing the broken parts.

There was a gun in his closet. It was no big deal; he lived in the city, in a first floor apartment on an alley and so he'd felt he should own one. It was a nine millimeter and he would use it to go after the beautiful woman who had pilfered chunks of his brain, put an end to her insidious theft before she did the same thing to someone else. There was a panicked instant when Rob couldn't recall where he kept the pistol, then he got a backwash of acidic relief when he spied it on the closet shelf and instinct said the gun was where it was supposed to be.

Rob took down the case, opened it and looked at the Smith & Wesson resting within the pre-cut pillow inside, a nice chromed piece that wouldn't rust and didn't require the care that a steel weapon did. He picked up the gun and hefted it; the metal felt cold and heavy in his palm and filled the air with the thick smell of cleaning oil. Another cut-out in the padding held a box containing bullets, each with a tiny cross-shaped indentation in its point.

Rob could see her in his mind's eye: impossibly long hair and black, black eyes, full moist lips, the skin of her shoulders and breasts smooth and dusky, like fine-woven silk.

Now if he could only remember her name.

☙ ❧ ☙

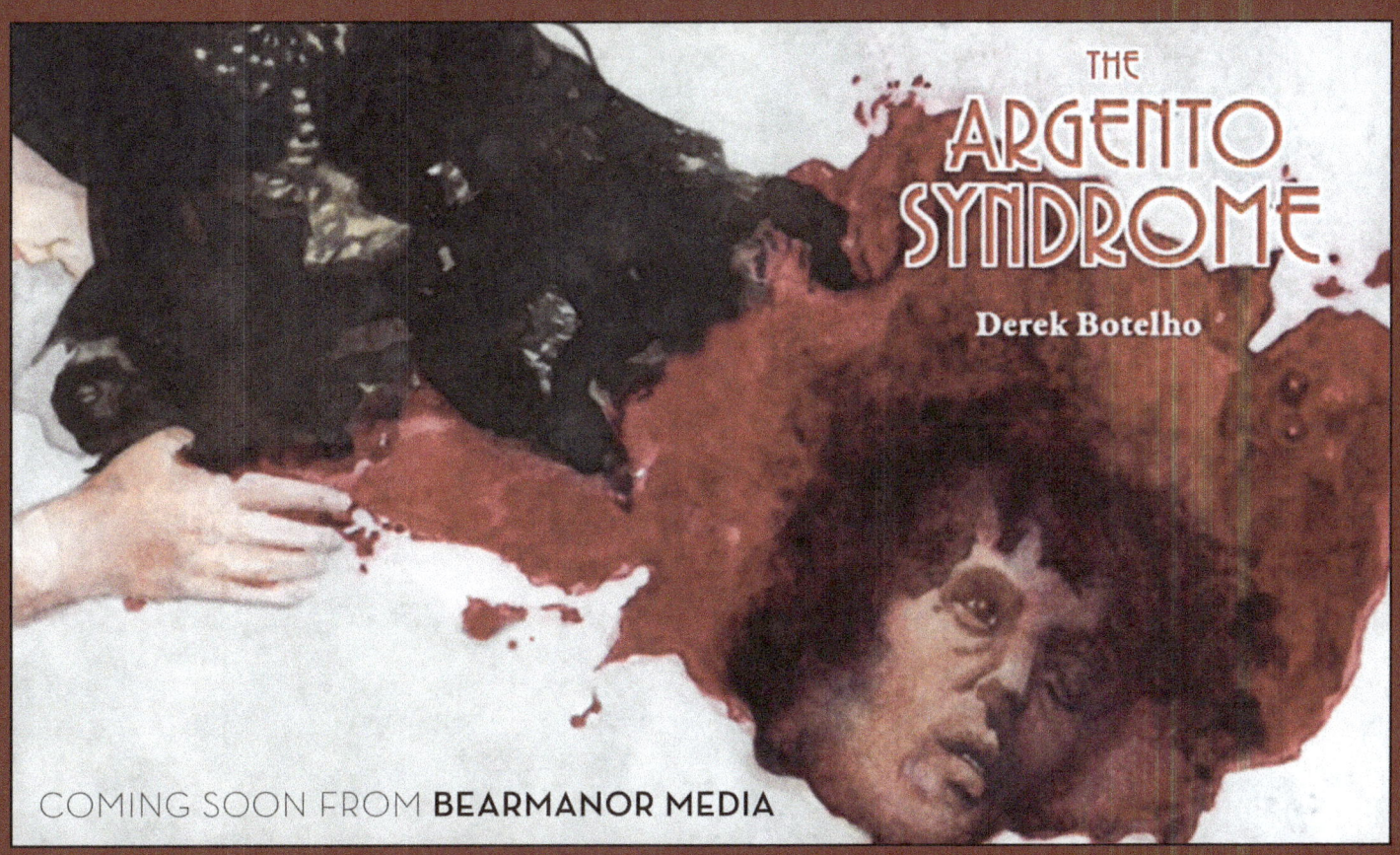

THE GIALLO GIRLS

By Derek Botelho

It could be argued that the Italian crime thriller sub-genre known as "giallo" is the Italian counterpart to the noir films from the U.S., as they both have roots in the pulp fiction of the 1930s and 40s, deal with murder and sexy dames, and have created legions of fans for both genres, respectively, for many divergent reasons equal to the ones they share. Giallo is the Italian word for yellow, and since the pulp crime thrillers in Italy had yellow covers they became known as "giallo." Mario Bava is credited with creating the genre with his 1963 film *The Girl Who Knew Too Much* starring John Saxon and Leticia Romain. Bava then followed it up with what I view to be the standard bearer for all gialli to follow, *Blood and Black Lace* with Eva Bartok and Cameron Mitchell. The opening of the film is just as memorable as anything that comes after as Isabella (Francesca Ungara) is chased through the woods outside the fashion house after work one night and brutally murdered. While the act is terrible, it is photographed and lit so beautifully that it takes on the sheen of the poetic. Bava would go on to heighten the sex and violence and practically create the modern slasher film with *Bay of Blood* in 1971.

The 1970s saw many a gialli courtesy of directors such as Lucio Fulci, Sergio Martino, Aldo Lado, and Dario Argento, whom all dabbled in the form. One of the most vital aspects of the giallo is the woman at the center of the story, whether good, bad, or other. Here is a primer to the femme fatale of this most Italian sub-genre. Their ultra-stylish hairstyles and clothes are only one aspect of their importance. As much as the

women in these films were deemed objects to look at, they got involved in solving the crimes, or committing them, and were as strong as any male figure. Of course there are exceptions. From child actors Lara Wendel and Nicoletta Elmi to the more sultry likes of Suzy Kendall and Edwige Fenech, here is a beginner's guide to some of le regazze in giallo (the girls in yellow).

Carroll Baker – Ms. Baker is an American actress most famous for Elia Kazan's film *Baby Doll* with Karl Malden and Eli Wallach, based on Tennessee Williams's one-act plays *Twenty-Seven Wagons Full of Cotton* and *The Unsatisfactory Supper*. Fans of her work in the U.S. and Europe would be surprised to know she made some dozen gialli. *The Sweet Body of Deborah* co-starring Jean Sorel was her first and one of the most well-known. This was followed with three films by Umberto Lenzi which formed a loose trilogy: *Paranoia, So Sweet, So Perverse*, and *A Quiet Place To Kill*. *Knife of Ice*, one the better gialli Baker starred in, was one of her last. *Baba Yaga*, while not a giallo was a fairly major film for the genre in Italy as it was based on a popular comic by Guido Crepax.

Daniela Barnes (Lara Wendel) was born in Germany and has worked extensively in Italy with a diverse group of talent. Lara started young, with a small role in *My Dear Killer* at the age of seven. Within a few years she would star in *The Perfume of the Lady in Black* with Mimsy Farmer, *Ring of Darkness* with John Phillip Law and Marisa Mell, and *Little Girl in Blue Velvet* alongside Claudia Cardinale and Denholm Elliot. She is perhaps best known for her role as Maria Alboretto in Dario Argento's *Tenebre*, as the young woman who is chased down by a manic Doberman pinscher and ends up at the murderer's home to meet with an untimely end. She has also worked with Argento's "protégé," Lamberto Bava on his film *Murder at Midnight* and one of Federico Fellini's later films, *Intervista*.

Florinda Bolkan – A truly striking actress in such Italian fare as *The Cage* with Tony Musante, and *One Evening at Dinner* (co-written by Argento). She is probably best known to genre enthusiasts from her two films with Lucio Fulci, *A Lizard in a Woman's Skin* and *Don't Torture a Duckling*. I prefer the latter of the two, where she plays Maciara, a witch unduly accused of murder in Lucio Fulci's masterpiece. The director's trademark gore effects were never used better than in a pivotal scene with Bolkan in this dark thriller about a serial child murderer in a rural Italian town.

Barbara Bouchet – Czech born and raised in California as a child when her family was forced to leave the country, Bouchet went on to appear on quite a few American television shows in the 1960s such as *Star Trek* and *The Man From U.N.C.L.E.* She also had a role in *Casino Royale* before going on to star in several gialli. Lucio Fucli's *Don't Torture a Duckling* and Emiglio Miraglia's *The Red Queen Kills Seven Times* were made back-to-back and feature great

in the annals of the abnormal there is no more erotic nightmare than the strange lusts of a...

"LIZARD IN A WOMAN'S SKIN"

Edmondo Amati presents
FLORINDA BOLKAN · STANLEY BAKER · JEAN SOREL
in "LIZARD IN A WOMAN'S SKIN" [R]
with Alberto De Mendoza · Silvia Monti · Mike Kennedy · George Rigaud · Anita Strindberg
and with LEO GENN · Directed by LUCIO FULCI · Music by ENNIO MORRICONE
Co-production: Apollo Films, Rome · Les Films Corona, Paris · Atlantida Film, Madrid
TECHNICOLOR® · An American International Release

performances by this unique actress. Prior to both she starred in *The French Sex Murders* with Anita Ekberg and Rosalba Neri. Also of note is *Amuck* co-starring Farley Granger and Rosalba Neri.

Nicoletta Elmi – The little red haired child star of several horror films, such as Bava's *Baron Blood* and *Bay of Blood*, *Who Saw Her Die?* for Aldo Lado and Warhol's *Flesh for Frankenstein* is perhaps best known for her role as Olga in Argento's *Deep Red*. Her angelic face, belied by a mischievous grin and piercing eyes, gave her an odd presence in these films that most child actors could never hope to attain. As a teenager, Elmi was in *Demons* for Lamberto Bava as an employee at the Metropol and is now a surgeon after leaving acting behind her.

Rosella Falk – With a compact resume, and large, expressive eyes, Falk was able to make a big impression in films of varying genres from directors like Federico Fellini (*8 1/2*), Robert Aldrich (*The Legend of Lylah Clare*) and Joseph Losey (*Modesty Blaise*), to a few gialli with Umberto Lenzi. Falk made several gialli: *The Fifth Cord* with Franco Nero; *The Black Belly of the Tarantula* with Barbara Bouchet and Giancarlo Giannini and *Seven Blood-Stained Orchids* alongside Antonio Sabato for Umberto Lenzi. Most recently, horror fans saw her in Argento's neo-giallo *Sleepless* playing the mother of a dwarf accused of murder.

Mimsy Farmer – Chicago native Mimsy Farmer, who is now a successful artist and sculptor, had an interesting screen career to say the least. Farmer began acting in her teens after being spotted by a talent agent. Early on she made quite a few appearances on television in such fare as *My Three Sons*, *The Donna Reed Show*, *The Outer Limits*, *The Adventures of Ozzie and Harriet* and *Perry Mason* amongst others. Her film work includes *Gidget Goes Hawaiian*, *Spencer's Mountain* with Henry Fonda and Maureen O'Sullivan, and *More* directed by Barbet Schroeder, which Farmer co-wrote. Italian horror fans will recognize Mimsy's icy

wife of Michael Brandon in Argento's *Four Flies on Grey Velvet*, her leading role in Barilli's *The Perfume of the Lady in Black*, and a leading role in *Autopsy* by Armando Crispino.

Edwige Fenech – This French born beauty may be the most representative of the women in these films. She's a gift to any photographer, still or film. Her work in such films as *All the Colors of the Dark*, *Strip Nude for your Killer*, *The Strange Vice of Mrs. Wardh*, *The Case of the Bloody Iris*, *Your Vice is a Locked Room and Only I Have the Key*, and Bava's *Five Dolls for an August Moon* put her in the center of the genre. Her performance in *Dark* for Sergio Martino is especially memorable as she is the victim of a satanic cult, which may not be what it seems. It's a fun work of paranoid horror. Eli Roth paid tribute to his love of these films and Ms. Fenech by casting her in a small role in *Hostel 2* as an art teacher.

Cristina Galbó – A Spanish actress best known for her horror films, and her role in the Spanish/Italian co-production *Let Sleeping Corpses Lie*. Other credits include two excellent gialli: Luigi Cozzi's *The Killer Must Kill Again* and *What Have You Done to Solange?* with Camille Keaton. Also of note is the great Spanish horror/suspense film *La Residencia aka The House That Screamed*, which seems a possible influence on Argento's *Suspiria*.

Ida Galli (Evelyn Stewart) – A veteran of two Mario Bava classics, *Whip and the Body* and *Hercules and the Haunted World*, Ms. Galli had her first credited film role in Fellini's *La Dolce Vita* and would later work with Visconti on *The Leopard*. Ida's work in gialli is equally as impressive. She can be seen in *The Sweet Body of Deborah* opposite Carrol Baker, *The Weekend Murders*, *The Case of the Scorpion's Tail*, *The Bloodstained Butterfly*, *Maniac Mansion* (more horror than giallo), *Knife of Ice*, *The Night Child*, and Fulci's *The Psychic*, which appears to be her last giallo.

Suzy Kendall – This blond, British beauty was a famous model by the time she dipped her toe into the acting pool. It's a shame she never received more plaudits for her efforts, as she is quite a good actress. Dario Argento's *The Bird with the Crystal Plumage* and Sergio Martino's *Torso* are her most well-known horror entries. Kendall also appeared in *The Penthouse* with Martine Beswicke in 1967 playing the victim of a bizarre home invasion.

Marina Malfatti – Largely unknown to even the most ardent giallo fan, Marina Malfatti starred in a great number of them, and some quite good with many other actresses in this list. As evidenced by her leading role in the erotic thriller *The Night Evelyn Came out of the Grave* directed by Emiglio Miraglia, Malfatti has a face the camera clearly loves. Marina worked with Miraglia again on *The Red Queen Kills Seven Times* as Barbara Bouchet's sister. A few of her other giallo credits include: *Seven Blood-Stained Orchids* with Rosella Falk, *All the Colors of the Dark* with Edwige Fenech, and *The Deep End of the Swimming Pool* co-starring Carrol Baker.

Nieves Navarro (Susan Scott) – Another Spanish actress and star of many gialli and spaghetti westerns. Susan's face will be instantly recognizable if not her name for films such as *Death Walks at Midnight*, in which she plays the lead as a fashion model who is given an experimental drug which causes her to have violent visions of murder. In a possibly unintentional nod to Mario Bava's *Blood and Black Lace*, the murderer has a weapon fashioned to fit his hand much like the murder sequence in the antique store in that previous film. Susan can also be seen in *Death Walks in High Heels* and *All the Colors of the Dark*.

Daria Nicolodi – Most notable is her work with longtime partner in real life and the cinema, Dario Argento. Their initial artistic endeavor was *Deep Red (1975)*, which was followed shortly by the birth of their daughter Asia. Nicolodi was a stage actress of some repute before making her

mark in gialli with Argento such as *Opera* (1987), *Tenebrae* (1982) and *Phenomena* (1985). Although her greatest performance is probably in Mario Bava's final film, *Shock* (1977) with her *Tenebrae* co-star John Steiner. Nicolodi recently teamed up with Dario and Asia for *Mother of Tears*, the finale of the "Three Mothers Trilogy" started with *Suspiria* in 1977, which Nicolodi co-wrote.

Rosalba Neri – This Roman beauty turned down an offer to study at the Actor's Studio in Hollywood and went to appear in large number of films and TV shows in Italy starting in her teens. She is probably most well-known for starring in *Lady Frankenstein* with Joseph Cotton and Mario Bava's *Hercules in the Haunted World*. Her impressive giallio resume includes Williams Rose's satanic sex cult film, *Girl in Room 2A*, *Smile Before Death*, *The French Sex Murders*, and *Amuck*, starring as Farley Granger's wife. Fernando Di Leo's *The Beast Kills in Cold Blood*, which was re-released as *Slaughter Hotel*, may be one of the best though thanks to the always-reliable Klaus Kinski and its strange setting of an asylum for seemingly sex addicted women.

Anita Strindberg – A staple of the giallo, the Swedish actress made a name for herself in genre films with a singularly icy allure. *Antichrist* co-starring Mel Ferrer and Alida Valli may be her most famous genre work. However, Strindberg starred in several of the most known gialli: *A Case of the Scorpion's Tale, Who Saw Her Die? Your Vice is a Locked Door and Only I Have the Key, A Lizard in a Woman's Skin* in near succession. Her last film in 1981 was Riccardo Freda's *Murder Syndrome*, a new take of the giallo, not a great film, but an interesting summation of the many things that defined them.

Marilù Tolo – While not the largest presence

in the giallo firmament, she does have some import for her work with Dario Argento, whom she dated and worked with, and her varied resume. Working with everyone from Federico Fellini on *Juliet of the Spirits* to Mario Bava on *Hercules and the Haunted World*, Tolo did a bit of everything, even working on *Charlie's Angels* in the U.S. Her gialli roles include an episode of Argento's series *Door into Darkness* in the episode "Eyewitness," the films *Night of Violence*, and *My Dear Killer*. She also had a memorable role as a nymphomaniac turned on by violence, billed as "The Countess" in Argento's period comedy *The Five Days*. Tolo's final screen appearance in the TV miniseries *Sogni e Bisogni/Dreams and Needs* also starred Daria Nicolodi and her daughter, Asia Argento in her first screen work.

While this list is not complete by any means, it does, I hope, shed some light on the importance of women in a largely male dominated genre and field. As with any horror film, the female is the driving force. Whether

she is the victim or one of the protagonists trying to break the case, if it weren't for the "fairer sex" these films wouldn't have their sex appeal and mystery. Of course, all of the fashions and hairstyles were mere dressing, as these characters were more than something beautiful to look at and were at times the object of desire and the brains behind the operation.

Taking the reins from Mario Bava as the biggest name in the giallo at the time, Dario Argento was one of the greatest proponents of putting women in these roles in his films. *Deep Red* from 1975 had Daria Nicolodi starring with David Hemmings as a journalist who is involved in investigating a series of murders. *Suspiria*, while not a strict giallo, had Jessica Harper as

the heroin, trying to solve the mystery of her new home, a German dance academy. *Tenebrae* again saw Nicolodi paired up, this time with Anthony Franciosa, to solve a series of murders in Italy. *Phenomena* featured a young Jennifer Connelly with a psychic link to the insect world, which she uses to solve a series of murders at her Swiss boarding home. More recently, Argento had Stefania Rocca playing a female police officer hot on the trail of a mysterious killer in *The Card Player* and his last giallo was well-titled *Giallo* and starred Emmanuelle Seigner opposite Adrien Brody in pursuit of a killer who held her sister captive.

The giallo had its peak in the 1970s and into the 80s, but it's one of the few genres still actively produced in Italy, and the interest in the genre is alive and well across Europe in several countries. *Eyes of Crystal* from 2004 was a detective film from Italy worthy of the genre, with some truly creepy moments and garnering quite a bit of praise. There are a few gialli coming out of Spain recently, such as *Shadow*, which was released in some territories in 2012. Interest in the genre has in a way never been bigger, with so many titles becoming available through video and other means and fans requesting the release of more obscure titles. For a while, even Netflix was streaming *The Fifth Cord* and a few of the gialli released by Blue Underground. There are rumors of Sergio Martino directing a remake of his own film, *Torso*. The signs are positive that we will see more beautiful women, knives, and mysterious killers for years to come.

❦❦❦

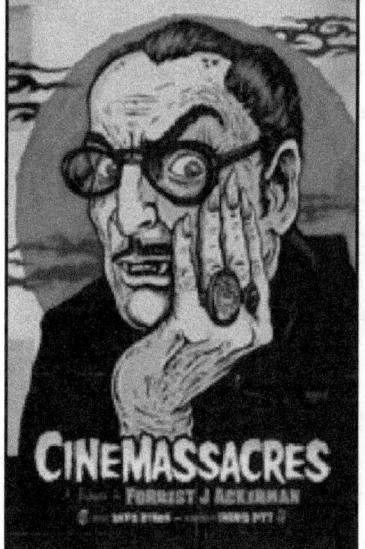

ASIA ARGENTO:

TOTAL ENTROPY

Interview By Derek Botelho

Born in 1975, Asia Argento has lived a lifetime in the public eye, being the daughter of director and writer Dario Argento and actress Daria Nicolodi. Never one to rest on her laurels and be famous for fame's sake, Asia has carved out her own distinct identity as a writer/actress/director/artist/DJ and, as some may or may not be aware, a musician. She has recently released an album comprised of music written and recorded over the last decade entitled "Total Entropy." On September 20, 2013 (her 38th birthday) Argento has started shooting a new film entitled *Misunderstood*. In a poetically cryptic manner, Argento would only reveal the following about her new film: "Details will come soon. It's a story about children set in 1984. My favorite actress in the world will play the role of the protagonist's mother. What I do is secret. SECRET." Asia talks about where her career has gone, where it may be going, and several things she keeps close to her heart.

DEREK BOTELHO: What is your first memory of a film set?

ASIA ARGENTO: The first time I visited my father on a set was during *Tenebrae*. I didn't grow up on film sets. I didn't visit one of my father's until I was nine and started working in movies. My father didn't like his daughters around; I think he thought we might be distracting. My first memory is someone shouting "SILENCE PLEASE!" and I'm holding my breath for the whole take because I am afraid to make noise.

DB: What was school like? I'm assuming most people in Italy knew who you were because of your parents. Did this make things difficult for you?

AA: I think kids were intrigued and they loved our horror Betamax video collection. We made a pact that if they came over to watch a scary movie, they weren't allowed to tell their parents.

DB: You've basically been writing your entire life. When did you start, and what did you write first?

AA: I've been writing poetry since I was five years old. At age nine, I published a small book.

DB: Then you acted in *Demons 2*. Do you have any strong memories of this shoot?

AA: I remember being in a car with fire and demons all around… and feeling a little scared.

DB: *The Church* came next. Although you were young, can you tell me anything about working with Soavi? He's a unique talent and creates some interesting visuals and set pieces, but not in the way your father does.

AA: He was very gentle and fun to work with. I don't remember so much of the shoot, but there were other kids and we were in Budapest and we had a lot of fun watching soft-core porn on the hotel pay-TV.

DB: After two horror movies in a row, you did a few dramatic roles (*Zoo* and *Friends of the Heart*). What were these experiences like after being in such fantastic and dark films as a young actor? Did you have to use part of yourself that you hadn't used up to this point?

AA: When I shot *Zoo*, I was 11 and it was my first lead role. I felt an immense pressure and responsibility. I won many awards for that movie. Shooting *Palombella Rossa* with Nanni Moretti was very hard because I was far from home and didn't have my family with me and felt very lonely. I would barely leave the hotel room. People thought I was a spoiled brat, but I was only depressed. I stopped acting in movies because of the shock until I did *Friends at Heart* at age 16. That was a big turning point for me. That's when I realized for the first time this was the job I wanted to do in life.

DB: Finally, your father put you in one of his films when you made *Trauma*. Since you had grown up watching your father work, do you think that prepared you for the type of director he would be?

AA: I was afraid he'd be severe. I was afraid to disappoint. But the experience was great and it brought us very close.

DB: After a few more films, you made *La Reine Margot*, which was a big success worldwide and was the first film I ever saw you in. Can you tell me about this film and what it did for your career?

AA: When I tested for the movie, I had no idea it would be such a big production. It was my first French language movie and I didn't speak French. I am not sure what it did to my career; I never know what movies do to one's career/life.

DB: Most people outside Italy, myself included, have never seen *DeGenerazione*. Can you tell me a bit about this project?

AA: It was a collective movie directed by young upcoming directors of horror/fantasy. It was the first short movie I ever directed. It was pretty weird and I don't know how it fit with the rest. Mine was surreal, a dream about masturbation.

DB: I consider *The Stendhal Syndrome* to be one of your father's best films and my favorite of everything you have done together so far. It's a very rough journey your character takes. What was it like preparing to become that person, who then becomes someone and something else entirely?

AA: It's my favorite movie that we shot together and the most challenging role. Maybe I was too young to play it (I turned 20 on the shoot).

DB: What were you processing in *Stendhal's* final shot, the one where you're being carried away in the arms of the police. It's very intense and poetic and reminds me of Michelangelo's "Pieta."

AA: I was processing the loss of my sister. Especially that primal scream when the police catch her. The final image

Photo Courtesy of Derek Botehlo

came to my father's mind the day before we shot, and I improvised the part of the dialogue when the character is making plans for her future before she gets caught.

DB: *Traveling Companion* and *Viola Kisses Everybody* got you some more international exposure and *Traveling Companion* won a lot of praise for your performance. Again, after working with your father, how were these two projects for you?

AA: *Traveling Companion* remains one of my favorite movies I've ever done. Working with a master like Michel Piccoli was such a great lesson of cinema. *Viola Kisses Everybody* was a comedy, which became a big hit in Italy. It was very challenging to play in such different movie genres.

DB: *Phantom of the Opera*… when you read that script and your father approached you about it, were you hesitant? That story has been filmed many times. What do you think your father brought to it that is special or unique?

AA: Actually, I was very enthusiastic. He had never done a movie like that before, a classic, a story that wasn't his. What my father brought was the opposite of Andrew Lloyd Webber.

DB: I know Abel Ferrara is a huge influence on your work and it shows in *Scarlet Diva*. What do you most admire about Ferrara?

AA: Working with Ferrara for the first time, I didn't have to follow the camera but the camera followed me, and so I encountered the joys of improvisation. Abel really pushes

you to the limit. He makes you think you're coming up with something, but he's manipulated your mind so you're doing what he wants from you. I loved how he directed the actors, and I learned a great deal from him.

DB: *Diva* is a very personal film. What was the impetus behind it?

AA: After working with Ferrara, who is one of my favorite directors, everything just seemed dull. I was agoraphobic and barely left my home. So I started writing a book. My father read a few pages and told me he saw a movie there. So I began writing it. Reality and fiction merged into my creative process.

DB: Now that you have children, do you want them to follow into the family business? Anna is old enough to be acting and asking to do this kind of thing. Has she shown any interest?

AA: Anna Lou wants to be a rapper!

(This interview is excerpted from the upcoming book *The Argento Syndrome* soon to be published by Bear Manor Media. Keep up with the project at: www.facebook.com/theargentosyndrome).

❀❀❀

Asia Argento ☦

Total Entropy

PEARRY TEO'S

BEDLAM STORIES

THE BATTLE FOR OZ AND WONDERLAND BEGINS...

WWW.BEDLAMSTORIES.COM

TWISTED SISTER

by Chris Marrs

Hannah closed the door to her private room and its wondrous window then shivered a junkie's shiver. Her knuckles turned white as she stood with her hand on the knob pondering the harm of one more minute. Just one more little peek wouldn't hurt.

No, be strong. Ava will be wanting her breakfast.

She let go. Caring for her bedridden twin was both a blessing and a burden.

She made her way to the kitchen but stopped short of entering to cast a forlorn look at the door to her room. There'd always be later but later was so far away. Brushing an errant strand of hair from her forehead, she moved into the kitchen.

Empty take-out containers littered the counter. Dirty dishes, some slimy with mold, filled the sink, and the smell of spoiled food hung in the air. She crinkled her nose as she dug in the cupboard for the instant coffee. There it was. Not much left, she made a mental note to order groceries. Maybe she'd clean the kitchen and take care of the laundry, too. Ava needed clean sheets and she was tired of rinsing her underwear in the sink. If she worked fast, she'd have plenty of time in her room before dinner. Not ideal but better than nothing. She filled the kettle with water, set it on a burner, and scrounged around for a couple of clean mugs.

While waiting for the water to boil, she made a grocery list, called it in, then started Ava's toast. The kettle whistled. The toast popped up. She grabbed the screaming kettle and poured. Water sloshed into the freshly rinsed mug and onto the counter. The thought of forcing herself to stay away from the room made her shake.

Concentrating on her task, she put the coffee and toast on a tray and walked through the living room of overstuffed furniture, doily covered tabletops, and an overabundance of knick-knacks. Underneath the lilac sachets lurked the dirty odor of mildew. Opposite the staircase, whose steps creaked under her feet as she started up them, was the door to her room. It beckoned from across the banister. She glanced over at it, wistful, then quickly continued before she caved.

A pictorial time-line of family history decorated the length of the hallway. She avoided looking at the photos as she passed them. Silly of her, but she imagined them talking and whispering about her, judging and blaming. Once past the gauntlet of family, Hannah exhaled and went through the door at the end of the hallway. A wave of heat enveloped her when she entered Ava's room.

Crust laden plates and glasses of scummy liquid sat on the part of the nightstand unoccupied by books. A TV and a couple of framed photos of her and Ava sat on a dresser. Inside were clothes that her sister would never wear again. A wicker chair stood in one corner. Hannah almost dropped the tray when she didn't see Ava lying on the bed. Then released a brief burst of relieved laughter when she realized Ava had wrapped the comforter around her so only her head stuck out. Really, where would Ava go? She wasn't able to walk.

Hannah set the tray on the chair and helped Ava into a sitting position. She arranged it on her lap and their eyes met. Soft blue to soft blue but Ava's were narrowed. Not a good sign.

"I heard you go into that room again," Ava said. Hannah started. "Don't look so surprised. I can still hear fine. That makes it, what, every day now since we moved in here. How many months is that? Six? Seven?"

A piece of lint on the sheet drew Hannah's attention and she picked at it. Her facial scars warmed as her face reddened. She wished she'd never told Ava about her room.

"Come on, help me out here. Is it six or seven?" Ava asked. Hannah's entire face now felt hot and she hunched her shoulders. "Thought as much."

Hannah sighed and stepped back, "Do you need anything else?"

"Turn up the heat. It's cold in here."

"How can you be cold? It feels like a sauna."

"You're warm because you can move around. I'm stuck in this bed all day long."

Hannah ran a hand through her long, yet sparse, hair. Bumps and valleys peaked and dipped beneath her disfigured fingers. *Not this again.* She looked up at the ceiling as if to draw strength from the cracked paint.

"If you'd let me take you downstairs or outside, you wouldn't be stuck in bed," Hannah said. Outside, now there was a scary thought. Hannah didn't know what she'd do if Ava actually agreed to go outside.

Ava snorted, "Like I'm going to sit in that ugly wheelchair and be gawked at like I'm some freak."

That was Ava, vain as ever. Everything was all about her, had been since they were children. Ava had been the head-cheerleader type who gadded about on their parent's dime while Hannah, the intellectual, toiled away in med school. And never mind the unfairness of Ava being lucky enough to keep her, their, perfect face intact. Granted, Hannah didn't want to go outside either but Ava didn't realize that, wheelchair or not, her beauty still held power. What Hannah wouldn't give to be able to walk outside without people cowering from her once they saw her face, her hands. A sour taste flooded Hannah's mouth.

"Fine, then, lay there for all I care." She stomped out.

"Come back," Ava said.

Hannah stopped. Maybe for once Ava really wanted Hannah to come back.

"If you don't come back and turn up the heat, I'll pinch myself. Hard."

"You wouldn't."

Hannah waited a minute. Nothing. A bluff, so she continued. Pain spiked across her forearm and dug into the muscle. Her breath hissed as she drew it in through clenched teeth. *Oh, that hurt.* The sharp pinching subsided then another spike jabbed the other arm. *Ouch, damn you.* It was pointless to deny Ava anything when she was in the frame of mind to use their connection. Shared physical pain, in Hannah's opinion, was a curse.

Defeated, Hannah went back into the room. Ava sat there, red marks on her arms and a satisfied smile on her face. Hannah turned up the thermostat, just a smidge.

"Happy now?" Hannah said as she left.

On her way back to the kitchen, Hannah paused in the living room. *Should I go into my room or finally clean up?* She shifted her weight from foot to foot while weighting the pros and cons then glanced into the kitchen. The heap of dishes in the sink really needed addressing but why was her hand on the doorknob to her secret room? Five minutes, that's all.

Her hand turned the knob, her heart sped up,

and anticipation fluttered in her stomach. Darkness hid the cobwebs that coated the corners and dripped from the ceiling. Her sock-clad feet whispered on the hardwood floor. Except for a scruffy kitchen chair and a small telephone table, the room was barren, the air dry. She stood before the heavy brocade drapes that hid the picture window. It was time.

Breath quickening, she gripped the edges of the drapes. Dust puffed into the air. A light sweat spread across her skin. Inch by inch she pulled them open, savoring the moment. Sunlight slowly stole into the room, caught the dust motes, and dissolved the webs. Hannah let out an excited breath and sat down.

The room used to be a den where the girls slept on a sofa bed whenever their parents brought them to see their Grandma. Farmlands used to cover the area surrounding the house, but over time, a small subdivision replaced the farms. This house was one of the last original homes. When their Grandma passed away, she willed it to the girls and they'd lived there ever since.

Across the street a cluster of shops, a restaurant, and a few professional offices replaced the field where Hannah and Ava had once picked wildflowers. Cars passed by at intermittent intervals, and people, perfect and unflawed, wandered the sidewalk. Her hand unconsciously went to the scars on her face. *If only.* As she watched the outside world, she rubbed the familiar knots of tissue.

Sun shone on the hair of a stunning blonde woman. A satchel hung from one slender shoulder as she walked, head high and shoulders back, to some unknown destination. Hannah imagined the woman was an accountant. She was on her way to meet her fiancé for lunch. They'd talk about the wedding, how many children they'd have, and which private schools their kids would attend. Everything was perfect and everyone was happy, loved, and normal.

The woman passed out of Hannah's sight but here came a gorgeous brunette with a lovely young girl in tow. The girl, her daughter, adored her mom for taking her out of school to shoe shop. Happy, she skipped along and chattered about her teacher, her friends, and her kitten. Soon Hannah lost sight of them too, but more beautiful people waited in the wings to parade through her private little show, her gateway to the outside world.

The doorbell rang. She jolted from her chair. No one ever stopped here. Then it bing-bonged again. Hannah bounced heel to toe, heel to toe. *Go away, no one's home.* Whoever it was leaned on the bell then knocked. She went to the window and pressed her cheek to the glass. A young man in a delivery uniform stood on the stoop, bags crowded around his feet. *Oh right, the grocery order.*

"I'm coming!" she yelled as she scrambled into the kitchen to grab the cash she'd set out and put on the glove she used to hide her hand.

Hannah opened the front door just enough to slide her hand through and give the boy the money.

"Let me bring these in for you, ma'am," the boy said. "It's no trouble."

"I'd prefer if you left them on the stoop."

"That's all right, I don't mind taking them in. It's kinda my job."

"Seriously, just leave them there. I can bring them in myself."

She heard him sigh, "If you're sure…" She didn't reply. "Okay, then. Have a good day."

There was a rustle of bags, then the creak of a porch step as the boy walked away. Hannah waited a couple of beats before she opened the door. The boy was almost at the end of the walkway when he turned around. She froze.

"You gave me way too…" His words faltered when he saw Hannah. "Much. You gave me way too much." He licked his lips and didn't come any closer.

She felt his gaze as it lingered on her scars. Revulsion and fascination warred across his face. It tore at her heart. Muscles refused to unlock and let her dart into the safety of the house. It had been too long since someone had seen her.

"It's okay, that's your tip," she said. Still staring, the boy didn't move. Hannah clenched her jaw. "Go on, get a good look at the ugly freak."

The boy cleared his throat. "Have you ever thought of a mask?"

That did it, the tension flooded from her muscles. She backed into the house, slammed the door, and leaned against it. Her heart hammered while tears slid down her cheeks in shame. Stupid of her to be upset, really, what had she expected, that she'd be welcomed back into the world with open arms? She brushed the tears away as she gathered the courage to open the door. The boy was gone.

Quickly, she retrieved the groceries and took them into the kitchen where she put away the perishable items. The rest would keep. After that little incident, she needed her room, needed to lose herself. That stupid, fucking kid. A mask, really? She imagined herself walking down the street in a Halloween mask or a balaclava even. Maybe she'd get one of those *Phantom of the Opera* ones. No, a mask was not an option.

Hannah stood in front of the picture window. The glass cooled her heated palms as she pressed them to it. Little smudges of fog outlined her hands and fingers like a used up aura. The late afternoon had brought a rush of people onto the sidewalk, mostly parents with children. Eager, she left the window, sat in the chair, and scanned the crowd. A stab pierced the webbing between her thumb and index finger. Ava, again. Lovely. Now she was stooping so low as to use their connection to get Hannah's attention. At least Ava had to endure the pain too. Knowing it would be futile to ignore her, Hannah shut the drapes, then went to see what Ava wanted now.

Ava sat propped on her pillows, a book in hand. A talk show, volume set low, flickered across the TV screen. Ava, an innocent expression on her face, looked up at Hannah.

"What do you want now?" Hannah asked.

Ava set down her book. "I need to pee."

Hannah bent down and retrieved the bedpan from under the bed. The cold metal made her shiver involuntarily as she slid it under the covers and got it settled under Ava. Nothing to do now but wait.

"It's too cold," Ava said. "I can't go."

"Don't play this game with me."

"It's not a game." Ava crossed her arms and glared at Hannah, who glared back. The minutes spun by then Ava broke eye contact. "I hate this."

Hannah tried to read her twin but wasn't able to figure out the shifting emotions that flashed across her face.

"I know. So do I," Hannah said.

"What's happened to us?"

"I don't know. I miss how close we used to be. Don't you?"

Silence.

A tear crawled down Ava's cheek. "This is all your fault."

Guilt squeezed Hannah's ribs until her breath hitched. Ava was right. Hannah was the reason her parents, after the death of the girls' Grandma, made sure they lived in the house they'd inherited instead of selling it. The reason they sent money once a month in exchange for the girls never returning to the world of country clubs and high-society they'd grown up in. The reason why Ava needed the wheelchair. The shame spread, forced its way into Hannah's throat. She choked it back.

"You can't imagine how sorry I am," Hannah said. "If I could go back in time, things wouldn't be this way, but I can't. Can't we start all over?"

Hannah walked over to the dresser and picked up an old picture. It was covered in dust but she showed it to Ava.

"Remember this?" Hannah said. She turned it back toward herself and studied the two of them. It'd been taken on prom night. They had their arms wrapped around each other, their eyes dancing with excitement, and carbon copy smiles gracing their pretty faces. "Remember how we used to be?"

"I don't want to remember. I don't want to start over," Ava said. "Just get out."

Stung, Hannah put the picture down, "Don't be like this. We can work things out. Maybe leave this damn house, together."

"I said get out."

"Ava…"

Ava reached a hand under the covers and brought it back out with the bedpan. *What's she up to now?*

"Get out!" Ava yelled then hurled the oval metal object at Hannah.

The clang of the bedpan when it hit the dresser and clattered to the floor rang in Hannah's ears as she dashed out.

~~~~

Thick, acrid smoke poured into Hannah's lungs. Dry, so dry, and hot; she choked on it. It stung her eyes until tears surged and spilled down her cheeks. The fire's heat baked her skin, cracked and blistered it. She tried to move, but she was pinned. Arms thrashed as she struggled to free herself. A scream made its way up her smoke clogged throat and jolted her awake.

Heart pounding, she untangled her legs from the sweat damp sheets and jumped out of bed. The scent of burning things still lingering in her nostrils, she turned this way and that searching for its source. Weak moonlight filtered into the room and bathed her dresser and bookcase in its silver glow. No smoke, no fire.

Shaking, she went to the window and opened the sheers. The meager backyard, blanketed with weeds and little else, looked monochromatic in the anemic glow. She pressed her forehead against the glass but the empty scene wouldn't banish the dream images. Maybe her room would.

Hannah went into the hallway. All quiet, her nightmare hadn't disturbed Ava, but she tiptoed into Ava's room anyway. In the dim light, the bed looked empty. Panic seized her and she remembered the last time Ava had fallen out of bed. Hannah rushed to the other side of the bed. *Please, please, be there. And please be okay.* She rounded the end of the bed. No Ava. A rustling filled the room and Hannah froze. It came from under the blankets. Slowly, she turned, eyes half shut against the fear of what she might see. Knuckles rapped against the wall as Ava flung an arm above her head and mumbled. Hannah looked at the empty space on the floor then the bed, and, relieved and a bit confused, she backed out into the hallway. She cast one last look at Ava's door before she continued downstairs.

The room's silence descended on her, weighted her down, as she stood in front of the drapes. She hadn't been here this late before. Where was the anticipation this moment, right before she pulled open the drapes, usually brought? Where was the tingle along her nerves, the heightened awareness? She paused, waited for the familiar rush that failed to appear. Maybe the late hour dulled her or maybe the lingering nightmare. Whatever it was, she didn't like it and yanked the curtains open instead of letting it deter her.

The sodium lamps painted the world orange and black and glinted off the windshields of cars parked along the street. Hannah sat and waited. No one walked down the sidewalk, no vehicles rushed to late night destinations. This was the perfect time to go outside, to feel the breeze on her face, and to feel normal. *No, what if someone came along? They'd see me.* But there wasn't a soul around. Should she? She started to rise then sat again. In her lap, she wrung her scarred hands. What was she thinking? Outside wasn't a viable choice anymore. All because of a frying pan left on a burner she'd forgotten to turn off.

Hannah had been tired, had been in the middle of studying for her final exams before starting her residency, and had fallen asleep at the kitchen table. The first tendrils of smoke had invaded Hannah's lungs and choked her awake. Blinded by stinging tears and burning lungs, Hannah had tried to put out the flames, but they'd already leapt to the grease stained wall behind the stove. She had started to run for the door when her spine spasmed like it was being ripped from her. It felt like a small explosion went off inside of her head. Her legs had given out and her cheek crunched as she hit the linoleum. She passed out.

Ava had been driving home from a party as the fire was awakening Hannah. The road was narrow, the ravine deep. The doctors said Ava, when she awoke, would never walk again. They said that Hannah was fortunate to be alive but they couldn't do anything about the scars she'd have. Hannah remembered the pain from the impact of Ava's accident. Ava claimed to remember nothing except a sudden coughing fit followed by the sensation of her eyes being gouged out.

If only Hannah hadn't been so tired, things would be different. They'd still be whole and Ava would still be…she'd still be, what? *Ava, she'd still be Ava.* Memories of sitting by Ava's bedside waiting for her to wake up played in Hannah's mind. Quickly, she shunted them aside. Even after all this time, the memories were too raw and painful to be examined.

Hannah looked out the window at the sidewalk still devoid of people, then at her scarred hands. Enough of this watching and wishing; life wasn't going to come to her. She'd have to go find it. The best way to start would be to give up her room, clean the

place, and, when she was ready, maybe invite a few of her old friends over. Little steps, little things to lead her back. Those ideas firmly fixed in her mind, she closed the drapes.

~~~~

Determined that today would be the day she cleaned, Hannah strode into Ava's room. Her heart froze for a beat when she remembered the image of the empty bed, but Ava sat staring at the TV. She looked over when Hannah walked in. Hannah tossed the clean sheets onto the chair.

"Sheet day," she said.

"I don't think so," Ava said.

Cranky from lack of sleep and not wanting a fight, Hannah ignored Ava and stripped the comforter and top sheet off the bed. At the sight of Ava's exposed legs, thin, pale, and lifeless, she subtly recoiled. A jab of guilt punched her in the side like a cramp. Ava shot her a look.

"Don't bother," Ava said. She gripped the sides of the mattress. "I'm not helping you."

"I'm going to do this whether you help or not." She lifted Ava's legs. Bedsores rose red and angry across the backs of them. The guilt wrapped around her torso. "Ava, you're going to have to lay on your side for a bit."

"Piss off, sister-dear. The sheets can rot for all I care."

"It's not the sheets. You have bedsores. Again."

Ava glowered at her. Hannah averted her gaze.

The anger and pain evident on Ava's face reflected Hannah's own torment back at her. Empathy rose to the surface. She ran her fingers through Ava's thick hair like she'd done when they were kids and Ava needed comforting. The blonde strands flowed over Hannah's twisted fingers as she tried to alleviate Ava's suffering. Ava jerked her head back.

"Don't touch me," she said, her voice low and the words almost a growl. Stunned, Hannah yanked her hand away. "I wish I'd never been born a twin." Then Ava laughed. It sounded cruel and mocking.

The words struck deep within Hannah but the laughter was worse. It brought forth all the insecurities Hannah felt, insecurities that she and Ava, in their own ways, shared. She hadn't felt so alone then, but now Ava didn't even want to be her twin. Unbearable. Sheets abandoned, Hannah ran from the room.

"That's right, run away." Ava's voice followed her. "Run to that room of yours. Dream your twisted coward's dreams."

Don't listen to her, block her out. But Ava's harsh words echoed through Hannah's mind. They twisted her guts until it felt like she might puke. Swallowing bile, she burst into her room. Forget her oath from the night before; she needed to be here. She took a few deep breaths and the nausea receded. Not stopping to savor that special moment before the curtains parted, she yanked them open and sat.

A smiling redhead walked into view. Hannah watched her. She was a doctor on her way back from coffee with her mom. They'd had a good mother-daughter bonding session, they cried a little and laughed a lot. She stopped in the middle of the sidewalk, knelt to pick up a penny, her lucky day, and burst into flame. Her screams, high and sharp, reverberated as she tried to beat out the conflagration. No one stopped to help. The flames engulfed her head and became indistinguishable from the red hair that curled and fizzled. They traveled to her face, arms, and hands leaving blisters that popped and turned black in their wake. Hannah jumped up and pressed her hands to the window as if the act would douse the fire. The woman was a pyre of flame. Without thought, Hannah ran from the room and out the front door. The urgent need to save the woman beat in time to her heart.

The heat of the day embraced her as cherry blossoms blew past trailing their soft sent behind them. She ran down the walkway and sprinted across the road. Instinct born of her medical training took over, and she pushed the burning woman to the ground. Using her body as a blanket, she attempted to smother the flames but the woman squirmed, kicked, punched, and yelled at her. Hannah blinked. The fire was gone.

"Get off me you crazy freak!" the woman yelled.

Hannah rolled away, confused. What happened to the flames? The woman stood, brushed the dirt from her skirt then looked at Hannah, her lips parted as if to chasten her. The woman's eyes widened. People started to crowd around. Hannah felt their stares, heard their whispers. The voice of a child, accusing her parent of lying—the boogeyman did exist—carried through the air. Humiliated, Hannah got up and bolted. The screech of tires and a car horn followed her as she ran across the road, back into the house, and the safety of *her* room.

Nervous sweat coated her skin and her breath came in ragged gulps. What possessed her to go outside? She went to the window. A knot of people stood facing the house, talking and pointing. She shut them out. They only confirmed what she already knew. She didn't belong with them anymore and to try to fit in would result in disaster. She kicked and connected with the chair. It clattered across the room as she let out a scream powered by rage and frustration. She picked up the chair, smashed it into the telephone table, cracking it in half, and slammed the chair into the floor. *Trapped, trapped, trapped.* A low moan rumbled out of her. What was the point? She'd never be able to leave the house. Or would she? The words of the delivery boy floated across her mind.

In her bedroom, she went to the bookshelf. On it sat a case. Inside nestled the scalpel her father gave her when she told him she wanted to be a surgeon. She lifted the lid and gently liberated the scalpel from its bed of velvet. Sunlight shimmied across the cutting edge. A bead of blood welled on the pad of her thumb as she tested the blade's sharpness. Perfect. She slid it into her pocket.

"What was all that racket about?" Ava asked as Hannah entered the room.

"I tripped over a chair. Nothing to worry about."

Ava studied her like she was looking for a lie and, not seeing one, said, "I hope you haven't come back to change the sheets. Not going to happen."

Stubborn Ava with her perfect face. A face that used to be Hannah's too and would be again. It'd be too easy. Hannah would pin, with her knees, Ava's arms to the bed and, slice, slice, slice, the perfect mask. She'd be able to walk outside again without having to bear the looks of horror.

Hannah pulled the scalpel from her pocket.

Ava's eyes widened. "What's going on?"

"Don't worry, Ava, this won't hurt us for long." And the pain would be worth it.

Before Ava had the chance to squirm away, Hannah swung herself onto the bed. Her knees met empty air, then the sheets, but she didn't notice. She made the first cut.

The scalpel skittered across an unyielding surface. Hannah's own scarred visage looked back at her from the mirror propped on the pillow. She screamed. Dots swarmed across her vision as a black bubble rose in her mind and popped, spewing the ichor of truth.

The bleeps of a heart monitor, and swoosh of a ventilator, filled the hospital room of her memory. Antiseptic, sharp and pungent, had permeated the room. Hannah remembered sitting in a chair beside Ava's hospital bed, remembered willing her to wake up. But while she'd held sentry, Ava slipped past her coma and into death.

Then had come a day of rain, and black umbrellas had kept the mourners dry during the graveside service. Umbrellaless, Hannah had stood on the fringe, the tears running down her still raw cheeks, invisible in the downpour.

"Ashes to ashes. Dust to dust," the pastor had said, and then Hannah reached down and picked up a handful of cold mud, dropping it onto the casket where it landed with a splat. Alone, Hannah had walked away from the gravesite. How she'd wished Ava was there to walk beside her.

"No!" Hannah came back to the present yelling at her image in the mirror. She jumped off the bed. "Ava is not dead. She's not!" Hannah picked up the scalpel and tossed it across the room. "I'm sorry, Ava. I wasn't really going to hurt you. Please forgive me? Please?"

Ava didn't answer. Hannah readjusted the mirror, remade the bed, and then Ava was there smoothing down her rumpled nightgown. The sight of her brought relief. Hannah wasn't alone anymore.

"I'm sorry," Hannah said. "Forgive me?"

"Only if you eat up here with me tonight," Ava said. "I don't feel like being alone. Chinese sound good?"

Hannah, lipless and scarred, smiled. "Yes, I'd like that."

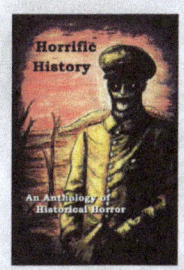

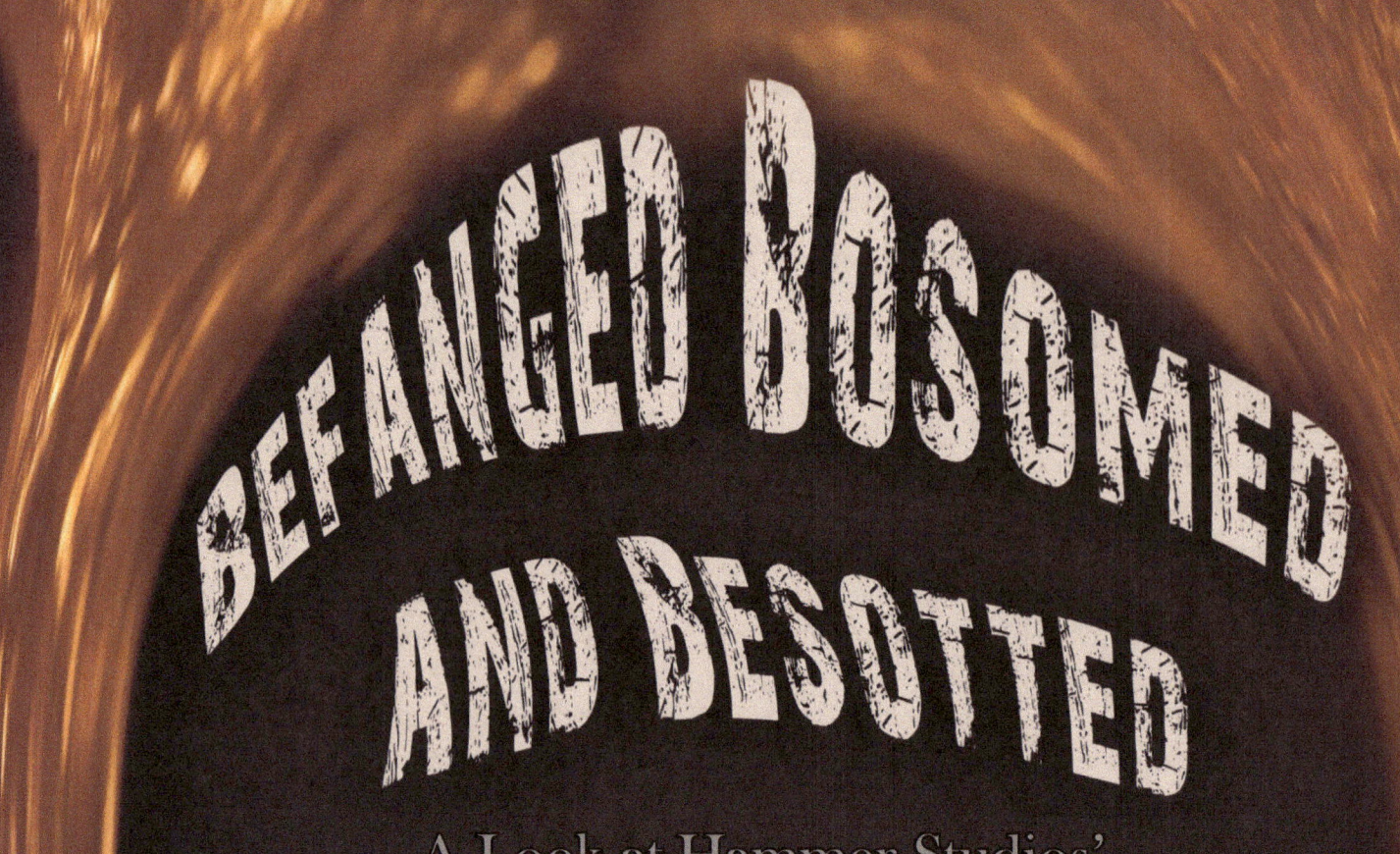

Befanged Bosomed and Besotted

A Look at Hammer Studios' Karnstein Trilogy

By
Jim Smiley

As penned by author J. Sheridan LeFanu, the fictional village of Karnstein in Austria was left depopulated by revenants, who continued to feed on the local townspeople in the surrounding area. These revenants were the specters of the Karnstein family, who returned after death to plague the living.

Intrigued? Hammer Studios certainly was, and they made a succession of three movies from 1970-71, all loosely based on LeFanu's "Carmilla." All of the screenplays were written by Tudor Gates, and every film had a different director, possibly leading to unintended changes in the texture of the movies. In terms of chronology, the last one released would be considered a prequel today, as it features the last living descendant of the Karnsteins, the Baron Karnstein.

THE VAMPIRE LOVERS (1970) BLU-RAY

Director: Roy Ward Baker
Starring: Ingrid Pitt, Peter Cushing,
Madeleine Smith.

The Vampire Lovers can be considered the best of the trilogy. This is the only one of the trilogy in which the undead countess, Carmilla, appears in most of the movie. In this movie, Carmilla appears to still have human weaknesses. She is dependent upon her unwilling donors for love, as much as for blood. To this end, she engineers an invitation to homes with pretty young women. Once in place, she starts to batten upon them. Her conquests are total: Love, blood and sex. At first, it is General von Spielsdorf's (Cushing's) daughter Laura. Laura, of course, expires, as Mircalla (Carmilla as she is known here) disappears. Exit Laura, and enter Emma Morton (Madeleine Smith). Toward the climax of the movie, Carmilla tries to escape with Emma. Once again, Carmilla has shown humanity, albeit of a twisted

variety. She is lonely, but the only way she can allay that is to take more victims, or make her victims into beings like her. Though Carmilla comes from a bad family, it is never made apparent if her evil is the product of her personality, or was forced upon her by the vampiric state. This film is easily the most polished of the trilogy, and at the time of its production no sequel was publically mentioned.

The Karnstein Trilogy can be remembered best for four things: female beauty, a questioning of existing mores, a return to a classical form of vampirism, and the advent of women as strong members of the cast. In none of the three films are there any women who are not lovely. Not only does this bring in young male moviegoers, it makes the man in us question. Even if it means my soul, can I strike down this beautiful young woman? This brings us to the next point, the questioning of mores. Carmilla is lesbian, but is that itself intrinsically evil? Or is the evil that she uses her beauty to lure both men and women to their doom?

It's interesting to note that the source of these films, "Carmilla," was written in 1871, some twenty-six years before the publication of *Dracula*. Before the release of the Karnstein Trilogy, "Carmilla" was largely forgotten, and most movie audiences got their vampire information from Dracula-themed works. "Carmilla" made lavish use of older conventions, where vampires can be destroyed by decapitation and inhabit old, decrepit castles and churchyards. They simply don't arrive at the opera in a tuxedo. Carmilla herself is out in the sun at times.

Ingrid Pitt's Carmilla commands almost every scene she is in. She seduces young women, a governess, feeds on who she will, and turns the inhabitants of a house against each other. Most of the men in the trilogy are brutal, vicious or stupid, and sometimes all three. Granted, the Countess is hundreds of years old and infernally clever, but the men have little to do but look confused. Even General Spielsdorf takes the word of Mircalla when his niece has been attacked. Carmilla changed the home dynamic into a matriarchy, and this might have upset conventional society more than the lesbian themes.

LUST FOR A VAMPIRE (1971), DVD

Director: Jimmy Sangster
Starring: Ralph Bates, Yutte Stensgaard,
Michael Johnson

Widely considered to be the least of the Karnstein Trilogy, *Lust for a Vampire* takes place some forty years after the last incidents of vampirism around Karnstein Castle. A traveling novelist (Michael Johnson) derides such talk, and investigates the castle. He finds something more horrific than vampires: privileged young ladies from a nearby girls' school. After some conniving, he is installed as a teacher at the school. One of the girls is new, and holds a certain hypnotic power over him. As well she might, being that her name is Mircalla. Girls begin to go missing. This is a standard plot device in such tales. Also, there must be a human turncoat, to act as the vampire's bodyguard. Mircalla finds such in the teacher, Giles (Ralph Bates).

Bad judgment is not a one way street in Styria, however. Mircalla finds herself having feelings for Johnson, and he seduces her in a graveyard. This is the only real objection I have to this movie: Sleep with a hot blonde vampire? Fine. Just don't inflict a horrible pop song on the audience. Please? In all fairness to Jimmy Sangster and his people, the execs from Hammer and the Rank Organisation threw the song in before letting even the director view it, and then would not consent to removing it.

In all, the movie has a studied, almost slow pace that contributes to a feeling of menace. There is no commanding presence of a Dracula here; it is the confused feeding of a recently risen vampire, who doesn't seem to know what she is. This serves to make Mircalla more a sympathetic character.

There is a feeling of disjointedness about the production, however, and the reason why only became apparent after some research: Sangster and the production crew were not involved in the editing of the film, either initial or final. In the final analysis, if one had to do without one installment of the Karnstein Trilogy, this would be it.

TWINS OF EVIL (1971), BLU-RAY

Director: John Hough
Starring: Peter Cushing, Mary and Madeleine Collinson, Damien Thomas

This movie participates in a bit of ethical reversal. The Church, in the guise of Peter Cushing's Gustav Weil (read it as 'vile'), is scouring the countryside for the witches who drain the blood from men's necks. In fact, Peter Cushing's hunting is so profligate that he would only kill more people when he destroyed Alderaan. He takes victims in order to save their souls. In fact, his ham-handed effort at disciplining his two nieces drives one of them into the waiting arms of Damien Thomas's Baron Karnstein.

Let us consider the Baron Karnstein. Last living descendant of a corroded aristocracy, he pines for the ability to directly serve Satan. After offering a suitably nubile human sacrifice, he gets his wish, and is turned Undead by his ancestor, Mircalla. Not one to waste a chance, the Baron grants Frieda fangs of her own. Frieda wastes no time in proving her worth by draining the Baron's wench.

Of the trilogy, the standard marriage relationship is only seen in this one. Gustav Weil's wife is downtrodden, and we feel an urge to hand her an axe when she finally has had enough of her husband abusing the nieces. Further, if Weil and his Brotherhood are the face of good, then where is the motivation to be 'good?' If one is to be condemned anyway, then why not follow 'evil?' If one follows the dictum that harm is bad, then Weil is a worse threat in both real and existential terms. After all, the Baron Karnstein is just being honest in doing what he wants, without pretense or apology.

Without completely ruining the movie, it is typical Hammer fare, with great sets and decent acting. The departure is in the unspoken question: Was the village better off with the Church, who was indiscriminately burning young village girls, or the vampire, who didn't victimize nearly as many? Is religious devotion best measured in pain? In all, a very pleasing change from many vampire films of the era, in which the Church was treated as infallible.

✹✹✹

LEAH JUNG: AN

Photo Courtesy of Christopher Vernale

Photo Courtesy of Christopher Vernale

INDUSTRY AND A CANVAS

By Joel B. Kirkpatrick

GRACING THE COVERS of twenty-six tattoo magazines, ad pages in thirty-eight print publications, a featured columnist in half a dozen magazines, a featured subject in numerous art galleries and art productions—our guest Leah Jung is also an actress, a singer/songwriter/producer, a model, and a legislative law editor.

Yes, that last item is correct.

Known equally for her stunning looks and the amazing art she wears on her very skin, Ms. Jung may be one of modern culture's best examples of "find your dream and live it." For some celebrities, this type of life is a literal bonfire—it roasts them alive. To more than survive it (to actually own it) is an achievement that elevates our guest to a level that some celebrities can only dream of. It is thriving in the smoke without perishing in the flames.

Joel B. Kirkpatrick: Let's begin with this: What's a nice girl like you doing in a magazine like this? Do you sometimes find yourself to be a victim of stereotypes? But, you really are about *erasing* clichés, aren't you?

Leah Jung (Favorite Nickname - *Leah my Love*): I am a sweet girl but not exactly wholesome and virginal. I love outrageous horror movies. I always have. I have a long interest in creepy, bizarre, R-rated things. Monsters, serial killers, and corpses—both re-

JBK: Who are your tattoo artists, and how do you and your artists arrive at the designs you so famously wear?

LmL: I have been tattooed by almost twenty artists all over the country! Most recently, Eric Brown from Impulse Tattoo in New York, and also Carl Grace from Seven Tattoo in Las Vegas. Usually I explain a specific idea and they draw it up for me, then we discuss the drawing before finalizing it. A couple of my tattoos are original drawings that I picked from the artist's sketch book. One tattoo I have is a simple stencil that matches one my best friend has.

JBK: We've learned that you once worked with a handful of tattoo artists, asking them to create designs of you in their artwork. We recently found one of them by Nick Whybrow and wondered what project you had planned for those designs?

LmL: I planned to have a collaborative "flash sheet" made of tattoo-able drawings of me. Flash sheets are displayed in tattoo studios on the walls or in books. Customers browse through these pictures to choose a tattoo or to get ideas. I was going to sell these sheets and donate the profits, but the featured artist, who really would have been the name that drove sales, dropped the ball after a drawn-out correspondence. It would have been a unique promotion for me and the artists. I am sad it didn't work out.

tattooed on me. One of them is vomiting blood. I swear way too much. Other than that, I am a nice girl. No criminal record, highly employable. I don't like fighting, drugs, or bullying.

JBK: How much of the intro did I get wrong? There were so many things to list, I probably left out quite a few.

LmL: I have actually been on about twenty-five tattoo magazine covers, four other types of magazine covers, two book covers, a few calendar covers, and I have three additional covers pending that may be released before this publishes. The ad page amount I cannot confirm or deny. I have had over a hundred photos published inside magazines, including editorials, features, event coverage, and advertisements. I have columns in three magazines. Another interesting fact: my Evian commercial is the most-viewed ad on the Internet in the WORLD for this year so far.

JBK: What is the significance of the Chinese lantern beneath your right arm? There is a person inside the lantern, and I would describe that design as a genie in a bottle trying to get out.

LmL: Yes, it is a little man in a lantern! He is Ebisu, the Japanese God of fishing and fortune. It represents being self-sufficient to truly reap the benefits life can offer you. Plus, at the time, I had recently started fishing and found it enjoyable and rewarding.

JBK: Do you still edit law documents for the New York Legislature? Most of our readers might imagine it too boring a job, for even a week. But what about it has satisfied you for more than five years?

LmL: I worked for the NY Legislature for over six years! I did not like it all. It is deeply boring to read law verbiage all day, but I was really good at it and it paid my bills while I invested in my other avocations. I quit at the end of last year, and now work as a model and at a tattoo studio.

JBK: Were you lucky enough to be editing documents that matched your own political opinion, or have you been faced with work that really rubbed your ideology the wrong way?

LmL: I read almost every bill that was drafted and every law that was passed in New York State. I was warned during my initial job interview that I would be required to read laws that made me uncomfortable and could not speak up about my personal opinions—"even things about molesting children," the HR rep told me.

JBK: In your music video for Heartless we believe we hear you singing the refrain, "I haven't got the time…" Those words sound blatantly biographical in the context of your public exposure. Are you working a normal job and going to school part-time in an effort to keep your celebrity fame from eating you alive? How do you balance the Performing Leah with the Normal Leah?

LmL: Biographical, yes. All my songs are inspired by my actual experiences. Sometimes if I re-visit lyrics after a period of time, certain lines in the same song are about two different scenarios. So, for the song Heartless in particular, someone I tried to date was not nearly as important or exciting as the other things going on in my life. I just did not have the time. Actually, I could say this about several people.

Photo Courtesy of Maze Photography

I work a normal job, kind of. I am regularly working at a tattoo studio for an artist named LaloYunda, who was in a half-dozen episodes of a successful TV show called Ink Master. I'll also work or audition as some kind of personality for something every week. I'll visit at least ten cities around the world before the year is over. It all seems rather normal to me.

JBK: You call yourself "monumentally jaded." Is that a natural defense now? What would you say to someone who gushed that you must be living the most perfect life?

LmL: For half my life I was awkward, introverted and emotional, and had my heart deceived an unimaginable amount of times. Now friends and strangers tell me how pretty I am (or the occasional "disgusting" from people who hate tattoos) in various poetic ways, a hundred times a day. To be stepped on and then put on a pedestal simply because I became more visually appealing makes me very numb to people's supposed feelings toward me. I hope I'll get over that eventually.

JBK: What is it like to browse the literally hundreds of images of yourself on the internet? Is it ever surreal to you?

LmL: *Thousands* of images. I mostly feel insanely honored. It feels real, it has incorporated itself into my reality at a rate that felt like a sincere progression. I definitely do not feel famous; maybe headed in that direction if I take those opportunities, but not quite. Depends on who you ask. A fan did recently get my autograph tattooed on his forearm; that guy definitely thinks I'm famous.

JBK: "Drink from this cold, heartless, cup of love" — your song lyrics from Heartless. Is that fame?

LmL: No, not at all. I don't think of myself as famous, so I certainly wouldn't write a song about it. "Cold and heartless" would typically reference a person. I needed the idea of love to be much more lifeless, yet still offer something that gives life. A cup of water came to mind.

JBK: Tattooing and Piercing Magazine has called you a singer who "…could take R&B to another level, without even having to make an effort…" What keeps you from making music your main focus?

LmL: They also called me the next Amy Winehouse. Come on now, not a chance, no way in hell. I'm sure they were just being nice. Besides my obvious lack of certainty about the appeal of my music… the main reason is that the magazines and clothing companies write to me much more often than the music producers. I am three songs into a partially self-produced EP that is going well.

JBK: Some of today's music stars have the misfortune of sounding just like everyone else being recorded. That certainly cannot be said of your voice, your style, or your lyrics. Who have been your influences?

Photo Courtesy of Sergio Royzen

LmL: Vocally: Fiona Apple, Jewel, Sarah Vaughn, Nina Simone. I have enjoyed many different genres. I like a lot of Scandinavian power metal, 80's music, female fronted dance-rock, and hip-hop to name a few.

JBK: This era of entertainment seems to create a new show for television (and new celebrity) every day. We know you love to travel, love to eat, are impossibly well read, are instantly recognizable and shockingly down to earth. Why don't you have three cable shows in the works already?

LmL: Hmm, I'm not sure. I come across extremely practical and humanized when handling high pressure situations, so I must certainly be a ticking time-bomb of celebrity meltdown and scandal. They have got to be ready to get this shit on video.

JBK: Have you been invited to do the voiceover for any audio books? (We learned recently that you would love to do that). Please be aware, answering this honestly might open the gates to a flood of such invitations…

LmL: I would really love to do that! I like reading and acting and... I wish I had a sarcastic joke about being a vain girl who likes the sound of her own voice.

JBK: Stephen King has said that he loves *Dark Discoveries* magazine, so he might call you up and ask you to record the audio for one of his books. Would you do it, and do you even like to read scary books?

LmL: Don't tease me like that. What a dream!

JBK: Let's talk books. What is your favorite read, if not still *Batavia's Graveyard*? (A monstrous, excellent story.) Do you keep several books going at once, or can you only read them one at a time?

LmL: Mmmm, *Batavia's Graveyard*: a narrative non-fiction about a mutiny. I like nautical history. And morbid history. I also really like shocking, smart stories like Chuck Palahniuk. Other favorites: *House of Leaves, Lord of the Flies, American Psycho, Lord of the Rings, Running with Scissors*. I am usually reading one book at a time; currently: *The Story of a Shipwrecked Sailor*.

JBK: Your most prominent skin design is a pirates skull and flintlock pistols. Is there a subliminal connection there between that design and your once-favorite book?

Photo Courtesy of Sergio Royzen

LmL: Yes, I read that book twice not long before I got that tattoo.

JBK: Which of these statements is most true: You studied classical dance for years. Or: You have an insanely natural talent to just wiggle and make it look professional.

LmL: Totally the second one. The wiggling is hit or miss though. Sometimes I really impress myself, sometimes the song ends and then I wince helplessly when I notice the curtains are open and someone may have actually witnessed that career-ruining embarrassment.

JBK: What is a normal day like for you? Does it take a small army to schedule your different appearances and activities? Are you a "handled" person?

LmL: I do everything by myself. I answer emails at red lights and eat standing up.

JBK: Modern tattoo art is not entirely the personal expression that most people claim, when you really consider the art itself. It is the artist's skill and desire that is being worn, and often only the suggested design of the wearer. In other words, you know what you want—but you get what you get. Which ink design was your first? How did that first session of ink turn into the love affair that you have now with body art?

LmL: Just like with any decoration, interior design for example, the furniture and fabrics being used were created by other people, but they still express a well-thought individual expression. Each room one of a kind. You have to respect the great tattoo artists of our time, because they really do bring our visions to life in a way we never thought possible. But you must also admire the wearer for their passionate decision. My first tattoo was a small black and purple sun between my shoulder blades. I really just believed it made me more beautiful. Then people start asking you about your tattoo, and you ask about theirs, and you look up "tattoos" online. The amount of resources are vast. I just love tattoos.

JBK: Do you have an ink design that you want to wear, but have not done yet?

LmL: I am collaborating with an artist named Chad Newsom to tweak a sketch he did that will eventually be tattooed on my knee—of H.H Holmes. I am also part way through my back piece, which is being done by Carl Grace. It will be a depiction of the Greek Mythological tale of The Sirens; some people call them Harpies.

JBK: What is your strongest desire that has not already become a part of your public persona? Are there secret parts of Leah Jung that the public cannot have, regardless their offered price?

LmL: My strongest desire is very public, because it involves an industry that requires me to put my supposed skill out into the public eye. I want to sing for audiences all over the world. Other than things entertainment related, I try to remain very private.

No one online knows that I have a boyfriend, that I am about to be an aunt for the first time, or the last time I was hungover. Maybe someday I will have to give up the luxury of privacy, but not yet.

JBK: Are there performance requests that you have not, and will not grant? What has remained your most outrageous project?

LmL: I don't like to do anything that's in-your-face sexual unless it is tasteful and passionate and extremely professional. I will never be bent over sticking my tongue out in a hotel room...well, not in front of a camera anyway, and certainly not for work. My nipples are not on the internet as far as I know. So, most of my "outrageous" photo-shoot stories are pretty anti-climactic tales involving abandoned buildings, below freezing temperatures, and biohazard risks. One time, Mae Richards and I thought we found a dead body in a swamp but we poked it a lot and found out it was just garbage wrapped in a tent.

JBK: Where is your favorite place to be completely quiet and still?

LmL: On my bed before I fall asleep, or on my floor stretching. I'm also quiet and still when I am on the subway, but that is not my favorite place to be.

JBK: Suddenly, you have a slow month (impossible— we know). You realize that you will be completely left alone to write. Do you have any urges to write a novel, and what would that be about? Or, if given this magical month, are you going to run to every amusement park that you can reach in thirty days?

LmL: I would visit one amusement park and three museums. At least five dinners with neglected friends. One trip, TBD. I would definitely write. Even if I just jot down short stories that I can later refine and compile into a cohesive novel. Likely something loosely based on my own experiences. I would spend a lot of time writing and recording songs.

JBK: Why is your favorite meal, one that someone else cooks for you?

LmL: Haha, I can only cook about five things myself. I am not much of a cook. But I love food. I am not a picky eater at all. I love trying new things. My all-time favorite is my Nani's Thanksgiving dinner. Oh my god, I die. She is my last surviving grandparent, but unfortunately, she is no longer able to cook.

JBK: You could totally whack a zombie to pieces without getting all girly about it, couldn't you? (This is the place where you get to tell the producers of *Walking Dead* that you want in the show.)

LmL: Fuck. Yes. Stone. Cold.

JBK: It is cliché to say, "The camera just loves her." But that truly is you, without the hyperbole. However, if anyone wanted to glimpse the shy side of Leah Jung, they would only need to watch the video for Heartless. A video-shoot is really nothing like a photo-shoot. Tell us how they are different. For which one do you "perform?"

LmL: I trailed off for a bit fantasizing about that zombie kill. Mmm, thanks for that.

Ok, the camera loves me. That is not completely true. I try to be photographed and filmed from certain angles. Also, if a photographer releases unflattering photos of me, I ask him or her to edit or remove them. However, admittedly, this doesn't happen often. I try to be myself during all my photo-shoots...even when

Photo Courtesy of JT Higgins

I am acting, I am pulling out emotions from the truth within me. The "performance" is a combination of things such as my use of angles and lights; my healthy lifestyle which allows me to be fun, alert and in-the-moment; and my attention to detail.

JBK: You claimed in a JournalStone.com interview to be the… Best in The World At: defining Leah Jung. That really puts you on the spot now, because we want to know—who are you? What are you going to be in ten years? Is Leah Jung even in control of LEAH JUNG ?

LmL: I'm just very private about myself to most people, so I don't think anyone knows me really, really well. My oldest friends and family can certainly describe the way I act in certain situations, but they usually throw in the word "unique" or "weird" because they are just not sure how else to explain it. So, it's not that I can provide an eye-opening definition of myself, it's that nobody else can come up with one either. I am very much in control of myself but I cannot predict the next ten years. New ideas and opportunities are presented to me on a regular basis. I just know I want to create various things to stimulate people's brains.

JBK: "…drink from this cold, heartless, cup of mine"—from Heartless. Your message to young women?

LmL: It is not a message for anyone to follow. It's meant to be vague and enigmatic. However you find it relatable, that's what it means.

JBK: Leah, thank you. Where are you going next? Are you going to get a magical month anytime soon?

LmL: Next weekend, Atlantic City, with my amazing hair-care sponsors, Beauty and Pinups. Shortly after that, some meetings in Las Vegas. Vegas means an opportunity for Carl Grace to add more to my back tattoo! November and December I'd like to see my family at least two weekends. If I'm lucky, one amusement park, and three museums.

꙲ ꙳ ꙲

The Unicorn (Art and Photogrphy by Jeff Foley)

Limited Editions

Mister October – An Anthology in Memory of Rick Hautala
Limited Edition   60 to 70 total

Featuring over 45 individual contributors, almost 800 pages, over 240k words, original Clive Barker artwork, over 30 illustrations.

"I have no doubt that readers will treasure this two-volume set. It is my hope that as you read, you will ruminate a little bit about the man for whom we all have come together within these pages." – Christopher Golden

On March 21st, 2013, Rick Hautala passed away. JournalStone Publishing is donating 100% of the profits from this two volume anthology to the Hautala family.

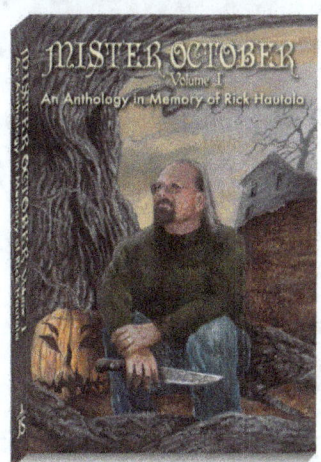

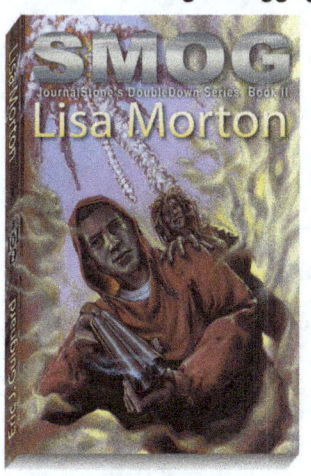

JournalStone's DoubleDown I – Limited Edition   100 total
Only the Thunder Knows – East End Girls

William (Billy) Burke and William Hare were two real-life, fist-fighting lowlifes who managed to stumble their way into infamy in Edinburgh, Scotland in the late 1820's, ultimately becoming Britain's first documented serial killers.

Seized by the vicious killings of Jack the Ripper, Victorian London's, East End is on the brink of ruin. Elizabeth Covington risks practicing medicine in the dangerous and neglected Whitechapel District and crosses paths with a man she believes is the villain.

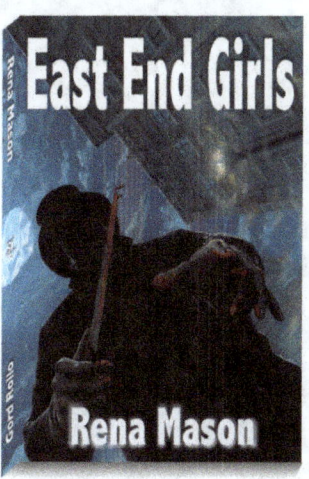

JournalStone's DoubleDown II – Limited Edition   100 total
Smog – Baggage of Eternal Night

JournalStone's DoubleDown III – Limited Edition   100 total
Dog Days – Deadly Passage

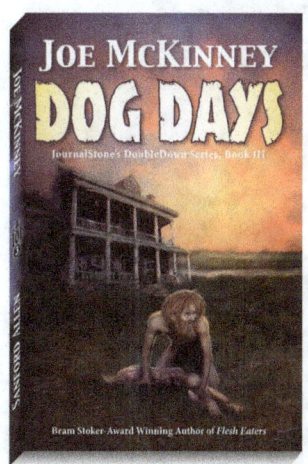

In Smog, it's 1965 in a Southern California suburb where everyone works for the aerospace industry. But something goes wrong with a rocket test and the smog thickens.

Charlie Stewart and Joey Third, are gamblers who obtain a sinister suitcase with a deadly mystery.

BONUS: Also included is Lisa Morton's novella, Summer's End, to be released October, 2013.

Dog Days: It's the summer of 1983 and in the swamps that surround Clear Lake a brutal and possibly super-natural killer is gathering strength, and waiting for the full moon.

Deadly Passage: Just after the American Revolution, the slave ship Lombard sets off from Africa. The death toll mounts as one by one the Lombard's human cargo dies.

THE FIFTY-YEAR KING

by Rhodi Hawk

Part 1: Catch

Clay awoke to the sensation that his left arm wasn't his.

His eyes blinked open. Thunder and lightning vibrated the windows and a damp breeze filled the bedroom. He slid his right hand over and stroked the left. It had no feeling though it seemed cool to the touch.

Then, like a sleepy Labrador, his left hand nudged back.

Clay lurched, knocking his head as he switched on the light.

Fia groaned and dragged the pillow over her eyes.

The arm just hung there. Uncooperative. It didn't look any different.

He lifted his shoulder, but that only hoisted it like a cow's tail just before the delivery of manure. He touched his left hand again. This time it didn't nudge back. He wondered if he'd dreamed that. The thing had probably just fallen asleep.

The phone was vibrating—*had been* vibrating all along. His fogged mind had believed it was only thunder in the windows.

That's what had woken him up, not his arm. A storm and a phone call.

Clay shoved himself to his feet, the left hand making a heavy smack on his leg, and snatched the phone from the dresser. Restricted number.

"Yeah?"

"Clay?" A woman.

He glanced at Fia, who was pulling herself out of bed and making for the bathroom. "Who's this?"

A pause, then slowly: "You don't recognize my voice?"

He did, but couldn't place it.

She was saying something like she was around and did he want—

"What the hell time is it?"

The voice said it was after midnight and did she wake him, though his clock read 3:42, and any idiot would know she'd be waking him.

It was Switch Day. A good night's sleep would

have been nice.

The room wavered as though it, too, had been sleeping, right down to the paint. He rubbed his eyes while holding the phone with his shoulder because he was still operating one-handed.

The voice on the phone kept talking, lilting, without any apparent need for so much as an "uh-huh" from him.

"Listen. Whoever you are. I'm hanging up."

She drew in her breath but he ended the call without waiting for her to respond.

He picked up the arm and let it drop. It was a piece of meat. But the veins were bulging, a promise that circulation would soon work its magic.

He'd been sleeping on it wrong and it had gone numb—not the first time, wouldn't be the last.

"Alright, then."

He set the phone on the dresser and his fingers came back sticky. A Dr. Pepper bottle lay on its side.

Cripes.

There came a low thunder boom. He looked for something to wipe down his phone, thumb-smacking his left hand like it was a can of chewing tobacco. The bedroom smelled like wet, dusty rayon. The sheer curtains billowed, revealing Cecropia moths clinging to the screen. From this angle, they looked like dried leaves.

Fia returned, wrapping herself in the pink silk kimono he'd given her six Christmases ago. "Who was that?"

"No idea."

She put on her glasses and squinted at the clock. "Well it's officially Switch Day." She paused. "Should we just get on down to the dip?"

"Can't do anything until daybreak. We've already spent all week preparing."

"Well maybe we ought to go back to sleep."

He shook his head.

"Me neither." She pulled her iPad from the dresser but her gaze was on the window. "There's those giant moths again. The pretty ones. What were they called?"

This was it. Switch Day. After all these years. After waiting his whole life. He sat down on the bed and pulled his right hand over his face. The left one was still out of commission.

Fia said, "Clay, honey?"

"Yeah?"

"What kind of moths did you say they were?"

He glanced at the window. "Cecropia."

"Seh—what?"

"It means 'face with a tail.' 'Cecropia.' Think 'serpent.'"

"Serpent? As in, snake?"

"Yeah, because the tips of their wings look like snake heads. Keeps predators away."

She shook her head. "That's an awful name."

He leaned back next to her on the bed and looked to where they clung to the screen, fluttering. More now that the light had been on a while. From this angle, you couldn't see the pattern on their backs. The eyes. The colors.

He said, "It's also the name of a king. Old King Cecrops."

"Hmm. Good king or bad king?"

"More or less good, but he was known for pissing off the gods. He reigned fifty years and they said the lower half of his body was shaped like a serpent. Again, 'face with a tail.'"

She zeroed right in, though he'd try to gloss by it: "Fifty years?"

"That's right."

"Spooky."

She was quiet a moment. "So I guess that means those moths have something to do with— "

He shook his head. "It would seem. No idea. I've spent my life studying every rock, weed, and bug on this property. Now here we are, Switch Day, right at the fiftieth year, and I don't know much more than I did when I was a kid."

"Well what's there to know, honey? You go down in there, flip the switch, and everything's fine for the next fifty years. Just avoid any spirits or trespassers."

He grimaced at the faltering in her voice. Poor Fia sucked at making light of things.

She busied her nerves, filling the iPad with pictures of Cecropia. "I should look up butterfly collecting when it's all over."

Her panties peeked from under the silk kimono. He walked his gaze over her, noting the crooked knobby toes, the long tan legs, the baby bump, the flat chest, the thin arms and thin nose, the glasses. He pictured what she'd be like with perfections only; no flaws.

She said, "Stop sizing me up."

He squeezed her leg.

Then she burst into a laugh, pointing at the screen. "Listen to this! *'Make a Butterfly Collection: Learn how to catch, kill, soften, and mount your specimens!'*"

He looked up at her. It took a moment, moving his mind back to Fia's compulsive Googling, and then the strangeness hit home.

Catch, kill, soften, mount.

They laughed. Hysterical, nervous, dread laughter.

Happy Switch-Day, pinned and pressed.

And then he stopped. Stopped dead.

That phone call.

That had been Vi on the phone.

Violet Stone.

None other.

He turned to the window as though she might be standing there now.

Ho-ly.

But she wasn't.

Shit.

His left arm was still dead. Still. Even now. Not even a tingle.

Vi Stone. Vi Stone.

Fia paged through images on the iPad.

He looked down. His left hand, the bastardized one, was gripping the cell phone. He was pretty sure the phone was supposed to be stuck to the dresser in gummed Dr. Pepper syrup.

"Fia," he said, and used his right hand to pry at the cell phone in his left.

"What, baby?" she said without looking up.

Lightning scarred the window. He pried at his fingers.

"Fia, honey." He pulled himself off the bed and yanked the fingers of his left hand, hard, and—

Pop!

His little finger snapped.

He felt nothing. Not a thing. The finger bent wrong, was surely broken, and the rest of the fingers on his left hand still wouldn't let go of the damn cell phone.

Which started ringing, from a restricted number.

Fia was staring at him.

"It's starting," he said.

She frowned at the buzzing cell phone. "Are you gonna answer that?"

"It's happening! Listen to me. Something's wrong. It's already started."

The iPad slipped to the floor. "Oh my God."

"Full swing. This is not a drill."

Fia jumped off the bed, feet shoved into sandals. "Tell me."

Vi's voice filtered up from the cell phone. His left hand must have answered the call. He had to grab it to keep it from putting the sticky phone to his ear.

He said, "There's a trespasser on the phone. My left arm's compromised."

Fia paused. "Your arm?"

He had to go down to his knees and press against the dresser to get control of the hand.

Fia made for the closet, then stopped. "I can't remember what to—on the phone, *and* one's got your arm? I don't know what I'm supposed—"

"Sure you do, baby. What's first?"

She breathed in twice, quick, without exhaling, then: "Keep cool."

She unfroze her steps and got the closet door open, then reached inside.

He slid to the carpet and mashed the arm against the dresser.

Through grit teeth, he said, "What do we do for an upper body compromise?"

But Fia appeared next to him in a crouch, the med kit open, the syringe filling. "Incapacitate, then secure."

Her tone was even but she had to be freaked. The needle went into his shoulder. The kit went sideways and the defibrillator tumbled out.

She squeezed him once, then was up and moving. "I'll call your dad and start loading up."

She paused. "I'm sorry. I—I forgot he—"

"It's OK. Just go."

The left arm was already slowing its fight. The little finger was ballooning in size, but he still felt nothing.

Catch, kill, soften, mount.

For some reason the words bubbled up in his mind. Weirdest wikihow ever.

Vi droned from the cell phone, now on the carpet. He couldn't pick out her words. That was all right by him.

~~~~

Fia returned, jeans and a sweatshirt replacing the silk kimono. The baby pressed at her waist band but she hadn't shopped for special clothes yet. "You ready for me to secure that arm?"

"Yeah."

She pulled a sling from the kit and slipped it over him, tying it snug. Very snug. She'd trained through that very method of securing a compromised limb, right alongside him, for the past ten years.

She picked up the cell phone and put it to her ear. He could hear Vi speaking though he still couldn't make out the words.

But Fia held the phone to him and shook her head. "I don't hear anything."

He frowned, taking it from her.

"It's been so quiet," Vi was saying, content to go on and on with no response. "I've been bored silly. I've been thinking of you, you know that? It's all I do. Even though you broke my heart, I keep—"

He ended the call and handed it back to Fia, pulling himself to his feet.

"If you can hear what that trespasser is saying, Clay, you're supposed to listen. We have to monitor what we can."

She was right, but it was too late now. "Let's load up and get to the dip as fast as we can."

"In the dark?"

"Yeah. It's against protocol but I don't think we have a choice."

Part 2: Kill

The house was at their backs, and to their right, lightning flashed over braided rows of threshed wheat. Fia drove. The Polaris caught the occasional raindrop in its headlights though the wet part of the storm had passed.

The compromised arm was bound snug. Even if the injection wore off, it would still remain secure. That was good, because Clay would be deep in the dip for the next several hours. He gripped the handle with his right hand and kept his eyes on the twenty-mile horizon where lightning skirted the hills below.

The dip was the furthest section of their property. It formed an awkward, sunken meadow of honeycombed rock and sinkholes, some of which were wide enough to swallow a Volkswagen, and all of which were perpetually flooded or a-stink with subterranean bogs. It gobbled up a full thirty acres of the homestead.

Clay was the first of his clan to have farmed the property, and the dip actually worked as a perfect run-off catch for the wheat fields. The soil was well-drained due to the slope, but it also held enough carbonate to wick water back up from the dip when things got dry.

The Polaris climbed to a small rise. Headlights angled toward the sky and for a moment, the land before them was black. But the Polaris leveled out, then nosed downward, and they were able to see six feet of mud at a time. From here, the grade would continue a subtle descent all the way to the dip.

A flash of lightning and it came into view. Or at least the fog bank that clung to it.

Fog over the dip. Even in a storm.

When his father was alive, anytime they descended this slope, he would ask, "What do we do if there's fog on Switch Day?"

And Clay would answer, "Use fans to create an artificial wind pattern, and if necessary, heat the area."

"How you gonna get fans and heaters out there with no electricity?"

"By being prepared. One week prior to Switch Day we put the generator in place, test for readiness. Clean and prepare the fire pits."

And they had, all week long, though Clay's father had missed it.

Down along the boundaries to the dip, Clay and Fia spent the week setting up the generator in a brand new shed. Made sure there was fuel. Stoked each fire pit with kindling, paper, and thick cuts of hardwood. The gear was packed as though for spelunking, including emergency extraction cables, head-strap LED lights, GPS, and back-up communication for when the cell phones lost their signals underground.

And of course they had stocked the medi kit. First aid, de-fib, and even tranquilizers in the unlikely event that ectoplasmic trespassers should find their way up from the deep down, underground P-trap, and slip into a world to which they did not belong.

Clay had spent thirty-two years training for this. For his father, the planning and drills spanned almost the entire fifty-year cycle. Hell yeah, they were prepared.

This was it.

Switch Day, October 20, 2013. The last one had been October 20, 1963, poorly managed by his grandfather. The next one would be in 2063. And Clay's children would be ready for that one, or his grand-children would be. He'd train them just like his father trained him.

Something glowed ahead. A faint but sizable ember, as though one of the fire pits had flamed up and was now dying.

Clay leaned forward.

The breeze was heavy, supercharged with ions and the smell of rain, and now he caught smoke.

The Polaris jostled to the source of the red glow and Fia pulled to a stop. Lightning strike. The old maple was burning, the one with the soft roots that marked the vent site, and there was still a pinch of ozone in the air. But the flames had already died back. Not liable to spread.

If it had been anywhere else he would have left it for now. But this was at the vent site. He didn't like it.

Clay got out and reached for the gear in the back.

Fia said, "Your arm's bound. Let me deal with the fire."

"No way. I don't want the baby near the chemicals. Just get the fire extinguisher out for me, if you would."

She retrieved it, and he checked the tree.

"Can you back the Polaris up to it for me? I want to get up on the back so I can get at it from a higher angle."

Fia got back behind the wheel.

A single yellow flame bloomed from the deepest bed of red embers, and winged insects were already mesmerized by the glow.

As a kid, whenever Clay walked passed this maple he could count backward from fifty and reach the dip by the time he got to one. There was no mistaking the boundaries: this side was sable-colored grass; the dip was always solid white. Snow in winter; fog any other time.

This was true on any given morning of Clay's life. He'd look out the window down the rise to a blanket of snow or fog. Always pure white. Once he'd watched a kaleidoscope of butterflies burst from the fog bank. It barely even shifted. Whenever there was a water surge, the dip would belch critters out into the fields. Crayfish, bats, minks, and more common things, too, like mice and fox squirrels—but in driving numbers.

The Polaris in its station, Clay told Fia to take the flashlight and walk up the road a safe distance, then he climbed up onto the rear and faced the strike zone. One puny fire extinguisher wasn't going to smother it cold, but it would reduce the risk of anything going wrong with the vent.

"Clay," Fia called from her position up the road.

"Yeah?"

"Do you think it's got something to do with the trespassers? The lightning hitting the tree like that?"

"Probably."

He stopped. His right hand, the good one, was tingling.

His leg, too.

He swallowed hard. A trespasser was still on board. That injection spared the arm but the thing was clearly working on the rest of him.

Just his damned,

fit-shittin,

sorry luck.

He wedged the fire extinguisher into his hip and used the one hand to hit the lever. Foam shot out in a stream.

The only other time anyone had heard of a body compromise was a hundred and fifty years ago, the year one of the great-grandpas drew the diagram. And even then the trespasser had seized a non-participant member of the family. It had used a poor old aunt's body to empty the kitchen of every morsel of food until the switch got flipped and the trespasser got vacuumed down the hill, into the dip, and through the P trap.

That's if the story was true. Clay took oral histories with a grain of salt.

Switch Day was supposed to be an all-day event. It took that long to get deep down through the passages to the switch site, then double back and get out.

But Clay was pretty sure that if he didn't at least get to the switch by just beyond daybreak, he wasn't going to be able to hold off the trespasser.

He covered the burning wood with foam, then let up. Checked the strike zone. The tiniest glimmer flared along the ground where the tree was anchored. Even as he stared, it pulsed red and went dark.

But then another faint light rolled beneath the packed ground.

He hopped from the Polaris and stepped toward the tree. Heat surged up into the soles of his boots. He backed off.

"Is it out?" Fia called.

"Just stay there, honey."

He circled to the back of the tree and stepped up on the root ridge, coming up behind the section that was still giving off heat. The sand-packed soil on that side of the tree was smoking.

He picked up his leg and stomped it with his boot. The ground gave way.

Clay lost his balance and dropped the fire extinguisher. An entire section of earth crumbled inward.

"Clay?" Fia called.

"Stay there!"

Lightning flickered, then again, giving over to continuous, uneven strobe.

The new hole in the ground glowed red. The maple's roots had tunneled into the granite shelf over the decades, and as the old tree came to the end of its life, its roots had shriveled back with rot. Now, they burned. And with the fresh dose of oxygen Clay just gave them, the roots swelled from red to full yellow flames.

From the Polaris, the cell phone rang.

The burning roots dangled over what seemed a bottomless pit in the dark. The gap didn't reflect sides or a bottom in the flashes of lightning, and from somewhere down below, a frigid, sulphured air current swelled.

Clay retrieved the fire extinguisher. He felt vibrations beneath his feet, and looked back at the tree.

Moths burst from the newly formed hole in the ground. Cecropia. Hundreds festooning the night. Their wings caught the lightning's illuminations, and their painted backs created an illusion of false predators—owls and snakes.

Clay frowned. Something was off. The fluttering wings organized into a concentrated entity, something of a glossy haze. In it, he could see himself mirrored. The fire extinguisher pinned under his elbow, his hand on the tree.

But also, somewhere within the cloud of moths, Clay could very clearly see a horse.

It moved. It was running. Advancing.

The thing's coat was white and silvery gray, and it had a black mane. But it was visible only in glimpses. Its movements unnatural. A projection onto the backs of the moths.

Clay recognized the horse—it used to belong to Fia. Long ago, when they were both in school, and he'd first noticed her. A girl from a nearby ranch riding her pretty white horse.

"Ashley," Fia said behind him.

He wheeled around. "Go back. You need to stay away."

She pulled her gaze from the horse to meet Clay's eyes.

He said, "That's not Ashley. Stay away from it. Stay away from anything like it."

She handed him the cell phone, which was once again transmitting Vi's lilting voice.

Fia said, "We're supposed to monitor them."

He took it from her and shoved the phone in his pocket. "Let's get geared up. We need to accelerate this."

He let it burn and fitted the Bluetooth into his ear as Fia helped him with his pack.

Violet spoke in that soft, continuous, intimate, drone. "It's funny how you think of so many things you want to say, and then when the time comes, you can't remember them all."

But Violet seemed to be coming up with plenty to say.

After high school, Clay and Violet had gone out a few times before Clay broke it off. They hadn't been serious but Vi took it hard. Weeks later, she died. She and a boy had gotten drunk and decided to race a train.

Tragic, is what it was. A waste. That's how he'd remembered it.

He'd felt guilty. He'd stopped seeing her, and therefore contributed to the state of mind she'd been in when she raced that stupid train. It fixed her as a tragic artifact in his mind.

But now he recalled that she was also a bad person. One of those really pretty girls with a mean streak. Otherwise he wouldn't have broken it off.

Somewhere along the line he'd killed the true impressions of her, and made her into that tragic mental artifact.

Catch, kill, soften, mount.

The white horse shifted abruptly so that it appeared further away.

It was in the moths. The way they moved.

"Get on back up the road now, honey," Clay said to Fia.

She turned with reluctance.

"Hurry for me," he said.

She quickened her pace up the road.

The moths were in a frenzy just beyond the tree. The snakehead illusion on their wings, the dried leaf undersides. The horse shifted into monstrous distortions within the rolling, writhing bodies.

Clay heaved the fire extinguisher and sprayed the burning roots, then continued up the tree until the thing gurgled and lost pressure.

He set it down. And the ground gave way.

The earth beneath his boots went soft and then

was just plain gone. Weightlessness. His stomach dropped. He was suddenly plunging in darkness. At length he hit solid earth, hard. It stole the breath from him. Gravel and hot foamy tree roots rained down on him. He realized he was sliding.

The vent, which no one had ever seen up close, not even on a fifty-year Switch Day, was apparently a two-way stream. The air vented upward, but water also coursed down on a slick cascading rock that formed downward-facing scales, polished by constant water and slime. He saw nothing but felt every hard shelf of rock as he rolled and slid, and kept slipping down, deeper and deeper.

The earpiece managed to stay in place, and the phone in his pocket kept its signal.

Vi went on and on the entire time. She never paused.

"If I had only known you were here," she was saying. "If I'd figured it out a little sooner, I would have climbed inside you myself, instead of him. I would have taken your hands. I'd wrap them around her throat. I would feel her screaming through your own hands."

When he finally stopped, he landed hard.

Part 3: Soften

His mind unfolded on wings of gossamer.

He saw himself down below. A memory of himself stepping to the brink of the dip with his father.

He felt himself drifting down, closer to the earth, taking a better look.

Clay and his father reached the fog bank and stopped. It didn't even rise as far as their knees but continuing any further wasn't worth risking a broken ankle.

Cotter said, "We'll wait until summer. Water table will be lower then."

"Yeah," Clay said.

He felt himself drifting closer, watching as though just over his own shoulder.

Cotter said, "Maybe then we can access that switch. Make some diagrams. See if it's something we can automate."

"Sure, Pop."

They had always said that. But the water table was never low enough to get through the labyrinth of rock and tunnels and drowning traps to get to the switch.

"Getting close," Cotter said. "A year and a half. You gonna be ready?"

Clay looked at him, no longer seeing himself from somewhere removed, but having somehow settled inside the memory of himself the way he was two years ago. "Of course."

His father said, "I'll be the one goin in. You'll have to be auxiliary."

"We've trained through every scenario."

"And we'll keep training until it's time. But I'll be the one going in. You've got Fiona to think about. I've got more experience."

Clay shook his head. "What experience? You were eight years old on the last Switch Day. Your mother never let you out of the kitchen."

"Goddamn it, don't argue with me!"

Clay paused. The older man's face was suddenly slick and gray, his lips tight. Cotter had been nearing retirement age and was fit as a fox. But in that moment, just as the sun was beginning its daily ritual of melting the vapors over the dip, Cotter Cowell looked twenty years older than he was.

Clay suddenly saw his father as he remembered him now, but at the same time he saw Cotter the way he actually was then, on that day, a year and a half ago.

This was the day his father had died. Right here by the dip. Fia was already on her way to work down the hill that morning, and Cotter had been coming over to help with the wheat crop.

Cotter pointed up the slope. "I was right up there in the house during the 1963 switch. In the kitchen. Eight years old. My father had been in the dip all day. Wore out."

"What went wrong?"

"He never told us. But he wasn't one to—" He stopped.

Clay said, "He was kind of an ass. That right,

Dad?"

"He wasn't the easiest man to know."

"He broke your mom's collarbone the night before."

Cotter nodded and went quiet.

Clay had wondered at the time why Cotter needed to ease the rough edges of his father's memory.

Cotter said, "On the day my father died, he told Mother that they were crazy. The—you know—the spirits that leeched up from the dip."

"Did you see any?" Clay asked, though he knew his old man had witnessed practically nothing.

"No, just my dad. But he wasn't one bit prepared. Guess he didn't believe it was true. He went about his chores that morning like it was any other day until the spirits started coming up the hill. By the time he got into the dip it was already good and dangerous."

"He flipped the switch, though," Clay said.

"Yeah. He must have. It all went back to normal. The dip filled up. He just never came out."

Abruptly, Cotter said, "I'm proud of you, son."

"For what?"

Cotter hesitated, then waved up the hill. "All that wheat. The crop looks really good. You never had anyone teaching you that."

"Four years plus grad school."

"Yeah, but you're smart, more than just book smart. Hard enough to learn all that. Even harder to take what you read about and *do* it, cold, without anyone showing you. You were supposed to be a scientist. You had that research on the what, the mold?"

"Mildew-resistant endosperm."

"What the hell was it you called your studies?"

"Theoretical production ecology."

Cotter laughed. "That's just a hoy mouthful. Don't expect me to ever remember it."

"Don't worry. Come on, we gotta get to work."

"I know why you left it. You did it for the family obligation. You didn't have to give away that mildew-free wheat thing."

Clay sighed, lifting a shoulder. "It's not like I handed it over. I sold intellectual property that will pay off in royalties over time. Not like I could have

subsidized the process. Patent goes through in a few years, prototype gets planted, someone else manages all that. In the meantime I'm just a farmer on the land I love."

Clay motioned his father to join him on the path, and Cotter finally started moving.

Cotter said, "We're all attached to this land. You know, with Switch Day and all. It's why my father named me Cotter, and I named you Clay. It's pride in these hills."

"Guess I'm lucky you didn't name me Volcanized Dolomite."

Cotter frowned.

Clay said, "That sure as shit would have gotten me picked on in school."

Cotter stopped. "You know what? You are one over-educated asshole son of a bitch."

But when Clay looked back at him, he was smiling.

This was why. On that last day his father *was* different. Cotter had always been brusque. He'd never before told Clay he was proud of him. He truly was softer. Already becoming the memory.

Capture, kill, soften, mount.

Clay tried to shake it off. Wake up. He needed nothing more from this memory. He certainly didn't need the next few moments, when Cotter took a knee on the dirt road, and Clay lunged for him. It had happened so fast. Cotter was gone before he'd even slumped to the ground, still on his knees with Clay gripping his arm.

Cotter had been fit as a fox. He truly had been. But at fifty-four, his heart gave out right there by the dip. Same property where he'd been born. It had been eighteen months shy of Switch Day.

~~~~

Fia was screaming for him. Vi droned on in the ear piece.

His body was screaming with pain, but he couldn't quite tell where. He unfolded himself from where he lay in a heap.

A light was wandering through the darkness. Fia's flashlight from a gap high above. He rolled, coughing, and found himself mostly intact.

"I'm here, honey, I'm OK." Then he muttered, "I think."

The left arm was bound tight in the sling. The dense feeling in his right arm had intensified, as had the left leg. There were pains all over, mostly in his head.

He pulled the cell phone from his pocket and silenced Vi's diatribe, then shone it over his head so he could see.

His pack had landed only a few feet away on the same ledge where he'd been dumped. Water coursed around him and spilled through gaps to a deeper pool below.

From up above at the surface, Fia's light found him. He shielded his eyes.

"God, I thought I'd lost you!"

She pulled the beam away and scanned the sinkhole. "There's a shelf. I think I can get in."

"Don't you dare."

He squinted at the spot where the flashlight wavered above, and knew he didn't have to worry about her trying. Though the underground chamber was vast, the opening along the top was barely enough to fit a small dog. She might get her leg through it, nothing more.

He did his best to get the LED head strap on though his good arm had gone clumsy.

"How'd you find me?"

"The GPS is tracking."

Preparation at work. Though he'd forgotten, she must have initiated it before they left the house. That was protocol.

"So where am I?"

"You're right over the P trap, if the diagram's accurate."

That was good news. It meant he was already very close to the switch.

If only his limbs weren't thickening with the sensation that something was trying to kick him out. In a few minutes he may not be able to walk. At least not according to his wishes.

He threw his gear over his shoulder and strapped it in place while striding as quickly as his awkward limbs would allow.

If he was this close to the switch then Fia was up there blind in the fog bank, sinkholes all around.

"Go on and start the generator," Clay called to her. "You can't provide support to me if you can't see. Get the fans going and the fires, then call my cell phone."

"Oh, God, please be careful," Fia said.

He moved as quickly as he dared. Careful was fine. Fast was better.

Clay switched on his phone and thumbed to the 1813 diagram. It displayed in a thumbnail image, more a comfort than a reference because he didn't want to take the time to zoom in. Clay'd had it committed to memory for years now. He also had paper copies and scans in varying resolutions on his computer.

The document dated October 20th, 1813 was the only real reference they had for Switch Day. It showed a diagram of the dip from two vantage points: aerial and cross-section. It showed where the vent was. This, at least, Clay and Cotter could easily find from ground level. But it also showed how the deep underground P trap prevented backflow—just like any other P trap in everyday plumbing—and how to reach the switch.

Finally, beneath the diagram, in careful handwriting, were these sparse notes:

> The lever must be set again when the water drains on the fiftieth year. The vent clears itself.
>
> The current semicentennial maintenance is complete as of this writing. The next occurrence shall be 20th October 1863.
>
> The maintenance work need not extend beyond the landowner, though a parent, offspring, wife, or sibling might assist without consequence. Any other would perish. This is surely true and confirmed. The landowner should keep good conscience.
>
> Encounters with spirits should be avoided.

That was it. No record of what *actually happened* on any of the Switch Days. And other than the 1813 diagram, the rest of the great-grandpas had written down absolutely nada. Clay did at least have some pictures of the men. Lots of pictures of his grandfather, at least. And an old one of Seneca Cowell, the 1913 gramp, standing in front of the grist mill down the valley where he worked. An ordinary laborer. No one outside the family ever knew that Seneca Cowell smoothly prevented fifty years of phantasmagoria during the 1913 switch, which was said to have taken no more than five hours, and during which, nary a single trespasser found its way beyond the P trap.

If Clay's body didn't give over to the trespasser he was going to beat the 1913 record by a wide margin.

Freakish though it was having the mouth of the vent crumble away and swallow him up, it had injected him deep into the dip. It probably saved him hours of picking and descending.

The LED provided all the light he needed. The rocks beneath his feet were slippery, though not as bad as the vent had been. These rocks had been under deep water and therefore had no slime coating like what had formed on the constant trickle of the vent. He was able to move fast by keeping his knees bent and his right arm out.

Somewhere in the darkness beyond the reach of the LED came the sound of Violet's voice.

She was talking just as she had on the cell phone. Droning on.

Then his LED light shone on something manmade. Just ahead, though the underground corridor continued on, there was framed timber on the left wall. It was shrouded by a fine, hairy network of roots. He drew nearer and saw beams spiked in place like in a mine shaft. And just beyond the opening, the beginnings of daylight. Purple and faint.

This was the entrance. Same as the diagram showed. Beyond the framed doorway there should be a spiral staircase that lead down to the switch.

Clay pulled away the root mesh.

The first thing he noticed was the crack along the ceiling that revealed the beginnings of dawn. Then he noticed hundreds of eyes staring back at him.

"Shit!"

He stumbled backward and they erupted. The sound was like fire whooshing to life.

Cecropia. Hundreds.

Half the colony burst into flight and funneled up toward daybreak. The rest remained in the cramped chamber with him. Each wing of each moth had a large, colorful spot that looked like a snake's head, right down to the eye.

He let the LED follow along the walls until he saw a man-sized opening chiseled from a layer of dolomite.

And from it came Violet's voice.

And then Vi herself was there.

She turned slowly as though she'd just ascended the spiral staircase, her face dreamlike, her head heavy on her neck.

But same as what they'd witnessed by the vent with Fia's old horse, Violet was only visible in boiling, fractured glimpses within a cloud of panicking moths.

She smiled when she saw him. She looked sweet and vulnerable. It was the same expression she'd held in the gallery of his mind. It would have been unfair to remember her as she truly was. Vi was never sweet nor vulnerable.

And while still holding that framed and mounted smile, her eyes widened into a look of madness.

Whatever Vi had been in life, this creature that she'd become, this trespasser, was something entirely different.

She moved from the carved dolomite into the chamber. The roiling, fluttering screen of moth wings shaped her face into grotesque distortions. The lower half of her body tapered off, the moth eyes glinting along her scales.

Clay had no idea what this creature was capable of. How deadly. But he was sixty seconds from the switch down that dolomite staircase. He just needed to get past her to reach it.

His leg gave out beneath him.

He rolled away from her, scrambling one-armed. But something moved from inside the numbed parts of his body. The trespasser.

Moths were pelting him. And in their wings he saw Vi drawing closer. But he also saw himself mirrored back. Roiling, distorted, he saw himself duplicated as if he had a Siamese twin.

He realized he was looking back at the trespasser who was trying to commandeer his body. Then recognition struck. His father.

Clay lunged past Vi for the opening. She screamed.

He hurled himself down the spiral shelves of dolomite. Vi poured herself after him. He was practically swimming at the rock, one-armed and one-legged, slithering and tumbling with Vi right there in his ear.

Suddenly, the staircase ended. The switch was nothing but a baton of rock. It was lying askew, and on either side were deep shafts.

Clay felt the cold, searing rake of Vi's nails. She gouged him deeply, down his spine, peeling away something he needed. The sensation was more painful than anything his flesh had known. And with it, some deep piece of him loosened.

He shoved the baton back in place.

A deep, hollow rumble shook the chamber. Then came a low whistle.

Vi tore at him again. He arched his back and swung at her, but his fist passed through moths in flight.

The whistle grew in pitch until it sounded like a train. Air vacuumed in a funnel down the shaft to the right of the switch. The shaft to the left now trickled water.

Clay felt the heaviness lift from his body. Except for the arm that was bound within the sling, nothing felt numb or heavy. The trespasser—his father—disappeared.

Vi, too, disappeared.

The Cecropia moths calmed.

But Vi's shrieking persisted a while longer. Despite the now-deafening whistle. Her voice transcended hearing. It filled his mind.

Part 4: Mount

Clay called Fia the moment he made it out of the staircase and back into the moth chamber. The signal seemed strong. He told her all that had happened.

That it was over. The dip was filling. The only thing left was to pick his way to the surface—the long way, this time; no going back up the vent. But the important thing was that the entities were safely exiled beyond the P trap.

"Do you remember, honey?" she asked, her voice small. "Do you recall what those entities are?"

"I don't know, babe. Nobody knows."

The earth rumbled beneath him, air pockets shifting to let back the water.

He said, "I have my theories about them. I think in terms of farming, so I see it as similar to how nitrogen cycles. When we're growing that grain out there, it needs things to survive. Sunlight, water, nitrogen from the soil. But wheat can't just take up nitrogen. It's got to be broken down. For that, there's fungus. Or microbes. They break it down. The nitrogen gets smashed and mashed into nitrites or nitrates, and then the wheat—"

He could hear her breathing. She said nothing, just let him talk, and though was vaguely aware that he was droning on, he followed through with the thought:

"Take my granddad who died in 1963. Figure him like a hunk of nitrogen—until he died. He went into the ground where the microbes started working. Somewhere along the way he became something else."

"The body decomposes, but—"

"No! I mean, sure. But I'm not talking about the *body*. I'm talking about the *soul*. You want to get technical with the nitrogen?"

"No."

"When it's floating around it's just a molecule made up of two parts nitrogen. N_2. But when the microbes work on the N_2, they break down that molecule and mix it up to make new ones. NH_4, NO_2, NO_3. And—"

"Shut up with all that!"

He laughed, even though she truly was getting impatient, and yet he couldn't stop himself: "My point is that during this process, the thing that was once a soul is broken down into its basic components. And then it gets smashed and mashed. That soul is still there, but it's something else. It's a cycle."

"No, it's not."

"What?"

She took a deep breath. "No, honey. It's the opposite."

"What?"

"We've recorded your theory already, and it's something like this: When a person's *alive*, a complete body and soul walking around, that's when they're the mashed-up version. I'm paraphrasing, but, remember? With all the N's and O's and H's. A soul *without* the body, *that's* the basic one. The pure element. Remember now?"

Clay felt an uneasy shift. "How you figure, honey?"

"I don't. *You* figured it out."

She was right. He'd thought it through, at least to this point. Right here in the dip.

His memory churned.

This was not the first time they'd examined this.

The things that resided beyond the P trap, those weren't souls.

It hadn't been the *soul* of Clay's father that had been trespassing. Nor had Violet's soul been here. The remnant that had raked her nails down Clay's spine—

The trespassers were cast-offs. Waste products. Effluvia.

Fia said, "That's the theory you've come up with so far. It's our starting point."

Clay became very still. And when he did, the rock seemed to waver around him.

"Clay?" Fia said.

Her voice rose. "Clay? Don't leave me again. Please. Where are you? Don't go."

He frowned, looking up at the gaps of daylight. "What are you talking about? I'm right here."

She caught her breath, held it.

He stared at the gaps in the ceiling of rock. "How long has this been going on, Fia?"

She didn't answer.

He said, "Come to the gap where I can see you."

"You're not where you think you are, honey. This is always a shock for you at first."

"Dammit, just, wave. Wave like you always do."

A shadow fell across the pour of daylight, the sun at her back. He could see only her silhouette. He frowned. She was wearing a heavy winter parka with fur rimming the hood and cuffs.

But though he couldn't see her face, the softened daylight formed a halo around her. The air shimmered where she stood. Ice crystals. There was snow up above.

And the halo that formed around her—he realized he was gazing up through water.

Fia was looking down into the flooded sinkhole. And he was at the bottom of it.

It was deep winter up there where she stood. When he'd entered the dip it was just into fall.

He swallowed. "How long have I been dead?"

"You are not dead. You are still coming back to me, honey. You survived." She paused, then added, "Barely."

"I survived."

"Yes. After you went in, you sent me to start the generator and the fire pits. Clear the fog. Then you fell out of contact. When I finally found you with the GPS you'd already managed to get to the switch. The EMS team had to hoist you out on a line. The dip was already filling by then."

She paused, and added, "You don't need to worry about them, if you're wondering. The EMS workers are fine. The 1813 diagram says you can't get outside help, but when they came to get you out you'd already flipped the switch. It was over by then. You all survived."

"Then what the hell am I doing in this damn sinkhole!"

"You're not. You're up here. You're in the house right now. And, part of you is also down there."

He looked at his hand, his feet, his left arm still bound in the sling. He felt no different. He could hear the dip groan as water pressed into crevices below. The P trap sealed.

"This isn't right," he said.

But it was. They'd been through this before. They'd been through this many times.

"How long has it been?"

Fia hesitated, then, "Just over two years. You have a daughter."

His throat clenched. He turned and charged back into the moth chamber. The Cecropia colony burst into flight.

Half of them fled up through the gap, the other half remained inside the crevice with him, frenzied. He watched their false eyes.

And through them, he saw her. Fia.

He saw what they saw, rising up, passing her, continuing toward a frozen, crystal blue sky. From above, the dip was a stretch of deep, white snow. Leading into it was a crude path of stakes roped together like the queue line for a theater. Fia must have put it there to find her way in and out.

He saw the entire spread of land on diving, turning, painted backs of Cecropia. A shared vision with the moths that had flown up above ground. All of them seeing with collective eyes.

They neared the house, finding it warm, and lit on the window screen.

Through the glass, he saw himself sitting in the bedroom. The body from which Violet had cleaved his spirit. His arms lay draped on armrests, his feet were perched on a small wooden rise. His head was eased back, almost empirical. But also vacant.

Actually, slack.

Down the hall he could see Fia's mother. She was pulling something out of the pantry for the little dark-haired girl. His daughter.

Fia said, "So. You remember. Now you need to get to work. OK?"

It had happened over and over again, every night for two years.

He said, "You can't keep on like this Fia, You can't be talking to me. I'm gone now. The entities are crazy. They don't--"

"Stop it!" She hitched her breath. "Alright? Can you take a moment? I will say it again. *You are not dead.* You are not going to become some wild, violent ghost. OK? You are alive. Up there in that house. You're still alive, unlike any of the others. You just forgetful sometimes."

She laughed without much humor. "I mean, come on. It's a little disorienting. Once we get through this part, you're just like—"

Her breath caught again, and she spoke the next words as though she were swallowing them. "You're just like you always were. Have you found your way back yet? To where we left off yesterday?"

Yes. He had it, pinned and pressed, hanging in the halls of his memory.

The confusion fell away and was replaced by a recollection of sheer, fever-pitched urgency.

He said, "I have forty-eight years left. To figure it out."

"That's it, honey. *We* have forty-eight years. That's right."

The relief in her voice was palpable.

He had a daughter. That dark-haired girl up there was going to grow up. And either she was going to be coming for this switch in 2063, or one of her children would. Forty-eight years from now, when his reign over this godforsaken, waterlogged dip was over. Maybe his daughter would be next. Unless they figured out a way to end it.

From up above, Fia said, "You've already worked some of it out, honey. You've got a fix on how pieces of the soul find their way. Or lose it. We'll keep on it. And once we beat this, you'll know how to come on out of the ground for me. And you'll come back home."

He understood. This was necessary if they were to break the cycle. An evolution of the legacy. This was how he needed to be.

He untied the sling, let himself go loose. He felt the water move around him. He let it be real that this part of himself now dwelled here.

Wild, alive, hardened, and strangely free.

Coma Chameleon:

The Further Adventures of the Cannibal Cats

by
Nancy Holder

Pffft, shah.

Pffft, shah.

Beepbeepbeepbeepbeep.

Pfft, shah.

Prolonging the agony. For Dwight, anyway.

Was Dwight sorry that he had dragged Angelo out of their Jag and told the gangbangers that his best and only friend in the world was the serial killer who had been butchering their women? Did he regret leaving Angelo there with them while he rode off scott free? Or was he still surfing the Net to find ways to kill Angelo, just in case he ever woke up from his coma?

Pffft, shah.

Pffft, shah.

Running his fingers along the hairs on his knuckles, Dwight sat in the pleather chair and stared at nothing—certainly not at Angelo—in the dimly lit private room at Cedars Sinai and smelled the roses. And the lilies and the orchids. He had read that florists sent the freshest flowers to weddings and the half-dead ones to funerals. Maybe that was for people who didn't have assistants to check up on these things. You did not fuck with the Cannibal Cats. You did not fuck with Dwight Jones. Well, except for when you did.

Angelo was telling people. That was the one thing we swore never to do. Of course he broke every other promise he ever made to me, so why would he keep that one?

Beepbeepbeepbeepbeep.

Pfft, shah.

Dwight and Angelo were rock stars. Angelo's original garage band had been The Tokers, and in high school he had been cool and handsome and rich. Dwight's dad had just beaten his mom to death and it looked like it would be Dwight's turn soon. Somehow, Angelo picked him to be his friend. Dwight still didn't know why. At the time, it had seemed like a life-saving miracle. How had it gone so wrong?

Here was how they had gone so cannibal: in high school in Iowa, Dwight had accidentally cut himself too deep during their second try at the blood-brother ritual, slicing across the veins in his wrist, and there was blood freakin' everywhere in the copier room. Call it karma, call it good eating: He slurped up the extra on impulse before he went to the hospital.

It was a very bonding experience, and *Angelo* had visited *him* in the hospital. So now they were even, right?

The taste for flesh came later, after Angelo accidentally cut off the wee littlest bit of the tip of his pinkie, just about the size of a pencil eraser, and Dwight had popped it into his mouth. It was psychedelically delicious. That was how they had talked back then in the early years. While they were planning their lives as cannibals: they would eat only women. Madonna. Nowadays Miley Cyrus would be on that list. It was their thing.

Cannibalism plus daddy issues plus dreams of rock star fame: they left Iowa and moved into a mansion the Grateful Dead had rented in San Francisco and everything happened like a dream: They were:

Superfamous

rich young

cannibals.

Which is information you didn't want to spread around, even if you weren't famous or rich. Or young, even.

So how many people had Angelo told? Angelo was the one who had wanted to go to Alcoholics Anonymous so they could stop devouring human flesh. It was a metaphor, he said. There were these steps, these stupid procedures, twelve in all. You had to confess your sins to another person. To your sponsor. Tell that starfucker all the terrible things your addiction had prompted you to do. Not so metaphorically speaking.

Angelo always pushed. He pushed so fucking *far*.

At the AA meetings you yammered on about what a loser you were and then when you were done the group always said, *Thank you for sharing.* But other than spilling his guts—now *there's* a metaphor—about the one and only secret they must not tell, Angelo didn't share. Angelo ate Alice, Dwight's one true love, without a second thought.

He ate the wife of their Japanese record label guy, who turned out to be in the *yakuza*. And he started writing a screenplay without even mentioning it. Went off to the Robert McKee story class alone.

That *bastard*.

Sitting in Angelo's not-so-private private room, sweating in his tight black leather pants, Dwight could hear the nurses murmuring in the hallway. Cedars Sinai got a lot of celebrities but the Cannibal Cats were off the charts. Back in Iowa, when he was clinically depressed and loaded to the gills with PTSD, Dwight had been too lacking in self-esteem to even fantasize about the level of fame and fortune he and Angelo had reached.

Whisper, whisper, whisper, said the nurses. *Tragic, tragic, tragic.*

There wasn't any music playing on his iPhone. Dwight had on his Bose headphones because he wanted to be left alone.

Pffft, shah. Angelo had been so handsome. Nurses were totally into victims.

Yeah, well.

Dwight studied all Angelo's get-well cards and the bouquets. Most of the flowers had been taken to other rooms, to cheer up other half-dead people. That was their manager's idea. Shay Gomez said there was more stuff lined up against the security gates at the Cats' Spanish Revival mansion in the Hollywood hills. Flowers, pictures, a lot of Teddy bears and candles. And bikini underwear.

Dwight's back was hurting from sleeping in the recliner and he was allergic to at least one of the flowers in the room. Shay kept telling him to go home and get some decent rest but how could he when

Pfft shah

Angelo might wake up?

Whenever Dwight did catch sight of the pulpy mass in the bed, his mind skipped the present track and rewound to the scene of the crime: Echo Park. He saw what had happened in a series of montages with a thrash metal backbeat—close-ups of the faces of the drug-dealing gangbangers as Dwight convinced them Angelo had been the serial killer butchering their women. Extreme close-up of the

necklace he, Dwight, had planted in the glove compartment of the Jag after the last murder. M-A-R-I-A in rhinestones, from the LA County Fair. He had taken it off the victim himself. He and Angelo had driven around in the Jag for a week with Maria's necklace in the glove compartment, and Angelo had had no idea Dwight was the real Echo Park Killer. And why? *Because Dwight hadn't told him. He had kept it a fucking secret.*

Dwight hadn't planned on killing a bunch of Hispanic chicks all by himself. But he had been under a lot of stress. Angelo kept dragging him off to the NoHo bungalow of recovering alcoholic hottie Carla M to work on his stupid screenplay. Which of course now was being optioned for six million dollars, with Carla M attached to finish it in the event that Angelo was now a vegetable. Even though the script itself was a pulpy mass of eggplant shit.

Dwight hadn't planned on killing Angelo, either, or hitting him with the gun—repeatedly— when he had dragged him out of the car. He'd just been so fucking mad that Angelo had told. Dwight's plan had only been to stun Angelo, leave him for the homeys, and drive back to Carla M's house to fuck her and then devour her, like the Cats did. All those nights of sweating on her retro-chic Naugahyde sofa in his leather pants, dozing and texting the president of their fan club while Carla M the genius ripped Angelo's horrible screenplay to shreds and helped him sew it back together like some Frankenstein monster. Listening as Angelo asked her to hurt his hideous dialogue and nonsensical plot even more.

So yes, he had set up Angelo. So yes, he had killed a lot of chicks and then arranged all the evidence to point to his blood brother. Write *that* up in a screenplay, they won't just option it, they'll actually make the movie.

His character flaw had been losing his temper.

Character arc: in addition to going to AA, Dwight had been advised by his own stupid sponsor, Lou S, who was a douche, to go to Codependents Anonymous. He said that Dwight had codependent issues, meaning that he adopted Angelo's reality as his own. Dwight looked to Angelo for how to behave, how to respond, how to dream. Lou S said if Dwight hadn't met Angelo, he probably wouldn't have become an alcoholic.

That being the metaphor, remember?

The fact that Dwight had worked so hard to frame Angelo was nothing short of a miracle of self-actualization. Finally, ultimately, he had not put Angelo's best interests before his own. Put that in your hero's journey. Arranging for Angelo's execution-by-gangbangers was proof that if you put the time in, went to your meetings and did your twelve steps, you really could get better.

So he had successfully convinced those bad boys in Echo Park that Angelo had murdered all those girls. But about halfway to Carla's he realized that all those Echo Park homeys equaled witnesses. And in Codependents Anonymous he had learned that *You are known by the company you keep.*

Him. He was that company. Angelo kept *him.*

His mind raced; he didn't think any of those gangstas black and brown would *tell* that Dwight Jones of been the one to give Angelo Leone to them—then each home-bro would have to admit he personally had been at the scene. But what if they did? What if one of them said, "Hello, lads, we can't take justice into our own hands like this? If Mr. Leone is responsible for ending the lives of our young ladies, the law will punish him."

So ultimately Dwight dialed 911 and told them that a bunch of gangbangers had forced the Jag to stop (guns, big ones, no, he didn't know what kind, he was a classic rock star, not a rapper) and dragged Angelo out. And he, Dwight Jones, had barely escaped with his life. Sure enough, cops screamed over there and leaped out of their squad cars just as a guy in an oversized baseball cap and all gold teeth was pushing a .357 Magnum against the back of Angelo's head.

Not one single authority figure believed for a second that Dwight had left Angelo there to die.

Who *hadn't* interviewed Dwight after that? It was like Siegfried and Roy when the tiger had mauled Roy, only without the gay part. The Cannibal Cats' new release went triple platinum

while Angelo clung to life in Intensive Care.

Shay sat Dwight down in the hospital cafeteria, teared up, and gently suggested that it might make sense to send out some feelers about a solo project for Dwight. Inside, Dwight was jazzed; on the outside he protested indignantly and told Shay he was shocked about the way his mind worked.

Shay said, "Angelo did. Just in case."

Just in case? What the fuck?

Yet another thing Angelo had not told Dwight: *I got a Plan B to bail on your ass if things go south.* Talk about *pissed.*

Now, alone in the room with the allergen flowers, Dwight stared at Angelo. Really made himself look. *Pffft, shah.* And *bleah.*

"Mr. Jones?" It was the neurologist. Again. "We have the results of the latest tests."

Dwight took a deep breath. "Will he regain consciousness?"

Will he tell?

~~~~

Discharge. Home. News helicopters and paparazzi and a police escort. Turned out Angelo's bruising and swelling were temporary. Ta da, Angelo was still handsome. Of course. Shay was all jazzed. The upscale mags wanted to do photo shoots of the two of them to go with their intense, in-depth interviews about the near-miss of the demise of the Cannibal Cats. The photos had been up in the air because taking pix of a messed-up celeb was in poor taste, even though, Dwight later learned, that Shay had already slipped some to *The Star.*

Angelo was awake and aware. There was no brain damage.

There was just one good thing, one ray of hope, as far as Dwight was concerned: Angelo had amnesia. He couldn't remember the beating or the ride in the Jag that led up to it.

Dwight didn't know how that would last, so he told Shay to go ahead and send out the feelers on the solo project. But three weeks had passed and Shay hadn't come back to him. Dwight had the sickening feeling that no one wanted a Dwight

Jones solo project. Angelo was the sexy one, the front man, the leader. It had always been like since they had left Iowa. Correction: Angelo had left. Dwight had *escaped*. Angelo and his trust fund.

Dwight and Angelo.

Shit, what the hell was wrong with him?

Dwight watched Angelo constantly, waiting for the telltale flicker of memory. He practiced the conversation they would have. He was not into confrontation, so he figured out his position: they had each done one awful thing. Telling was as bad as leaving Angelo to die. Therefore, they were even. So that meant they should start over. But had Angelo told anyone else? Had his sponsor told anyone else? There hadn't been any blackmail texts or emails labeled I KNOW, at least none in Dwight's inbox.

"Hey, " Angelo said one evening. It was balmy and beautiful in L.A. Just like almost always. "What about this one?"

The two were sitting on the balcony of their mansion, smoking a joint and looking at resumes of backup singers. Everybody wanted the Cannibal Cats for concerts; Shay said their first appearance should be a charity gig for something anti-violent.

"Hmm?" Dwight leaned over. The chick was edgy-looking, black hair, black eyes, piercings. "She doesn't look anti-violent."

"But she does look tasty." Angelo grinned and ran his finger down the center of her headshot. "I haven't had anyone to eat since…" He drifted off, and his sharp profile melted into the shady darkness.

Oh, God, he's remembering. Dwight's heart pounded so hard he heard the rhythm in the soles of his feet. *I smashed him in the head. That's all he knows. He blacked out then. He was unconscious when I pulled him out of the car.*

I think.

"Dwight, I keep thinking…" Angelo turned toward him. By the orange light of the joint, Dwight saw Angelo's eyes. They were shiny. "It must have been so terrible for you, thinking I had told my sponsor. I probably scared you shitless."

Dwight took a breath…or tried to. He was suddenly so dizzy he was afraid he was going to fall off the balcony. Here they were. Here it was.

"Then I lost control of the car when we were driving in Echo Park. I was so high. Carla gave me this shit in the kitchen I'd never had before. I don't even know what it's called. I went totally psycho, man." Dwight gaped at him. *He's lying to me*, he thought. And then, *He's lying to himself.* And then, *Maybe he actually remembers it that way.*

Hanging his head (so that Angelo couldn't read the terror on his face), Dwight tried to think of a response. He was completely unprepared, and stoned to boot. None of the conversations he had had with himself had gone like this.

"I-I'm sorry, dude," Dwight blurted. Which wasn't what he had been about to say. Actually, he still had no conversational plans.

Angelo moved, and the moon caught the metal of the staples in his scalp. They had shaved off all Angelo's glorious black curly-perm hair. It was growing in now and it looked a little hipper short. Edgier, like Sting. There was more gray in it, too. Dwight had let their stylist shave his head again. Shay said his baldness made a statement: *When Angelo is wounded, I am wounded.*

Angelo reached for the bottle of Jack Daniels on the little tile table between them. The fragrance of liquor hit the air as Angelo tossed back. He still had a sharp chin line. Dwight had a little bit of a middle-aged wattle. Surgeon said he'd better come in sooner rather than later. Dr. Mehta was on retainer.

Angelo held out the bottle.

"I'm alive, I'm home, and no one knows," he said. "I swear it."

Dwight could take the bottle and whack him over the head with it.

Forensic evidence.

He could grab Angelo and push him off the balcony.

And possibly fail.

Shitttttt, shah.

~~~~

So what was he going to do? What the fuck was he going to do? For years—decades now, even—Dwight had worried that Angelo's arrogance would tip someone off. Then he'd been positive that Angelo had told.

What could Dwight do, leave? Where could he go? Where could either one of them go?

"We should talk to that girl singer," Dwight said one afternoon, after they got through the hangover part of the day. They were sitting at the breakfast bar. Maria, their maid, had made them some salsa. Fresh chiles, onions, cilantro, tomatoes. It looked kind of like Angelo's head after Dwight had beaten him with the gun. "We could use some sexual tension."

Angelo picked up a tortilla chip and scooped salsa into it. Popped it in his mouth. Drank some Dos Equis. He had lost weight. He look gaunt and sexy. Dwight had stress-eaten for months.

"We probably shouldn't eat her," Angelo said. "People will know we auditioned her." He caught Dwight's eye. "I *will* eat something," he said. "I know I have to keep up my strength." Crunch crunch crunch. Head cocked, hair growing in. Angelo had eyes that women drowned in. No wonder they had left their underwear by the security gate.

Angelo swigged back his beer, smiled brightly, and raised up the empty. Amazingly, not one of Angelo's teeth had been chipped during the episode. That was how Dwight would think of it now. The episode.

"Grab me another?" he asked Dwight.

"Okay," Dwight said, but he wondered if he was being codependent. He always waited on Angelo. Always. He didn't think Angelo had ever gotten up off his butt to grab a beer for Dwight.

But Angelo had just come out of a coma. How do you tell someone like that to get his own beer?

Dwight's bare feet slapped on the tile as he went into the kitchen. He was wearing loose shorts and Bag Balm. He either had to face facts and get some new black leather pants or lose some weight. He had stress-eaten in the hospital cafeteria, developing a serious Gummi Bears habit. He figured he had gained ten pounds on Gummi Bears alone.

He opened the fridge, grabbed a beer and was turning around when he heard Angelo's ringtone. His cell phone was on the counter. As Dwight shut the door with his hip, Angelo grabbed his phone. Earlier in their careers, they had hired assistants to do all this shit. But it was hard to be a cannibal when guys lived for poking through your garbage can.

"Yeah," Angelo said, putting the phone to his ear.

Dwight carried the beers back to the breakfast bar and idly popped a tortilla chip in his mouth. Maybe it was a magazine. Or Shay, with some more concert ideas. For *both* of them.

"Wha…*what*…?" Angelo's mouth dropped open. He went white. Stared at Dwight and pressed END.

Something in his voice made Dwight's guts twist. Maybe one of the gangbangers was threatening to come forward. Maybe the cops had done a little research on the M-A-R-I-A necklace that Dwight himself had bought and planted. (If they had it. What if they had it? No one had said they had it.)

Dwight grabbed the phone and listened. To a dial tone. He hit *69 and the number connected.

"Angelo, what happened?" Shay asked.

"It's Dwight," Dwight said. "What do you mean, what happened?"

"We must have got disconnected. Listen, Jesus, you are not going to fucking believe this. They want you to sing at the Superbowl!"

Angelo shook his head. His face was slack—he'd literally aged ten years in ten seconds. Okay, maybe five. He almost had a wattle.

"Hang up on him," Angelo said.

"Shay, that is fucking awesome. Let me call you back," Dwight said.

Shay said, "Cool, man."

Dwight disconnected and stared at Angelo.

"We have to say no," Angelo said, and looked up at the stars. "My voice is shot."

"Wha-*what*?" Dwight blurted.

Angelo opened his mouth. Squawking came out. Horrible, breathy rasping that sounded like someone was beating him to death.

"I've been singing when you're out of the house," Angelo said. "And this is the best it gets.

I haven't wanted to face it, man. I'm done. It's the end of us." Tears streamed down his face.

Dwight just stared at him.

"Lip synch," Dwight said, digging all his nails into his chubby thighs.

"I have too much integrity," Angelo wept. "I could never do that to our fans."

But you could do it to me, Dwight thought. *Without even thinking twice. Or apologizing.* His brain pounded inside his skull. Waves of complete and total apeshit fury surged through him. If this had happened to him, he would not be telling Angelo that it was the end of them. He would be discussing which tracks he would mouth the words to so that Angelo's rockstar lifestyle would not be threatened.

Dwight didn't know what to do, what to say. How to stop himself from bashing Angelo's head in all over again.

He turned away from Angelo and stared through a window at their illuminated back yard… and that was when he saw Angelo's reflection. His weeping blood brother was grinning through his tears.

Dwight went completely still. Angelo got up. He moved toward Dwight with less awkwardness than he had been moving before. He moved like someone who could get his own beer.

He said, "I *know* Dwight. I know."

Dwight stared at the glass. Handsome Angelo looked possessed. He looked like he was about to tell Dwight that his time was up and they would be going down to hell together now.

"You *know*?" Dwight croaked.

Angelo nodded. "I know."

"Jesus," Dwight pleaded, and he was about to launch into a long unplanned begging session when Angelo interrupted him, as he often did, and said:

"I know that you've wanted out for a long time. I could see it. Shay could *hear* it. Your heart hasn't been in it, not for *years*."

"Uh," Dwight said. His head jerked and cheeks stung like he'd been slapped. And pushed over the balcony.

"But Shay's sure that no one else has noticed it. Not yet," Angelo said. "This way we go out on top, man."

You asshole, Dwight thought. *You* do *know. And you are fucking with me.*

Dwight turned and faced his blood brother. Angelo looked like the Virgin Mary, the way he stood there all glowing with the glory of his suffering. He put a hand on Dwight's shoulder and Dwight's knees almost buckled.

"And, well, I got one word for you." Angelo cocked his head thoughtfully and beamed at Dwight. "If things go as planned."

Angelo did beam, yes he did, but there was malice there. Behind-the-eyes cruelty glittered like Dwight's father's eyes when he was drunk and violent. There was cagey sharp triumph. There was the monster Dwight had always suspected lurked inside Angelo, but had never quite caught a glimpse of before. The selfish, self-involved cannibal who fed off him.

"What's that word, Dwight?" asked Angelo. Angelo, with his sharp cannibal teeth and fingernails like knives?

Payback? Dwight shut his eyes.

Pffft…shah. His own life on life support.

Angelo patted Dwight's cheek.

"Comeback," he said. And he held out his empty beer bottle to Dwight. "We'll make a comeback, bro. But it might take years."

Years of fetching Angelo's beers. And being nervous. And wondering.

Dwight took Angelo's fucking empty. Opened Angelo another beer.

Got him some more chips and salsa.

"You're too good to me," Angelo said, settling back into his chair. "You'll always be too good to me, Dwight. It's who you are. It's what you do."

Dwight sat across from him, taking it all in. Figuring it all out.

Pffft…shah…

"Could you grab another bottle of Jack, Dwight?"

While Angelo prolonged the agony.

⚘⚘⚘

RICHARD MATHESON TRIBUTES

"An End, A Middle, A Beginning:
Richard Matheson and His Impact"
By Jason V Brock

RICHARD MATHESON... Most may not recognize his name, but his legacy—*I Am Legend, Trilogy of Terror, What Dreams May Come, The Night Stalker, Bid Time Return to name but a few*—that is another matter.

If there was one writer who most accurately reflected the zeitgeist of a post-World War II, post-technological America—even world—it would likely be Matheson. One could argue—not unreasonably—that perhaps such a designation should go to Ray Bradbury (*Fahrenheit 451*), or Robert Heinlein (*Stranger in a Strange Land*), or even Rod Serling (*The Twilight Zone*). All exemplary choices, however the fact remains that only Matheson captured the post-modern angst and everyday existential crises that came to predominate the general mindset of the "common person" in the mid-to-late 20th century—not only in content and execution (hallmarks of his oeuvre include the intrusion of the extraordinary into the machinations of the everyday, a strong feeling [especially in his earlier output] of paranoia, and an overarching desire to acknowledge the spiritual side of mankind [mostly in his later works]), but with respect to media representation (he wrote for film and television, as well as short fiction, novels, and even song lyrics [he was a musician] for Perry Como), and thematically as well. He presented these scenarios in lean, unromantic prose, with an expansive imagination, a keen eye for detail, and a rarely matched deftness at creating characters one could believe, even when couched in a fantastic setting.

Where Bradbury was a grand metaphorical writer whose conceptions and fancies predicted many aspects of what was to come (Bluetooth earpieces, casual rocket travel, far-reaching issues concerning privacy and access to information, and so on), his subtly alarmist notions were softened by his writing style: poetic, lyrical, full of longing for things, places, and people whose time had bloomed and vanished. Another futurist, Heinlein was by way of contrast more hard-edged—perhaps too much at times—his ideas frequently centered on the negative side of human nature, and the potential violence inherent therein. Serling, meanwhile (although a titan in television, he was never a great prose writer; he was also at one time Matheson's employer, initially recommended by Bradbury), was a champion of the underclasses; preoccupied with social justice and tugged by a similar thread of wistfulness one finds running through many of the works of Bradbury. In some ways, Serling, Bradbury, and Matheson were similar not only in their worldview, but also in their thought with regard to humanity overall; the misty-eyed reverence for their respective childhoods extolled by the former two writers was a signature only shared between them (exemplified in productions by Serling such as "A Stop at Willoughby," and by Bradbury in novels such as *Something Wicked This Way Comes*). This latter facet was not a trait shared by Matheson (or Heinlein), whose creations skewed toward a clear-eyed realist's appraisal of their protagonist's reactions and circumstances, as opposed to the magical wondrous/love conquers all of Bradbury, or the beatific downtrodden of Serling. This lack of nostalgia, yet cautious optimism (and hope) that there is more to the plight of humans, is another one of the things that separates Matheson's writing from his contemporaries in the multiple genres he explored (western, horror, science fiction, mainstream literary, with brief forays into nonfiction). Excluding writers working outside of a strictly America-centric milieu (such as Borges, García Márquez, Kafka, and others), of the myriad authors of the era from circa 1930 until the present, we have a number of instances of fascinating creators—from singular phenoms such as Harper Lee (*To Kill a Mockingbird*), to wordmills like Stephen King (*The Dead Zone*), to cottage industries a la J. K. Rowling (*Harry Potter* series), and of course, the previous examples of Bradbury, Serling, and Heinlein. Yet, in spite of Matheson's relatively modest output—he was never a "bestselling" author and not excessively prolific by most metrics—he was nonetheless unusually important. His anxieties, at their core, strike at the heart of social ennui in ways that none of his colleagues ever did (to include the ill-fated scribe, and dear friend of Matheson's, Charles Beaumont [The Intruder]).

Matheson was born February 20, 1926 in Allendale, New Jersey. Of Norwegian descent, early on he found solace in the world of ideas and writing (as a bulwark against an alcoholic family life), and, after an honorable discharge from the Army in WWII (he had contracted trench foot after seeing action), he secured a degree in journalism from the University of Missouri. Like most neophyte writers, he struggled to find his place, his voice. He was off to a good start, selling his first short story, "Born of Man and Woman" to esteemed editor Anthony Boucher for *The Magazine of Fantasy and Science Fiction* in 1950. During this time, honing his craft, he penned his first novels. One of these, *The Beardless Warriors* (released in 1960), was a mainstream effort—and a good one—about his experiences in the war. He continued to write books, all the while submitting to any other markets that he could, which at that time even included a few more pulp appearances. In this manner, he was slowly building a reputation, and he was heartened by a kind letter from a writer he deeply admired and would later befriend—Ray Bradbury. With Bradbury's encouragement (both in his prose writing, and with his unsolicited endorsement of both Matheson and Beaumont to assist a beleaguered Serling with scripting duties on *The Twilight Zone*), Matheson continued to woodshed, and began breaking new ground as his thoughts matured about what he wanted to say. To this end, his personal demons—paranoia, fear of insanity, dread of unintended scientific repercussions, the dangers of modernity—began to be addressed directly in his work.

A breakthrough occurred in 1954 with the publication of his dystopian vampire epic *I Am Legend*. Here, Matheson's hard-bitten style peeled away the lyricism of Bradbury; the metaphors and scenarios from this seminal piece resonate as strongly today (perhaps more so) than when the publisher presciently declared about Matheson on the book's back cover that "You may be in at the birth of a giant." There had not been anything like it at the time, and it swiftly brought Matheson deserved acclaim.

The follow-up book was another speculative masterpiece—*The Shrinking Man* (1956). In this novel, more (and different) notions about science, man's place in the universe (a theme that Matheson would revisit often in later works), and society bubbled to the fore, and with astonishing results once again. In this effort, Matheson was able to adapt the book into script format, thus demonstrating another talent: the ability to adapt work into another medium. He was ahead of his peers in this respect (with the notable exception of his dear friend Charles Beaumont [*The Intruder*], a writer of immense talent and promise whose life was cut short far too early), and it was then that he was tapped by Rod Serling (along with Beaumont) to lead the Twilight Zone stable of writers. Later, Roger Corman would demonstrate much keen insight and hired both of these luminaries to adapt his Poe films (*House of Usher*, *The Pit and the Pendulum*, and so on).

By this time, Matheson was not only a successful novelist and screenwriter, but also a devoted husband and father. His output still continued to touch on themes and concepts that his friends' work did not. These friends, known later as "The Southern California Writer's Group," but internally simply referred to as "The Group"—included as members not only Matheson and Beaumont, but also William F. Nolan (*Logan's Run*), George Clayton Johnson (*Ocean's 11*), John Tomerlin (*Challenge the Wind*), and by extension Ray Bradbury, Robert Bloch

(*Psycho*), and many others.

As his career accelerated, Matheson turned away from writing short fiction, and increasingly wrote film and television (for the likes of Dan Curtis [*Dark Shadows*], and later Steven Spielberg [who filmed Matheson's adaptation of his short story *Duel*]), though he continued to work on novels, exploring his passions and obsessions with intelligence and an open mind. Of this middle period, several of the standout books center on the ideas and thematic possibilities of the uncanny intruding into the everyday (which has become the operative norm in most speculative dark fiction), the importance of the magical, the transcendent power of love. Along the way, his outlook seemed to have changed, and he became less insular, less self-focused, and more encompassing the mystical aspects of life and the unexplained. He seemed to evolve away from the darker leanings of his earlier works and embraced a more expansive world view that yearned to believe in something greater than the self, than things science alone could substantiate. This evolution also separates Matheson's output from his peers, acolytes, and adherents. He continued to develop his gifts, his intellect, his skills and pursued his muse until he died—not as an elder statesman of literature (though he surely was), or some seeker of greater truth (which also suits him), but as a renegade in the realest sense—a genius able to articulate his changing humanity, and seeking to understand himself and others as best he could.

This is what defines an artist: How they use their talent and power to the betterment and service of others, whether through acknowledging our shared dilemma of consciousness, our collective astonishment of deeds good or bad, and our need to believe that we never truly end. Artists are the portals of a form of immortality that we can all tap into, albeit most will require their shamanistic assistance. Richard Matheson is still here—in his creations, his descendants, his ideas. He has shown us a way, and enriched us all in the process.

Isn't that what becomes a legend most?

"Rich"
By William F. Nolan

HE WAS A CLOSE AND DEAR FRIEND for over half a century—one of The Group's "inner core," along with so many others lost through the years: Chuck Beaumont, Ray Bradbury, Charles Fritch, Chad Oliver, Robert Bloch—all no longer with us.

Eventually, death takes everyone; it's an unsettling, yet natural part of the lifecycle. But death is never easy, never fully integrated into our psyche: We are never quite prepared for the loss of a loved one.

And Rich was loved. By me. By his family. By his friends—indeed, by the countless thousands who read his books and stories and savored his films.

I knew at 87 he was in fragile shape—the result of several major operations; I knew he was in pain; that he could no longer really walk; that his days of swimming for exercise in his backyard pool were over; that the visits I made to his home—shared laughter, warm memories—were no longer possible. All this I sadly accepted—but the news of his death, the finality of it, the dark truth of it, hit home, struck a blow… I told myself: Rich is gone. He will always be alive in the hearts of those who cherished him. That's important; that's what counts.

And his work is still with us… the novels, the plays, the stories, the films: They will survive.

A final warm salute, then, to a master, a decent man, a good soul…

To Richard Burton Matheson: Rest easy my friend.

"Meeting Richard Matheson"
By John Palisano

DRIVING MY JEEP north on the 101 freeway on a perfect February morning, it began to sink in. I was meeting one of my all-time heroes, Richard Matheson. I'd been asked by the HWA to videotape his acceptance speech for *I Am Legend*, which had won the 2012 award for Vampire Novel Of The Century. I'd known about the taping for weeks, but had to keep mum. It wasn't going to be announced until the Bram Stoker Awards a month later. I kept my mouth shut, but I was thrilled to be part of something so monumental.

Let's put that in perspective. The weekend prior, I'd videotaped Red Carpets and other events leading up to and including the Academy Awards. I met many celebrities and movie stars, but meeting Richard was going to be a whole lot more fun for me. This is a man whose accomplishments are amazing. His imagination has given us so many unforgettable stories.

Richard lived inside a cozy, gated community, where a guard called to confirm I was coming. I navigated winding, hilly roads, eventually finding his driveway, marked with a big R x R sign. He and his wife. The man who wrote *Somewhere In Time* and *What Dreams May Come* obviously had just as much heart as his characters.

I parked and got out my tripod and Hi-Def video camera. There was a man waiting at the open front door. I heard Richard say, "Is that John?" I walked into a handsome living room and found Richard sitting on a couch. We shook hands. "Nice to meet you," I said. I'd met him at signings before, but doubted he'd remember me.

"Did you find the place okay?" he asked.

"Oh, yeah. I put it into my iPhone," I said.

"Like a GPS in the dashboard?" Richard said.

"It's all in the phone. It's got a list of directions, or you can track yourself on a map."

He dug it.

"Sit down. Do you want anything to drink?"

"I'm okay," I said. "Thanks."

"Well let me know if you change your mind." He still had those amazing blue eyes that seemed to take in everything.

He asked me what exactly we were doing, and I told him it was for the HWA's award for Vampire Novel Of The Century for *I Am Legend*. I asked if he wanted to sit where he was.

"If you don't mind," he said.

"Of course not," I said. The lighting and background looked great.

I rolled the camera and Richard talked about how, in the military, he'd snuck reading *Dracula*, and that he got the idea for *I Am Legend* by thinking: what if there were more than one vampire? He then thanked the HWA for the award and then we stopped rolling.

"Do you want to see it?" I asked.

"Yes."

I handed over the camera. He reviewed the footage, and seemed satisfied.

After it was over, I said, "Is it okay? Do you want to do it again?"

"No. I'd just say the same things all over again. It's fine."

We both laughed.

"They don't start movies right anymore. The whole beginning part of the movie has nothing to do with the rest of it," he said.

We talked about *War Horse* where the first thirty minutes of the movie shows the horse digging rocks out of the ground, but the story really starts after that.

He said, "I worked with Steven years ago."

I nodded. Of course. He helped launch Steven Spielberg's career with the amazing *Duel*.

O Brother, Where Art Thou? comes up, and he says, "The Cohen Brothers make some fine films. Watched *Fargo* three times. What are they doing next?" I wasn't sure, but we both agreed we admired their craftsmanship and bravery in not taking the easy path.

"George Clooney is the epitome of confidence." I mentioned that it was hard to believe he could pull off his passive character in *The Descendants*, but he had.

"We have a great theater here." He mentioned the community playhouse.

I told him about working the Oscar weekend, and how it was surreal, that the photographers were treated poorly.

"Did you interview people?" he asked.

I shared with him a few of the names I'd spoken to.

A rat ran across the yard. "They had to redo the roof a few years ago and the rats went everywhere in the attic. They're just surviving. The government up here started trapping coyotes, which me and my wife didn't agree with. We found one in a trap, but couldn't get it out. We called and they came and got it out and it limped away. It kind of looked back at us like, Hey, thanks a lot!"

He mentioned his home. "Our backyard is a park now. They were trying to get it made into condos, but a bunch of people saved it. Now it's a park."

I asked if he ever went for walks or explored it.

"I used to, but now my health is too bad. My daughter does when she comes out. She takes Emma for walks."

Richard mentioned traveling to the Bram Stoker Awards. "I would probably go to Salt Lake, but my health is poor. I wish they'd have a convention up here!"

Concerning the last *I Am Legend* film, he said, "I wish they would have shot my novel. They haven't yet. They're making a sequel. Somehow they're going to find a way to bring him back to life."

I commented that the movie business is silly. "I don't know if that's the right adjective for that!" Too funny, and right on target.

He remarked that they changed too much on *What Dreams May Come*, and concerning *Hell* House he said, "I didn't like it at the time, but now I've seen it a few times, and it's better than I thought. Some of these things are better with time. A guy in New York is making a musical of *Somewhere In Time*. He keeps sending me the songs. There's an annual convention for *Somewhere In Time* where people dress up in costumes. They sell out the whole hotel. It's in October."

He mentioned an unrealized symphony he'd been working on for years. "I haven't touched a piano in twenty years, but all the themes and melodies are in my head. I just have to work them out."

I was surprised to learn he was a musician.

"I was first in line to write *The Birds*, as well," he said. "I went in to the office and none of the agents showed up. It was just me and Hitchcock. I said, 'I don't think you should show the birds.' And he went, (using Hitchcock impression) 'Nooo!' – and I think that was it for me on that job. Not showing things is scarier. The scariest scene in the film is when the birds are pecking through the door."

I told him that I thought the scariest part of *I Am Legend* is when they are calling Neville while he is inside his house, before we see any of them. He nodded.

He thanked me for coming, and I rose to shake his hand, said thanks back, and told him I hoped we'd meet again.

"Thank you. Drive safely," he replied.

"Bye-bye, Emma," I said, but she was passed out on the floor. I left the house and drove away. I'd met a true legend, and as I headed back down those chaparral-lined roads toward the freeway, I imagined the symphonies in Richard's head bouncing off the rocks, echoing through his neighborhood and spilling across the freeway.

Now, a year later, I picture Richard where dreams go, conducting and thrilling the afterlife with his stories and music, painting his imagination inside every soul he touches.

"Richard Matheson"
By Joe R. Lansdale

Richard Matheson, like Ray Bradbury, changed our culture. People may not even know him by name, but the many programs and stories he wrote are so much a part of pop culture his presence and impact are undeniable. I see it in films and TV, books and stories, and even commercials. He is one of my heroes as a writer. He was imaginative, clever, and he wrote a good modern style of clean, swift prose. He has taught so many of us so many lessons about writing. He will forever be missed, but his impact will continue not only with his stories, but with all the writers he has influenced.

"On Matheson's Passing"
By Stephen King

We've lost one of the giants of the fantasy and horror genres. From The Beardless Warriors, his brilliant (and largely unread) World War II novel, to The Incredible Shrinking Man and all the wonderful Twilight Zone scripts and stories, Matheson fired the imaginations of three generations of writers.

Without his I Am Legend, there would have been no Night of the Living Dead; without Night of the Living Dead, there would have been no Walking Dead, 28 Days Later or World War Z. Matheson wrote the script for Steven Spielberg's extraordinary film, Duel, and created one of the most brain-freezingly frightening haunted house novels of the 20th century in Hell House.

He fired my imagination by placing his horrors not in European castles and Lovecraftian universes, but in American scenes I knew and could relate to. "I want to do that," I thought. "I must do that." Matheson showed the way.

In addition to that, he was a gentleman who was always willing to give a young writer a hand up. I will miss his kindness and erudition. He lived a full life, raised a fine family, and gave us unforgettable stories, novels, TV shows, and movies. That's good. Nevertheless, I mourn his loss. A uniquely American voice has been silenced.

ON I AM LEGEND — " a lesson..."
By Jack Ketchum

Neville's been alone in his fortress for a whole year now. He fumes with anger and aches with loss. He's the loneliest creature on earth. Human life -- indeed all mammalian life -- appears extinguished. His research into the vampire bacillus has stalled so completely that he trashes his microscope and stays dead drunk for two days. On the third day he stumbles out to the porch and sees a miracle.

A dog.

A mangy, crippled, half-starved dog. Alive in the sunlight.

"To Neville," says Matheson, "that dog was the peak of a planet's evolution."

You can understand why.

He tries chasing him and calling him and cajoling him but that doesn't work. The dog's terrified of him.

You can understand why.

The dog probably thought he was the loneliest creature on earth too.

And Neville can only wonder at what he must have gone through in order to survive for this long.

Finally he gets hold of himself, calms himself down and tries the obvious. Food. Drink. Good raw hamburger out of his freezer, a bowl of milk and a bowl of water. Hamburger is dear and in short supply but there's plenty of dogfood in the deserted markets so he gathers it up. Over time the dog becomes the entire focal point of Neville's life as he tentatively and nervously takes his bait while Neville at first watches him through his peephole then ventures outside to his porch sitting silent and still, getting the dog used to his presence, inching closer and closer at each feeding, getting him slowly used to the human voice again. Good dog, that's a good dog, good boy. Delighting in him.

Then one day the dog doesn't show -- and Neville's frantic. He searches everywhere. For three entire days he's gone and when he does reappear his eyes are glazed and his legs wobbly and it's clear that not only he's been through hell out there but probably he's dying. In the dog's weakened state Neville manages to snatch him up and bring him inside. But now the dog's trapped in some unknown place and truly scared out of his wits.

He hides in some blankets Neville arranges for him under the bed, refusing all food and drink, snapping at Neville and whining and at dinnertime he hears a hideous crying and runs to the bedroom and there's the dog digging frantically at the linoleum floor. Suddenly he knows what's wrong. "It was nighttime and the terrified dog was trying to dig itself a hole to bury itself in."

This singular night is a horror of a new and different kind. Neville can't even begin to sleep for the sounds the dog's making beneath the bed so he switches on the bedside lamp and at that the dog panics even further, getting tangled up in the blankets and yelping and scrambling to get free so Neville reaches in and grabs him snarling and snapping inside the blanket and holds him firmly but gently in front of him on the floor talking to him all the while, good dog, we'll take care of you, you'll be better soon you'll see for easily over a hour until at last the dog subsides and Neville exposes his poor scarred matted head and strokes him, scratches him, pets him, speaks to him.

"The dog looked up at him with its dulled, sick eyes and then its tongue faltered out and licked roughly and moistly across the palm of Neville's hand.

"Something broke in Neville's throat. He sat there silently while tears ran slowly down his cheeks.

"In a week the dog was dead."

On that line the chapter ends.

And I remember thinking -- what simple, straightforward, devastating writing. What a double sucker-punch to the gut and heart.

And these finally have become the horrors that most interest me as a reader and as a writer. Not the vampires howling outside the door but the yearning and loss inside. The quiet survivals of feeling, empathy and compassion. The courage to bind and bond which life permits us access to for only so long but which heals us and makes life livable and allows us to go on.

When Neville emerges from the incident with the dog he emerges a changed man. The drunk has gone. His rage has gone. He's much the better for it.

And that's the lesson.

You beat horror by reaching out beyond it. By contact.

Then you go on.

☃☃☃

DOUBLE X CHROMOSOME

By Yvonne Navarro

Babes Doing It Better...
or Just as Brutally

Well, crap!

I have no idea what to write about for this third installment of Double X Chromosome. This issue carries the full theme of "Women in Horror," and y'all (thought I'd throw a little Southern accent in) already know I think that is just *so* clichéd. I don't even have a title yet for this issue's installment, and I'll be damned if I call it "Women in Horror."

Women in Horror. Horrible Women (one of the dumber suggestions I got for column names). Hmmmm...

If I can't decide on a title, at least I can come up with a topic. How about those women who have, or could have, or should have, inspired entire chunks of horror fiction?

The ~~softer~~ female side of serial killing?

DeadTimes

yvonne navarro

I won't bother going into the whys and hows of female serial killers and murderers—God knows I'm no psychologist. Half the time I can't figure out why I do certain things, or why one of my dogs decides to poop in the house, or why the bird suddenly bites me. Don't even get me started on the whims and wiles of my husband. And I'm not going to stick only with ladies who kill, because sometimes you don't need to wield the weapon yourself to be oh-so-high in the rankings.

Let's just make a list—in no particular order—and see what we come up with.

Countess Elizabeth Bathory (1560-1614). If the name of this Hungarian babe doesn't sound familiar, you've been living on way too much television... and even then I don't see how you missed her. Convicted of the murders of 80 young women in 1610, her true body count is estimated to be well over 600. The locals thought she was a vampire, and for good reason: she bathed in the blood of her victims because she thought it helped her stay young. I've used the dear dead Countess myself in two projects, once in a double section of my novel *DeadTimes*, and the other in a story called "die Blutgrafin" in the *Buffy the Vampire Slayer* anthology, *Tales of the Slayer, Vol. I.*

The Witch Bitches (1690s). Who were they? Glad you asked: Elizabeth Parris, Abigail Williams, Ann Putnam, Jr., Mary Warren, Mary Walcott, Elizabeth Booth, Sarah Churchill, Elizabeth Hubbard, Mercy Lewis and Susanna Sheldon. These fine examples of female insanity ranged in age from 11 to 25 years old at the time witches "afflicted" Salem, Massachusetts. Their testimony included lies and fits thrown at home or in the courtrooms, and without ever physically picking up any weapons, they helped send a lot of innocent men and women—including many of their own relatives—to the gallows. Their evil deeds have popped up innumerable times in history and fiction, including my own book (again), *DeadTimes*. For all the talk about how well-behaved children were "back then," all I can say is these kidlets could've used a good dose of my Mom's favorite saying: *"I'm going to count to three..."*

Vera Renczi (?-?). Rumored to have been born in 1903, this enchanting woman had an invisible hitchhiker—that great, green monster called *Jealousy*. Her father tried to thrash it out of her when she was a child because she killed her dog rather than see it given to someone else. In adulthood she killed her husband for being unfaithful to her; killed her ten-year-old son because not only was she afraid that he would betray her, but that he would soon grow up and hold other women besides herself; one more husband; and then thirty-three more men, some married, because she couldn't bear to think of them holding another woman after having embraced her. Lovely Vera's case was so notorious that in addition to the articles and books she inspired, there was even a Pulitzer prize-winning reporter, Otto B. Tolischus, following her trial. Good thing he didn't follow her home.

Sister Credonia Mwerinde (1952-?). This pyromaniac masquerading as a cult holy leader trapped her followers in a pyrotechnically-rigged building called "The Ark" in Kanangu, Uganda and burned them all alive. There are differing figures out there; some reports cite the death toll as a staggering 738, with 530 people found inside the building and the remainder of bodies found at other cult locations. Sister Credonia was reported to have left before the conflagration, and a warrant was issued for her arrest in 2000. She has not been apprehended, and currently walks free. Perhaps she's building up another church following. Perhaps she's handing you change at your favorite store. Comforting, eh?

Amelia Dyer (1837-1896). Apparently in days gone by there were places called "baby farms" where a girl or woman who discovered herself in unfortunate circumstances could pay someone to take an unwanted child off her hands. Sometimes a woman did so only because she couldn't care for the baby at the moment, but she intended to get things right with her life and claim her daughter later. Such was the case for Evelina Marmon, who handed her week-old daughter Doris over to a woman named Amelia Dyer along with a £10 adoption fee. Dyer had advertised that she was looking for a child to adopt, and although she was older than Evelina expected, Dyer talked a good game about loving children and having a beautiful place to raise her. Dyer left with tiny Doris Marmon and after traveling to a location not even close to where Evelina believed them to be going, Dyer and her daughter Polly tied white edging tape around the baby's neck and strangled her. Eleven days later Amelia Dyer was arrested; although she was convicted of only one murder and hanged on June 10, 1896, history showed that she—and her daughter, who was freed for some still unknown reason—are believed to have killed hundreds of infants.

Belle Sorenson Gunness (1859-1908). This strapping six-foot-tall woman is estimated to have killed between 25 and 40 people, starting in my old

stomping grounds of Chicago. Why? Everything in the records points to money. She burned buildings to dispatch her children, husbands (one on the only day on which two, count 'em, *two*, insurance policies on the man overlapped), stepchildren, adopted children, and numerous suitors responding to her newspaper ads. The disappearance of the suitors began to arouse suspicion, and a fired handyman in love with Belle would not go away. One night, her home was completely engulfed by fire (yeah, go figure). In the ruins were the bodies of all three of her children as well as the headless corpse of a woman weighing about 150 pounds and five-foot-eight at best. All the dead were later found to have ingested legal doses of strychnine. To make a long story short, eventually the handyman claimed she had enlisted him to help her escape and placed her own bridgework next to the dead woman in an effort to prove that the corpse was her. Experts disagree, but the general consensus appears that Belle Gunness escaped to Los Angeles as a rich woman. Although it was never proven, ultimately she is thought to have died while awaiting trial under the name Esther Carlson. The charge?

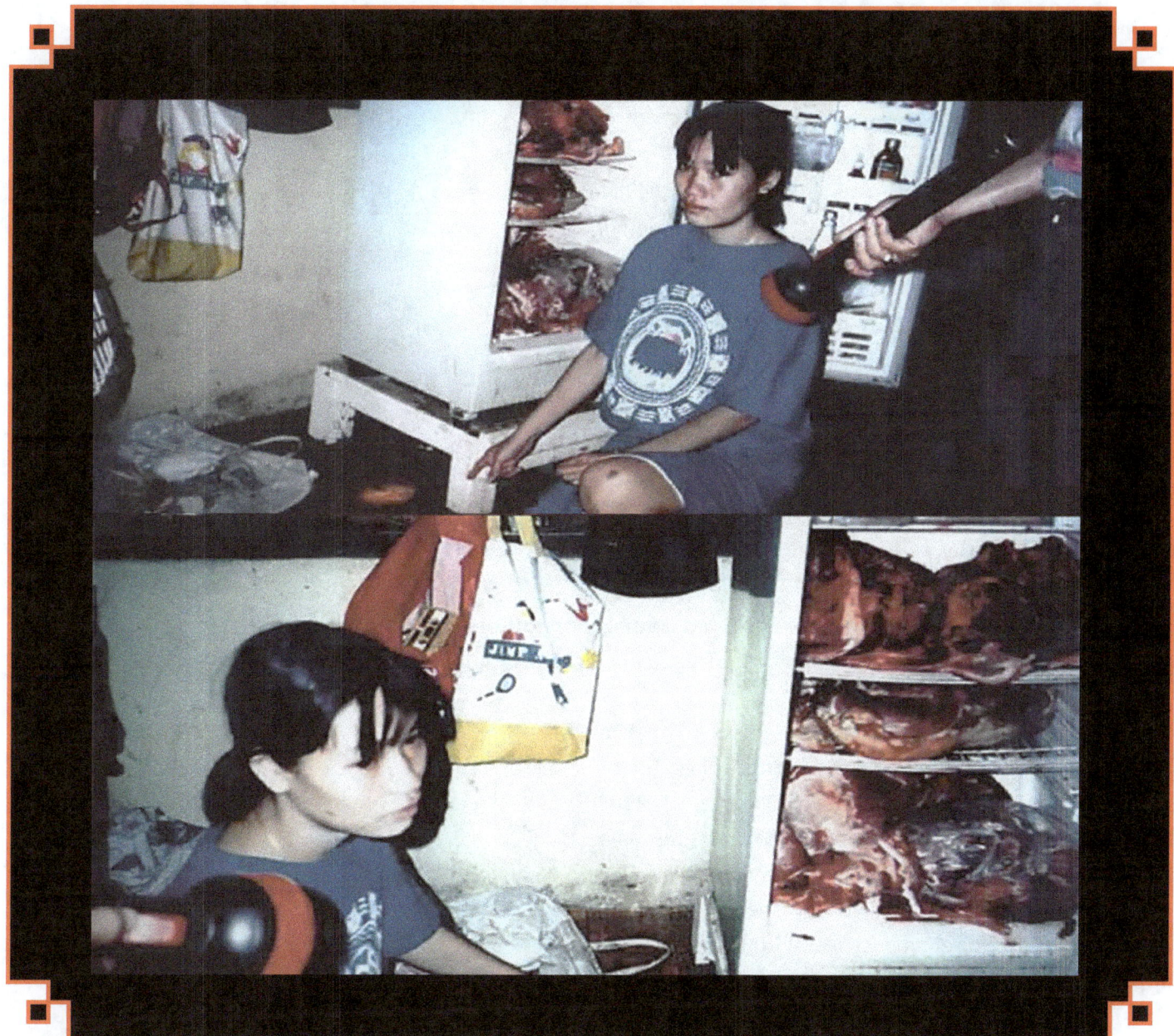

Poisoning a man for money.

??? What's up with these pictures? you ask. (You know you did.) Hey, if you need proof that horrible women are alive and operating well in the present, put this in your cranium file under *Recent Cases*: In January 2012, Indonesian police arrested a 29-year-old Philippine woman for killing and eating more than thirty girls, plus her own husband. She chopped up the bodies and kept the leftovers in the refrigerator. The word "leftovers" is mine because, you know, she'd been cooking and serving the, uh, goodies to friends and relatives at parties for quite some time, and they all thought the food was great. This unidentified psychopath (Indonesia is apparently too embarrassed to release her name) said she'd do it again given the chance; convicted and in prison, she bit off and swallowed a finger from the right hand of a guard.

Y'all be sure to enjoy all those free appetizers in the hospitality room at the next convention, you hear?

Yvonne wrote her own female serial killer story, called "Lifeline," which was published in the HWA anthology, Robert Bloch's *Psychos* in November 1997.

Comments? Questions? Suggestions? Yvonne Navarro can be reached via her website, Facebook page, or at her Dark Discoveries email:

yvonne@journalstone.com.

WHAT THE HELL EVER HAPPENED TO...?

Robert Morrish

An interview with Alan Rodgers

By Robert Morrish

Past installments of this column have profiled a variety of authors and editors. This issue's subject is notable for achieving prominence in the horror genre as *both* an author and editor.

ALAN RODGERS first achieved renown in the horror field when he became the inaugural editor of *Night Cry* magazine in 1984. *Night Cry* was a horror fiction digest launched by Montcalm Publishing as a companion to *Rod Serling's The Twilight Zone Magazine* (where Rodgers had previously been Associate Editor), running for eleven issues, with the final issue appearing in Fall 1987. Mixing original fiction with classic reprints, *Night Cry* quickly became a venue for some of horror's biggest names, publishing work by the likes of Dean Koontz, Robert Bloch, Ramsey Campbell, F. Paul Wilson, and David Schow, to name a few.

As a writer, Rodgers also arrived on the scene with a bang, with his "The Boy Who Came Back From the Dead" tying for the Bram Stoker Award for Best Novelette in 1987. His first novel, *Blood of the Children,* was published by Bantam Books in 1990 and three more novels appeared from Bantam: *Fire* (1990), *Night* (1991), and *Pandora* (1995). Two further horror novels followed – *Bone Music* (Longmeadow, 1995) and *Her Misbegotten Son* (Wildside, 1996) – and Rodgers also compiled the collections *New Life for the Dead* (Wildside, 1991) and *Ghosts Who Cannot Sleep* (Wildside, 2000). Outside of the horror genre, he published fantasy novel *The Bear Who Found Christmas* (2000) and science fiction novels *Alien Love* (2002) and *The River*

FROM THE EDITORS OF ROD SERLING'S THE **TWILIGHT ZONE** MAGAZINE

NIGHT CRY

FALL 1986 $2.95

DEAN R. KOONTZ
SNATCHER
from the author of
STRANGERS

ROBERT BLOCH
THE CHANEY LEGACY

J. N. Williamson • George Alec Effinger
John Skipp and Craig Spector
Avram Davidson • A. R. Morlan

Display until Sept. 6

of Our Destiny (2002), but hasn't published anything at book length since 2002.

Sadly, the last decade of Rodgers' life has been beset by tragedy. In early 2005, his infant son, Anthony Sterling Rogers, died in an accident. Then, in 2012, he suffered a series of devastating strokes, which have left him partially paralyzed and in need of regular medical care. He has improved somewhat, but his recovery remains very slow.

The following interview was conducted with the assistance of Amy Sterling Casil, mother of the late Anthony Sterling Rodgers, who remains close friends with Alan.

DD: How did you initially get involved with *Twilight Zone* magazine?

AR: When we got out of college, my (now ex-)wife and I went up to New York to look for work in the publishing business. My ambition was to edit a science fiction magazine. She managed to get work opening the mail and such for *Hitchcock's*; I found a job proofreading junk mail. Which wore thin after just a couple months. I sent out a couple hundred resumes, and one of the interviews I got was with *TZ*. Where Ted Klein hired me specifically because I knew a lot about science fiction. What Ted knew and worked with was horror; he thought, I guess, that having a SF person on staff would add balance. I don't know. We had lots of disagreements—most of them pretty friendly. I wasn't much of a horror reader back then. Didn't like being scared, and couldn't imagine what anyone would see in it.

Which is pretty much the same way I felt when Ted announced that he was leaving the magazine and recommending that I replace him. Management, unfortunately, thought I was too young—and I was young, truth to tell. Eventually they ended up hiring Michael Blaine for the job, and giving me *Night Cry* to soothe my ego.

Now, *Night Cry* wasn't just horror, but *very* horror. To edit it I had to learn to enjoy being scared. That was a strange couple of weeks, I'll tell you. To enjoy being scared I had to admit being scared—and every nightmare I'd ever had, all the big and little

fears that I avoided instead of facing—all of them came to get me.

Yeah, I know that sounds melodramatic and unreal. But it's true: I had two solid weeks of nightmares before I came out on the other end.

DD: *Night Cry* ceased publication in 1987, after 11 issues. Do you think the magazine was given a fair chance to succeed? In hindsight, is there anything you would have done differently with the mag? Any interesting anecdotes from those days come to mind?

AR: Yes, it was. I think a year would have been fair. We went 11 issues instead of four, a lot longer than I would have anticipated. As far as anything I would have done differently, if I had known who my friends would have turned out to be, I would have bought stories by them. We spent time looking for stories from the hot writers at the time. That's how I got to be a Ramsay Campbell and Dean Koontz fan during that period.

The town of Green Hill has a horrifying secret...
Blood of the Children
Alan Rodgers

"The Boy Who Came Back from the Dead." (For chronology, I wrote it while Ted was in process of leaving *TZ*. Took about six months.) I wrote most of *Blood of the Children* while I was still at Montcalm.

While I was at *Night Cry*, I wrote every morning standing on the subway writing by hand in a spiral notebook. That's how I wrote "The Boy Who Came Back From the Dead."

DD: It seems like your big breakthrough was "The Boy Who Came Back From The Dead" in *Masques II*. Would you agree with that? How did that story come to be written and published in *Masques II*?

AR: This was the first complete horror story I ever wrote. I came up in love with comics, and it was definitely the story where I looked up and suddenly knew how to write. It ended up in *Masques II* because Jerry Williamson asked me for a story. Jerry Williamson had been asking me for work for quite a while. I wrote this story on the subway and I knew it was right for the book. It has turned out to have been the right choice since then, and I'm glad he asked me.

DD: Let's talk about *Blood of the Children*. Obviously that was the first novel you had published. Was that the first novel you'd written? What was involved in the writing and selling of that book?

AR: I did one partial before *Blood of the Children*, and sent it to Lou Aronica over at Bantam. (Sent to Lou partly because he was my wife's boss and would break my legs if I sent it elsewhere, and partly because I'd known, liked, and respected Lou for years.) Lou convinced me that I should set that book aside and do something different for him. I sent over a handful of ideas (*Fire* was another of them) and we decided that the first thing I should do was *Blood of the Children*. (Note: *Blood of the Children* frightened even hardened horror writers and editors.)

DD: How did the idea for your 2nd novel, *Fire*, germinate?

AR: The idea part of the book was something I'd

In fact, that's how I met Dean Koontz. I really liked his work and I started talking to writers, to find out who knew him. Then I was able to talk with him about his work. It was a privilege to publish his work, and I've read everything he's written since. He's a great man and a great writer.

DD: Did you get the chance to do much writing while you were working on the magazines?

AR: Sort of. I didn't do any writing at all the first year I was there. After that, though, I knew that magazine editing wasn't something I could do for a lifetime, and that I had to work on my fiction if I was going to have a career that lasted more than a few years. So I started writing, steadily, every morning during my commute. I wrote ten thousand words of something very "skiffy" that's still in my trunk, and then I wrote been kicking around for years—partly a response to Greg Bear's *Blood Music*, partly a response to Lucius Shepard's *Green Eyes*. But it was too skiffy, and I'd already decided I didn't want to grow up to be a science fiction writer. The sort of thing I do isn't commercial at all when you try to sell it as science fiction. So the idea just sat there, stewing, till I looked up and realized that it'd be a really nifty thing to use in an apocalyptic end-of-the-world novel. After that it only took me about two days to sketch out *Fire*.

DD: Between 1990 and 1995, you published four novels with Bantam. Tell us about how your relationship with that publisher came to an end.

AR: My ex-wife Amy Stout had been working for Bantam during this time. She received the position because I was offered the job first, but I preferred to do *Night Cry*. When her position was terminated, I was also between books, so I didn't continue with Bantam, but I continued writing and working with my agent.

DD: Bantam ran a fairly big publicity campaign for *Fire*… how did that book sell? Was it your best seller?

AR: It sold very well, and it was my best-selling novel. It sold a couple of hundred thousand copies, which was a good performance for a horror novel at that time.

DD: You said the following about your third novel, *Night*: "I started working on this book with the thought that God isn't dead, and it isn't that he doesn't love us, either. It's just that he wants to give us room enough to be ourselves, even if that means we screw up." Coming between *Fire* and *Pandora*, both of which had SF trappings, *Night's* philosophical subject matter seems decidedly different. What prompted that book?

AR: was thinking about the ideas that are important to me when I wrote *Night*. The subject and characters and voice are more like what I grew up thinking about in the South. Thinking about more spiritual things or

the big questions of why we are all here encouraged me to write that book. Angels and demons and what motivates them; spirits with uncertain motivations or very clear motivations, and where our souls might go were the topic of *Night*.

DD: Your first three novels with Bantam were published in less than two years, but then four years passed before your last novel with them was published. Why the long delay?

AR: To be honest, Bantam was unhappy with my sales even though afterwards, they were good in retrospect, and they wanted to give me another chance and re-launch me with *Night*, so that was the time period that it took.

DD: That final novel with Bantam, *Pandora*, was something of a science fiction/horror hybrid. I'm

speculating that your parting of ways with Bantam was due to *Pandora* not selling as well as hoped… if that is, in fact, the case, do you think the fact that *Pandora* straddled a couple of different genres may have in some way contributed to the lack of sales?

AR: I think you're right. Sci-fi and horror mixed together is not really a good plan. Each sells to different audiences in different ways. It's hard to sell to both at the same time. I like the book, but that was my mistake.

DD: After leaving Bantam, you had your first hardcover publication with the novel *Bone Music,* from Longmeadow Press in 1995. How did that deal come about, and why did you only publish one title with them?

AR: *Bone Music* is a challenging book, and my agent Kay McCauley sold *Bone Music* to Longmeadow. It

She was the government's best-kept secret.
Now the lid is off….

17

PANDORA
An epic novel of horror by the author of *Fire*
ALAN RODGERS

was always envisioned as a one-title sale. We kept the paperback rights and I later reissued it as a paperback with Wildside Press.

DD: After *Bone Music*, you went on to publish four more novels – *Her Misbegotten Son, Menace: Battle Mountain, The River of Our Destiny*, and *Alien Love* – as well as a *BattlestarGalactica* tie-in, co-written with Richard Hatch. Tell us a little about each of those books and how they came to be.

AR: I was able to do these books when I was a partner with John Betancourt at Wildside Press. We were able to release them as paperbacks, and they are all related to prior stories or books, whether in the Lovecraftian milieu or related to the aliens in "The Boy Who Came Back From the Dead." I actually did not write the *BattlestarGalactica* title. I enjoyed working with Richard Hatch very much, but Amy Sterling Casil, who is a science fiction writer and familiar with the series, has more of a sci-fi bent, so she wrote the book with my permission with Richard, although she is credited as "editor."

DD: Although you mentioned earlier that you didn't want to become a science fiction writer, it does seem like some of these latter titles were more on the sci-fi side of the ledger… did you make a conscious decision to stop writing horror and try the science fiction field, or…?

AR: No, I really didn't. All of the science fictional elements in my stories, I think you will find, have to do with the "alien" or other, which is a horror-like concept. And sometimes it was easier to sell science fiction than horror.

DD: Since publishing *The River of Our Destiny* and *Alien Love*, both in 2002, you haven't published anything further, to my knowledge. Did you stop writing?

AR: No, I haven't stopped writing. Before I became ill in 2011, I wrote 6 novels. I continued to write stories in the Lovecraftian world and published those regularly until I became ill.

DD: Tell us a little about those unpublished novels.

AR: *Smoke* is a novel set in a similar world to *Night*. It tells the story of Tom Candy and the "Dark Man" who appears in several other stories. It has a similar voice to *Night* and shares the Southern setting, which is where I grew up. I have also written several young adult books, including *My Best Friend is a Dragon*, about a little girl attending school along with a dragon in Manhattan, and two books about kids in a wizard's school who confront Cthulhu-like beasts.

DD: You had a strong publishing relationship with Wildside Press for a while… is there any particular reason that came to an end?

AR: I was partners with John Betancourt at Wildside Press from 1999 to 2005. My son died in an accident at home in January 2005. While I was ill after that terrible event, John Betancourt and I dissolved the partnership. The majority of the previous Wildside catalog became Alan Rodgers Books. Because I have never promoted Alan Rodgers Books, many people are not aware of the large number of titles I put into print while partners with John at Wildside, and after that time. The majority of the business consists of library hardcover editions of hardcover books with critical introductions, including a number of classic horror authors like William Hope Hodgson and Bram Stoker. I also discovered a love for 19th century fiction, including classic children's authors.

DD: Tell us a little more about the "Alan Rodgers Books" publishing imprint.

AR: Alan Rodgers Books is my publishing business. It currently has more than 2,000 titles in print, and is primarily a reprint publisher of classic titles that I selected, edited, and directed in preparation for quality library and trade paperback editions, in addition to some living authors including Bruce Holland Rogers, Adam-Troy Castro, and Amy Sterling Casil. I was very glad to have been able to re-release some author-editions of books by writers like Brian McNaughton. Alan Rodgers Books is still publishing books, although on a modest scale. The titles are primarily reprints, because they sell in modest, yet consistent numbers. This is not good for living authors, but is very good for classic reprints to continue to be available to readers and libraries.

❦ ❦ ❦

A Darkened Screen in Seattle

By Richard Dansky

Video games are perhaps the only creative medium where the genres are defined, not by content, but rather by mechanics. One generally doesn't talk about science fiction games; one discusses FPS and open-world sandboxes. The genre of the narrative is essentially secondary, as what matters most is how the player interacts with the world.

That being said, horror (and its near relation, dark fantasy) are malleable types, and can adapt themselves to almost any play style. First person shooters trace their lineage to *Doom*, after all, which reaches literally into Hell for its setup. *Limbo* is a moody 2-D sidescroller, while *Wasted Land* brings Lovecraftian elements to turn-based strategy, and so it goes. Name the genre, and there's a horror in it. Name a mechanic, and game developers will find a way to make it scary.

A quick look at the horror-themed games shown at the recent PAX conference in Seattle demonstrates that this line of thinking is alive and well. From fast-paced actioners with AAA budgets to hyper-stylized 2-D indies, the range of horror titles shown was impressive in its many styles and approaches. One thing that held true across the board, however, was that nobody seemed interested in doing the same old, same old.

Perhaps the highest profile horror game shown off at PAX was Warner Brothers' *Dying Light*. Another entry in the "infected zombie apocalypse" subgenre, the game falls neatly between *Mirror's Edge* and *Left 4 Dead*. By day, the protagonist scavenges a destroyed world and dodges relatively powerless zombies; by night, the real monsters come out and turn the tables on the remaining humans. The cycling of play style—scavenge by day, hide by night—and enemy responses constantly adjusts the challenges players face; writer Haris Orkin says "it's like two games in one" and that it's more "gritty and real" than his previous zombie effort, *Dead Island*.

Lines to play the game often reached well over an hour, with the fluid freerunning style making for a faster gameplay experience than the usual zombie slugfest. The freerunning also allowed the integration of a stronger vertical element, opening up new corridors of mobility for players previously rare in the genre. Created by Dead Island masterminds Techland, the game is slated for a 2014 release.

Also making a strong showing in the zombie category was *State of Decay*, described by one of the folks manning its booth as "GTA with zombies." An open-world experience with more emphasis on moment-to-moment survival than on mowing down undead hordes, it's now available on PC as well as console via Steam.

Tucked into the Sony booth was the eerie ghost story *Rain*, a product of Sony's Playstation Developer C.A.M.P project. Players take on the role of what appears to be the shade of a small boy, wandering the monster-haunted streets of a city under an endless downpour. Only the rain gives him shape; getting under cover renders him invisible to the beasts that would otherwise tear him apart. Heavily implied is an *Ico*-like relationship with the ghost of a small girl whom the protagonist only glimpses in the demo. Visually, the game is striking, presenting a haunted version of the everyday world free of the distorted grotesqueries of a *Silent Hill* or *Resident Evil*. Moody, atmospheric and alluring, this platform puzzler will be available October 1st as a Playstation Network exclusive.

Over on the indie side, the booths might have been smaller but the ambitions just as large. Blurring the lines between entertainment and real-world concerns was the much-discussed *Neverending Nightmares*. With an art style and sensibility clearly indebted to the works of Edward Gorey, the game is deceptively slow-paced but deeply disturbing. The player avatar "awakens" from one horrific nightmare only to find himself trapped in another one, and another, and another. While the Gorey reference would seem to imply a certain level of humor, in reality it works to heighten the horror, as the stylized characters indulge in acts of brutal violence and self-mutilation. The slow pace also heightens the dread, as the nightmarish sense of impending doom that pervades the scenario is amplified by the characters' inability to move just a little faster.

But the game is more than just a slow-motion creepfest, as it was inspired by designer Matt Gilgenbach's personal struggles. He's up front about this as well, saying, "With *Neverending Nightmares*, I try to capture the true psychological horror I've endured when battling obsessive-compulsive disorder and depression."

The extensive developer diaries Gilgenbach posts on YouTube provide real insight into his approach and creative process, as well as outlining where some of the game's most disturbing imagery comes from.

Currently, *Neverending Nightmares* is planned for release on Mac, Windows and Linux, with a Kickstarter to fund the full project well underway.

More energetic but just as stylized was *Contrast*, a gorgeously decadent looking action-adventure title from Montreal-based Compulsion studios. It's the story of a little girl named Didi, told with a twist—the adults in this world appear as shadows, and Didi's best friend Dawn—who is invisible and may be imaginary—has the ability to jump back and forth between shadows and the real world. In one particularly striking sequence, Dawn leaps from back to back of the shadows of carousel horses in order to reach an otherwise inaccessible balcony high above the cobblestones. Writer Alex Epstein describes the game's setting as "a shattered, hallucinatory world of film noir cabarets and carnivals," which, combined with the player's ability to literally change the landscape for shadow-Dawn by moving light sources, makes for a unique and visually striking set of challenges.

With the new generation of consoles about to hit, budgets for AAA titles increasing and mobile platforms making up an ever-increasing chunk of the market, the gaming landscape is in a state of flux unparalleled in recent memory. That being said, if these five titles are representative, the future looks bright for games that stick to the dark side.

ONCE UPON A NIGHTMARE YA HORROR

By Amy Shane

Throughout time we have had some powerhouse female authors, such as Mary Shelly, Shirley Jackson and Anne Rice. However, it hasn't been until recently that the young adult market has taken on horror titles penned by women.

These new writers are forging their own paths, causing others to move over and let them pave the way. Kendare Blake, Robin Wassermann, Victoria Schwab, Kate Quinn, and April Tucholke are among the newest on the YA circuit. They have shattered the ties that bind, setting stones for other authors to follow. They've captured the market by breaking into the paranormal scene and are moving straight into horror. These women have become role models to our youth, teaching the younger generation of today not to be limited by society's image of how anyone should be portrayed.

Horror is finding renewed popularity through such mediums as television shows (like AMC's *The Walking Dead*), movies, books, and magazines, changing the way horror is viewed, and how it is represented. Women actors and authors are breaking the mold, forcing previous expectations to take a passenger seat... proving that even in the deepest recesses of a woman's mind, horror has a place.

In this issue, I had the privilege of interviewing the *Girl of Nightmares* herself, Kendare Blake.

Kendare has set a new benchmark with her successful horror novel, one that is written from the perspective of a boy. She is the author behind the Y.A. horror series *Anna Dressed In Blood* recently optioned for a short film by the Fickle Fish production company, and Girl of Nightmares, while her newest book *Antigoddess* has just hit shelves.

Amy Shane: First off, why horror and why a ghost named Anna?

Kendare Blake: I grew up on horror. Stephen King, Anne Rice, Bret Easton Ellis, and Poppy Z Brite. I loved the twistedness and the gore and to hell with happy endings. Then I got older, and I started writing different things, literary things, adventures, etc. But after working on two back to back literary projects and a slew of literary short stories, I missed the blood and guts. As for why Anna, I don't know. She showed up: "Anna Dressed in Blood." And I thought, well, she obviously kills people. Someone ought to go kill her.

AS: Do you feel any resistance, being a woman writer in the industry, or do you feel that you have been welcomed in the genre?

KB: I haven't felt any resistance. And in the YA community, we're mostly women anyway, so while there isn't much horror in there, "Anna Dressed in Blood" has enjoyed an extremely warm welcome, for which I'm grateful!

AS: Do you feel that you have broken the ties and constraints that bind women to traditional writing in the horror genre?
Kendare: I don't think a lot about constraints binding women. Because, eff that. Some girls like gore. Some girls like the dark. No one could write

pretty entrails like Poppy Z Brite, and he did it back when he was a woman. Women can be as sick, as gritty, as anything as they like. No other possibility has ever entered my mind.

AS: How do you feel about deviating from what is expected of a female writer and becoming the writer you are today?

KB: "Anna Dressed in Blood" was written in a male POV. I've heard that the voice is true. That's what I hear the most—that people are surprised that I'm a woman, not because of the violence, but because they bought that my narrator was a dude. I don't know what that says about me. When I'm writing I'm thinking as a writer, not usually as a woman writer. Except for when it comes to writing about female characters. That's where a lot of the pressure is. Everyone wants strong female characters. But I'm getting off track; it's detrimental to the quality of the work for me to think about "expectations." I always try not to.

AS: How has the industry treated you as a horror author?

KB: Fantastically! I was invited to join the Horror Writers Association, and very welcomed there. I've had the pleasure of meeting and talking with horror master Jonathan Maberry, who was a champion of my work before we met and is an all-around interesting novelist and straight-shooting person.

However, I have heard some disturbing stories from author friends and acquaintances, so I know that hurdles and ugliness do exist. It seems strange to me that horror would ever be a boy's club. Sure, more men are serial killers, I suppose, but Lizzie Borden used an axe, man. An AXE. And Jamie Lee Curtis would take only so much crap from Michael Myers before, well, you know. Horror is a universal experience. Scary things are scary, regardless of what you've got going on downstairs.

AS: Were you brought up with horror movies and books?

KB: Yes. I lived on the "Nightmare on Elm Street" movies. "Genius." And "Scream." I need something with an interesting hook in my horror fare. It can't be just a slasher flick. I know everyone's very excited about "You're Next," but if it isn't something more than a standard home invasion, I'm going to be disappointed. I want weird. I want ambiguity. I'll even accept a little bit of dumb, as long as you were very ambiguous about the previous 75 or so minutes.

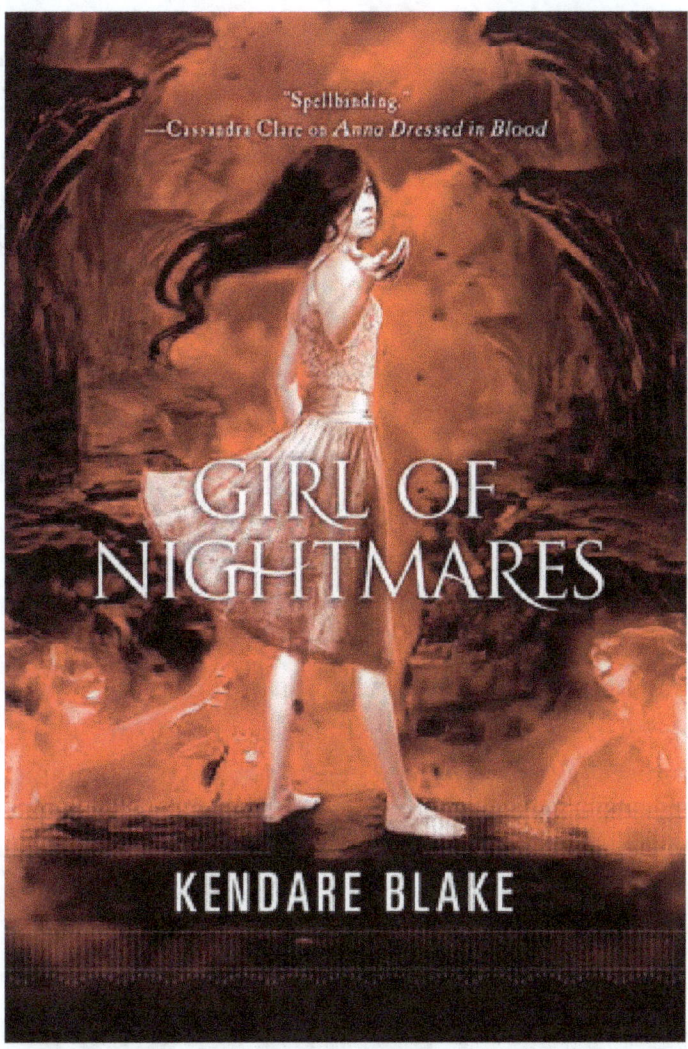

"Spellbinding."
—Cassandra Clare on *Anna Dressed in Blood*

GIRL OF NIGHTMARES

KENDARE BLAKE

AS: Have ghosts, horror, and the paranormal always been part of who you are, or is this a newfound passion?

KB: I'm tempted to say it's relatively new. I don't know why. It's a complete lie. Even when I was writing literary, I was helping my best friend with her Master's Thesis on Jeffrey Dahmer and Ted Bundy. Ghosts are new. I never thought I'd write about ghosts. And I don't know if I ever will again.

AS: Is there another horror book on the horizon for you?

KB: Someday. Yes. I've been turning back to it. My new stuff, *ANTIGODDESS* (The Goddess War) has a lot of darkness and gore, and nasty violence, but not so much fear and horror. And the series I'll write after that... feels like more of a creepy saga. But, just last night actually, I started to think about all the horror elements I love, and what I'd like to work with. So it's coming around again!

⚜ ⚜ ⚜

THINGS THAT BITE

Legends and Folklore of Supernatural Predators

By Jonathan Maberry and David F. Kramer
Bram Stoker Award-winning authors of THE CRYPTOPEDIA

1. HELL HOUNDS

The dog isn't always man's best friend.

Wolves have been around for sixty million years. Except for tropical rain forests wolves have inhabited every kind of habitat in the world, from the frozen arctic to the dusty steppes to the deep forests. Currently there are thirty-two remaining species of wolf. Twenty-four of these species exist in North America and the remaining eight can be found in Eurasia. The smallest and rarest breed is the Mexican Wolf (Canis lupus baileyi) and the largest is the bigger varieties include the Russian Wolf (Canis lupus communis; a declining population found in Central Russia) and the MacKenzie Valley Wolf (Canis lupus occidentalis; found in the Northern Rockies and parts of Canada). Many other species, including the fearsome Dire Wolf (Canusdirus) have become extinct.

About one hundred thousand years ago, the wolf genetic line split and the first proto-dogs emerged. Science is still trying to sort how exactly how and why dogs emerged from wolves, and there is a huge knowledge gap between the original schism and the earliest records of domestication, which date back to 17,000 and 14,000 years ago, during the late Upper Paleolithic--man began the process of domesticating dogs. The jump from wild wolf to domesticated dog is unusually fast in terms of the normal process of evolution. One theory is that juvenile wolves became separated from their pack and mated with other juvenile wolves, an event that resulted in the establishment of different behavior patterns than those of the mature pack. Such behavioral changes influenced the animals' interaction with their environment and that resulted in developmental differences. Within a few thousand generations these new creatures no longer acted like wolves, and from there the dog emerged, with other changes caused by alternations in diet, interbreeding, and other conditions.

Dogs, from the start, have been transformative creatures. Dogs are virtually unique among animals in that new varieties or breeds of them can be created in sustainable form within a generation or two. Consider that in 1873 there were only forty known dog breeds while today there over eight hundred recognized breeds, ranging from the almost-not-even-there one pound Chihuahua to Zorba, an English Mastiff cited by the Guinness Book of World Records as the heaviest and tallest dog ever in with a weight of 343lbs and measured over 8 feet from nose to tail.

This transformative and malleable nature is reflected in much of the folklore surrounding both dogs and wolves, and that includes the ability to deliberately change shape so common in werewolf legends. Myth and legend is filled with dogs, ranging from the noble wolf of Jack London tales to the hyper-intelligent Lassie and Rin Tin Tin to demonic hellhounds and wolfmen. Dog stories, like dogs themselves, seem to come in all shapes and sizes.

2. MONSTER DOGS

There have been monstrous dogs in folklore since the ancient Greeks. Cerberus, the three-headed guardian of the underworld should probably be given the role of de facto pack leader, but other notable canine creatures abound. In both Egyptian and Eskimo cultures Dogs were believed to be guides to the afterlife. The Greek Goddess of the hunt, Diana, was thought to ride with spectral hounds who would locate lost souls. And generally the Greeks thought dogs could foresee evil.

Often dogs are believed to be omens of either good or bad luck. In Russia a dog howls by an open door, it is considered an omen of death; and in central Europe a dog howling during a child's birth is supposed to signal an unhappy life for the child. In several places around the world there was on belief that dogs are witches who took animal form and that they howl when other witches are nearby. In England and France it was believed that if a dog howls three times in a row and then stops is supposed to signal the moment of a death; and all through Europe and Colonial America that hearing a dog barking first thing in the morning is thought to be a sign of misfortune. In Ireland, a strange dog digging up your garden means illness or death is on the way. In Ireland, Scotland, and the deep American South folks still say that if a dog sleeps with its tail straight out and its paws turned up, bad news is on the way, and that the direction the tail is pointing indicates the direction from which the bad news will come. And you'll find these beliefs worldwide thanks to immigration and cultural blending: A dog running between two newlyweds is an indication of many fights between them to come; if a dog runs between a woman's legs, the husband should have reason to doubt her fidelity; if a dog runs and hides under a table, expect a strong thunderstorm to occur; a dog scratching or rolling on the ground for a long period also means rain will come; a dog howling for no reason is thought to be howling at ghosts. The same holds for dogs that suddenly stare at something in the room no one else can see.

Conversely, in England it is a sure sign of good luck to have a strange dog follow you. And in Western Europe having a black and white dog cross your path while you are on the way to a meeting means good luck at the meeting. In Europe, a person bitten by a wild dog should eat a sandwich consisting of hairs from the dog and rosemary, leading to the cure for hangovers known as "the hair of the dog that bit you." In Scotland, a new friendship will follow a strange dog coming to your house.

The color of a dog is supposed to indicate the darkness of its soul, and some black dogs are thought to be embodiments of unquiet souls, whereas others are thought to be protective guides to travelers. Black poodles are placed on gravestones of German clergy who did not follow their religion too closely.

Seeing three white dogs together is considered good luck. A greyhound with a white spot on its forehead is considered good luck. And white dogs have been used to sniff out evil of all kinds, from witches to vampires.

The broadest range of hellhound tales come from Great Britain, and frequently over the last thousand years there have been tales of packs of ghost hounds roaming the countryside. These hounds foretell death or disaster. To avoid spotting them, a person should drop face down onto the ground when they hear the dogs coming. The most feared of these is black spectral dog called the Barghest, and is considered to

be a harbinger of death.

In Scotland and Northern England there is a very old legend of massive hounds that haunt the sites of battles and lap up the blood of the fallen. These Blood Dogs coalesce out of morning mist on the day after a battle and then slink around the field, digging in the dirt to get at bloody seepage, and often feasting on the bodies of the unburied dead. Blood Dogs have gray bodies, dark red eyes, and hot breath that can scorch the earth. Despite their hulking size the Blood Dogs leave no mark on the ground and their baying sounds like the wind.

The Scottish version of the story differs slightly from the English version in that the Blood Dogs only fed on English blood and it is hinted that they are the ghosts of Bonny Prince Charlie's hunting hounds.

Of course the most famous fictional hellhound tale is The Hound of the Baskervilles written in 1902 by Sir Arthur Conan Doyle, which is also the most famous case of the legendary Sherlock Holmes. In the novel a killer plays on the local myth of a spectral hound as part of his twisted scheme. Though the story is, ultimately, a straight mystery with no

supernatural elements, it was written in the style of the late nineteenth century gothic horror stories. The various film versions of Hound also go for shocks and frights to keep the viewer wondering whether this is a ghost hound or not.

3. MONSTER DOGS IN FOLKLORE

Adlet: Among the Inuit peoples of Canada and Alaska there is an ancient legend of a race of bloodthirsty were-dogs called the Adlet. The Adlet race began as the hideous offspring of an unholy union of an Inuit woman and a monstrous red dog that was very likely possessed by a demon. This blasphemous sexual encounter bred creatures that were half human and half dog. The Inuit mother essentially gave birth to a "litter" of five of these creatures. Aghast at what she had brought into the world, she bundled them onto rafts made from whalebone and animal hides and set them adrift in the frozen artic waters.

The infant dog-creatures did not perish from the cold, however, but rather crossed the ocean and came ashore on the banks of one of the European countries (the legends don't specify which). According to the mythology of the Inuits it was this pack of vicious monsters became them the progenitors of all of the white races of Europe, which explains (according to the) why there are so many tales of monsters and shapeshifters in white European culture.

Either the tale of the mother setting them adrift is wrong or the Adlet somehow managed to return, but there have reports for centuries of Adlet attacks— monstrous doglike creatures who attack hunters or villagers and feast on their flesh and blood.

Barghest: The Barghest is the 'hound' behind *The Hound of the Baskervilles* (1901). In legend it is a monstrous hound that came out of the shadows to chase victims down country lanes. At times it has been reported baying in the forest near a home where someone is doomed to die. The howl of the Barghest can be heard on the moors and in the fields in the dead of night.

In some Yorkshire tales this hellhound actually chases down its prey and kills them with savage teeth, though when the bodies are found the marks have mysteriously vanished. In the West Country the hound's baying is enough to freeze the heart. In southern England the hound is more omen than predator, but is still counted as an evil creature in league with the powers of darkness.

Beast of Gevaudan (Also Le Bête de Gevaudan): The Beast of Gevaudan stands as one of history's most documented and believed monsters. Resembling a large wolf, the beast terrorized the Auvergne and South Dordogne regions of France between the years 1764 to 1767, and is believed to have killed nearly 100 people, mostly women and children. Witnesses who lived to tell of the creature described it as roughly wolf-like, but as large as a cow and with a huge barrel chest, a prehensile tail and a mane of fur around his head and shoulders. The beast was said to be able to leap thirty feet in a single bound, and would sometimes pounce the life out of its victims.

This was not some piece of rural folklore that could be easily dismissed. The number of deaths was shocking and eventually the beast came to the attention of King Louis XV, who ordered that the creature be tracked down and killed.

Theories abound as to the exact nature of the monster. Certainly it could be any of a number of wild predators, a hyena or other canine not natural to France, but brought back from distant lands by travelers or a circus. After the first few killings it was unlikely anyone would step forward to claim ownership, and therefore responsibility, for the monster.

Cryptozoologists speculate that it might have been some hyperthyroidic mutation of either a dog or a wolf; a mix of a large hunting dog and a wolf; or perhaps the last lingering member of an otherwise extinct species such as the monstrous Dire Wolf (Canis dirus). Or it could be a lingering member of Mesonychid, an order of predatory mammal that bore resemblance to wolves and which became extinct during either the Paleocene or Eocene ages. Though wolf-like in appearance, Mesonychids were actually more closely related to both Artiodactyla (mammal-like goats) and Cetacea (whales and their kin).

Whatever the beast may have been, its three year reign of terror did come to an end, though no hunter was ever able to put the creature's head on his trophy wall.

Black Shuck (also The Doom Dog): This is a brutish ghost dog reported in the coastal areas of Essex, Norfolk and Suffolk. Like most British Hellhounds the Black Shuck has fiery eyes that radiate real heat and it is as large as a full-grown horse. Depending on who is telling the tale (and what they might have been drinking before the encounter), the Black Shuck sometimes walks on all fours, sometimes floats on the mist, and sometimes just moves through the air without apparently moving its body. Mostly it looks like a normal, if large and red-eyed, dog; at other times it's just a hulking body with no visible head. Though the Black Shuck has been encountered on lonely roads, places of executions, and at crossroads, its regular 'haunt' is the graveyard.

Cadejo: In folklore, as in life, things are seldom black and white, however when it comes to the Cadejo, a monster dog from the legends of Salvador, Nicaragua, Costa Rica, Honduras, Guatemala and southern Mexico, they really are. If you see a white Cadejo good fortune is heading your way; if you see a black one, you're pretty much screwed. The white one will protect you through an otherwise dangerous journey; the black ones eat you. In both cases the creature is the size of a cow, with shaggy fur, cloven feet, and burning eyes.

The creature gets its name from the Spanish word 'cadena', meaning 'chain', because the monster is often depicted dragging a long chain behind it.

Legend has it that there are three distinct types of black Cadejo. One –the worst of all—is a true incarnation of the Devil and encounters with Old Scratch just don't end well unless it says 'Spotless Saint' on your birth certificate. The second kind is a flesh-eating monster –which isn't much better in the short term since you still die, but the long-term advantage is you don't get dragged down to Hell. The third kind is a half-breed offspring of the first two (and, yes, this puts a new spin on 'bestiality'). Thought frightening and dangerous, a strong or well-armed man can kill this last kind.

Cerberus: HE was an enormous doglike monster with three heads (or, if you read Hesiod instead of Virgil or Homer, fifty heads). The central head was shaped like a lion's, and the flanking heads looked like dogs. The monster had vast powers and aside from three sets of teeth as long as swords, a mane of writhing snakes, clawed feet, poisonous saliva, and a ponderous mass, it had a whipping serpent's tail that could smash a man's bone to jelly.

Only a few heroes in all of Greek myth were ever able to defeat Cerberus: Hercules (who had to lure him out of Hades as one of his Twelve Labors); Orpheus (who charmed it to sleep with sweet music from his lyre); and the combined team of Aeneas of Troy and Bybil of Cumae (who lull it to sleep with a magic cake). Everyone else was apparently far less successful.

Church Grim (also Kirk Grim in Scotland, Kyrkogrim in Sweden or Kirkonwäki in Finland):

It's unclear whether the Church Grim is a great black dog that sometimes takes the form of a small, hunchbacked human, or the other way around. In either case the creature appears in both English and Scandinavian folklore and is believed to be a protector of churches. However it is commonly believed that the Grim is the penitent spirit of a sinner who rings church bells and does other service as part of its centuries-long penance for a life of terrible sin.

In other legends the Grim is believed to be the ghost of a black dog deliberately buried on church grounds so that it would rise from the grave as a guardian spirit.

Cu Sìth (also Cusìth): A hellhound of the Scottish highlands, that is as big and strong as a bull and fiery eyes. Unlike most monster hours of the United Kingdom, the Cu Sith is dark green rather than black, and has long shaggy hair like that of the highland cattle.

Despite its size the Cu Sith is an absolutely silent hunter, however it sometimes announces its presence –or boasts of a kill—by uttering three immensely loud barks that can be heard for miles and even far out to sea. Some folktales insist that this bark was its way of giving fair warning that it was coming, which gave villagers the chance to hide their womenfolk. The Cu Sith, whose name means 'fairy dog', was believed to capture women and carry them off to a sìthean (Fairy mound), to serve as wet nurses for the daoine-sìth (fairy children).

A variation of the Cu Sith, called the Cooshee, appears in the game Dungeons & Dragons. In myth there is a feline version of this monster called, appropriately enough, the Cat Sith.

CŵnAnnwn: In Wales there are very old legends of the "Hounds of Annwn", the spectral hunting dogs that rode out with the Wild Hunt. Annwn is a spiritual realm of fairy, and depending on who is telling the tale, the Hunt and its dogs are either benevolent (and really indifferent to the human world) or they are bloodthirsty and vicious and prey on humans. One should note that after the settling of Christians in the Celtic lands much of the fairy world was suddenly deemed to be Satanic and evil.

The Hounds are most commonly heard on the eves of St. John, St. Martin, Saint Michael the Archangel, All Saints, Christmas, New Year, Saint Agnes, Saint David, and Good Friday; though other tales say that they most often appeared on the Solstices and the Equinoxes. Many believe that the CŵnAnnwn served another and more regular purpose, which was to escort the souls of the newly departed on their journey to the other side of death (be that heaven, hell, or some fairy realm). In the darker versions of the folklore, the CŵnAnnwn are frequently seen in the company of a haglike witch called Matilda of the Night (Mallt-y-Nos) who was always up to no good.

Dip: In Catalonia there are very old tales of a monstrous hellhound called the Dip that is both a servant of the devil and a blood-drinking vampire. As with many creatures from Catalan folklore, the Dip is lame in one leg and the limp is the only thing that allows potential victims to outrun it.

Gwyllgi: A gigantic spectral mastiff from Welsh

legend, often called the Black Hound of Destiny. It is generally encountered on dark country roads and terrifies unsuspecting travelers with fiery red eyes and a breath like the fumes of hell.

Gytrash: A giant spectral hound from northern England that preys on travelers. This creature can apparently shapeshift and has been known to take the appearance of a donkey or horse, though usually it appears as a hound. The Gytrash is either a bit schizo, subject to moods, or there are different kinds of them that have different dispositions because in some tales the creature leads lost travelers back to the correct path while in other tales it leads them astray and then eats them.

The variation of this monster reported in Lincolnshire and Yorkshire is always hostile, according to legend, and this version (or perhaps subspecies) has eyes that burn like hot coals. The author Charlotte Brontë wrote a compelling scene about the Gytrash in Chapter 12 of Jane Eyre: "As this horse approached, and as I watched for it to appear through the dusk, I remembered certain of Bessie's tales, wherein figured a North-of-England spirit called a *Gytrash*, which, in the form of horse, mule, or large dog, haunted solitary ways, and sometimes came upon belated travelers, as this horse was now coming upon me. It was very near, but not yet in sight; when, in addition to the tramp, tramp, I heard a rush under the hedge, and close down by the hazel stems glided a great dog, whose black and white color made him a distinct object against the trees. It was exactly one form of Bessie's Gytrash -- a lion-like creature with long hair and a huge head …with strange pretercanine eyes…."

North Country Hellhound: In the late eighteenth and early nineteenth centuries there was a rash of animal murders in the mountainous country between Northern England and Scotland. Hundreds of sheep were found dead, their throats torn out and their bodies drained of blood. At the scene of each killing the farmers and investigators found numerous prints like those of a very large dog. Now, up to this point the story is gruesome but not actually weird, because

wild dogs do roam those mountains and hungry dogs have certainly been known to dine or a sheep or two. But here's the kicker: according to paranormal investigator Charles Fort, the sheep were drained of blood but none of their flesh was eaten, and there was not enough blood on the ground to explain the total exsanguination. Hounds that kill just for blood? Yeah, that's creepy. No solution to the mystery has ever been found.

ShunkaWarak'in: Among the Ioway native peoples the ShunkaWarak'in is an ancient legend of a wolf-like creature that will attack humans as well as animals. Spotted frequently on the Great Plains by Native Americans and settlers as well during the late 18th and well into the 19th Centuries, the ShunkaWarak'in was known for sneaking into a campsite or village to hunt for dogs. Its name even means "carries off dogs".

The ShunkaWarak'in had oversized forelegs and shoulders, giving it a stature more like a wild boar than a dog. When one of these creatures was killed it supposedly cried out in a voice that was eerily human.

There is a longstanding rumor that a settler killed one at the end of the 19th century and mounted it before donating it to a tiny museum located in a grocery store in Henry Lake, Idaho…but the specimen has since vanished.

Waheela: A lupine cryptid that has been reported many times in the Northwest Territories of Canada, particularly in the Nahanni Valley. Ivan Sanderson (1911-1973), the noted naturalist and cryptozoologist believed that the Waheela might be a surviving example of a kind of 'bear dogs' known as amphicyonids, which lived during the Late Eocene to Late Miocene. The creature was believed to be a solo hunter, which is one of the many reasons this creature bears some striking resemblance to the Inuit legend of the Amarok.

Yardley Yeti: Since early Fall of 2005 there have been a number of sightings of a strange dog-like creature roaming the fringes of various Bucks

County, PA towns. The creature looks like a mix of dog, jackal, and kangaroo, and was dubbed 'The Yardley Yeti' by newspaper columnist J. D. Mullane (Bucks County Courier Times). Other folks are calling it The Lower Makefield Lurker (or Lower Makefield Monster), the Bucks County Boggart, and the New Hope Hyena.

Lower Makefield Police Chief Ken Coluzzi said that his department had fielded several reports about the creature. Chief Coluzzi told me: "Some called it a cross between a dog and a hyena. Others said a wolf dog, and others said it was a sick looking fox like creature. Others said a coyote."

Now here's where this story gets even weirder...I've not only seen it, I've taken photos of it. Considering that I write books about strange creatures, it seems wonderfully appropriate that I got a chance to not only see the thing, but to photograph it. My wife, Sara Jo, and I were visiting the Michener Art Museum in New Hope, PA on October 30 of 2005. We had our camera with us (a Minolta D-Image digital). In the parking lot we saw a very odd-looking creature moving among the parked cars.

It was brownish, with some gray, with an unhealthy-looking coat. The creature moved very quickly. Never aggressive in any way. It didn't even take notice of us other than to continue moving away from us. It moved out of the parking lot and across the tracks of the Ivyland-New Hope line before finally disappearing into some brush. It made no sound, and didn't even react when I made some noise to try and attract its attention. At a guess I'd put it at about 35 pounds, give or take.

Various website postings have included speculation that it's a cougar (not a chance); that it's an unknown species of fox (doubtful); that it's a coyote (maybe); that it's a dog (possibly –but a dog of what species mixed with what-other species?).

On various cryptozoology websites, such as www.cryptomundo.com (the leading theory is that the creature is a red fox with mange, but when I showed the pictures to veterinarian and exotic animals expert Adam Denish, DVM, he said that it was definitely not a mangy fox. In fact he told me, "Frankly, I don't know what it is."

So...the mystery continues.

☙☙☙

Michael R. Collings

Sitting at breakfast the other morning with my son—a multiple-bestselling author of horror and all things dark—we took a break from watching my granddaughter toddle about the restaurant playground to talk-shop, as it were.

"I should write something about zombies," I said, then added, "but I really don't care for them."

Since he was in the middle of writing volume two of *The Colony*, his multivolume zombie-apocalypse epic, it took him only a moment to respond: "Zombies are easy. They are simply a force of nature."

That triggered several thoughts.

The first and most immediate was that he was essentially correct. As generally portrayed—and I'm thinking specifically here of several prevue clips for the film *World War Z*—the figure is precisely that: a force of nature. Hordes of zombies surging down the streets of New York resemble nothing so much as an avalanche, a tidal wave, an enormous mud slide that wipes out anything and everything before it. Only in this case, the avalanche, the tidal wave does not merely destroy; it adds incrementally to its mass by transforming living humans into similar forces of nature, the aggregation growing larger, stronger, more unstoppable with each foot, each yard, each mile.

That sense is augmented in much contemporary fiction by a subtle shift in the assumptions concerning *how* zombies happen. In earlier fiction, there were general two possibilities: one was that the zombie was a result of arcane and exotic rites performed over the dead—and occasionally upon the living—to transform them into creatures whose will was entirely subordinated to the master, to the creator. More often than not, the creator would be explicitly connected to some form of voodoo, giving the whole situation supernatural, quasi- or fully religious overtones. The quest was rarely to eradicate the zombies(s) *per se*. What was important was to kill the master and thereby simultaneously destroy the spell, the magic, the charm that gave life to the walking dead.

The second option was much simpler: the zombie simply seemed to appear. How it rose from the grave was secondary to the fact of its rising. In this case, the quest was to remove that aberration and restore humanity to a balance between life and death. This alternative was less common than the first, primarily because it diffused focus from one individual who could be definitively removed, thus removing the danger, to something less directed, more difficult to work with. In essence, however, the question of source becomes irrelevant; the zombie simply *is*.

In much contemporary zombie fiction, on the other hand, the zombie is neither the result of a renegade meddling with the laws of nature and trying to control them nor an anomaly, an assertion to make a complex plot work. It is instead a literal force of nature. No serpent-wreathed, painted-faced necromancer need chant by the flickering light of a jungle bonfire to raise the ravening dead. There is simply a mutation, for example, in a hitherto benign virus, often frighteningly communicable...and the zombie-menace is born.

The figure becomes no different than—and often a metaphor for—the threat of a naturally occurring pandemic in a world so tightly connected that if one man sneezes in Los Angeles, the next day the virus might be killing thousands in China.

There seems good reason for this sense of the zombie's force—both literal and figurative.

Two seminal works of science-fiction/horror appeared within about a decade of each other. The first would introduce readers to an irresistible force of technology; the second, to an irresistible force of nature. And both would be picked up as metaphors for the powerlessless of individuals in a society that had seen the destruction of all sense of order, harmony, hierarchy, and control by the horrors and the violence of the Great War.

In 1920, a Czech playwrite, Karel Čapek, introduced the word 'robot' into English and a score of other language with his play *R.U.R*— subtitled *"Rossum's Universal Robots.* With the word came the characters—*robots*, stemming from *robota*, meaning 'compulsory labor,' and *robotník,* 'a peasant owing such labor.' Initially, the characters were what would today be more accurately called *cyborgs* or possibly *clones*; but the image of artificially constructed, mechanical, human-like entities rapidly became more negative than positive, evolving into quasi-horror stories such as Brian W. Aldiss's 1958 "The New Father Christmas." Rather than individual robots subservient to humankind, the construct transformed into phalanxes of identical units, marching lock-step over the remains of human civilization...the technology that had created mankind's helpmeet overgrowing its original intent and ultimately replacing humanity.

Instead of salvation, irresistible defeat.

The figure continued, spurred on by the imagistic power of Nazi propaganda, by the burgeoning of automation in the mid-century decades, by the popularization (and trivialization) of the robot on television and in films (think, Robbie the Robot from *The Forbidden Planet*), by the wholesale incorporation of the figure into several decades of highly sophisticated science fiction stories and novels, and culminating—perhaps—in the entire Terminator mythology with its multiple films and apparently ageless characters.

And in each, humanity confronts something of its own making, something cataclysmic that destroys, superseded supplants sentient man.

Truly, an image of fear and terror.

The *horror* initially lacking in Čapek's robots entered literature just over a decade later. In 1929, William Seabrook published *The Magic Island,* a fictionalization of his experiences in Haiti and elsewhere that introduced Western readers to zombies. Several years later, the novel became the basis for the first major zombie film, *White Zombie* (1932), starring Bela Lugosi. Not particularly well received at first, the film gained in stature over the years and has been instrumental in forming the contemporary zombie. The zombie became a comicbook character in the 1940s, made the transition to full-scale horror novels with Richard Matheson's 1954 *I am Legend,* and emerged as filmic hero/anti-hero not only in multiple wide-screen versions of Matheson's story but even more influentially in George A. Romero's 1968 *Night of the Living Dead* and its many sequels.

By the turn of the millennium, zombies—and the specter of the dreaded Zombie Apocalypse— had become key images in horror, whether expressed in novels, in stories, in comic books, in films, or, as recently demonstrated by *The Walking Dead,* on television.

Zombies, in this sense, are almost precisely parallel and *oppositional* to robots. They almost exclusively inhabit horror, while robots remain largely in the domain of science fiction. Both creatures, however, reflect to an identical underlying fear—the fear of helplessness, of isolation, of powerlessness in the face of something antithetical to the individual as individual and to humanity at large.

The earlier sort—the robot—almost inevitable evolves into a technological nightmare. No matter how subservient it might seem at first, it always carries the hint of danger...so much so that Isaac Asimov was forced to define specific laws governing robotic behavior to protect the integrity of human life. It is not coincidental that many of his stories, and even more stories written *after* his, concentrate on real or apparent contravention of those Three Laws. Often plots revolve around understanding how the robots have both broken and kept the Laws.

The slightly later zombie almost inevitably evolves into an anti-technological nightmare.

There are a few exceptions, of course. Patrick Freivald's serio-comic *Twice Shy* (2012) and *Special Dead* (2013) in part defuse the inherent terror generated by zombies by making them the central characters—the *heroes*—of the two novels: almost but not quite typical high school teenagers with just a small aberration...an insatiable hunger for living human brains. The comedy in the novels grows from efforts to treat them as 'normal'; the horror rests in the understanding of just how far from normal these children are.

But most zombie novels concentrate on the creatures as non-human (but once-human), nearly non-sentient (but once fully sentient, which is where the greatest empathy for the zombie emerges), and utterly anti-technological. The zombies are a mass, a horde, a mindless crush with no ambition other than to consume living, healthy human tissue.

There may be attempts to find a 'cure' for the zombiism, but in most cases there is none; the cause defeats the best science has to offer and the only possible response is to quarantine the infected.

The consequence of this anti-technological twist—this essential horror—is that most effective novels do not deal with the zombies. They concentrate on those threatened by them. As soon as a zombie is adopted by the reader, gains the reader's sympathy, becomes someone the reader can empathize with, the stories tend to verge into the comic...as with Jeff Strand's YA horror, *A Bad Day for Voodoo* (2012).

In Joe McKinney's multi-volume treatment of a zombie apocalypse, it is significant that chronologically the first key event in the story, *Dead City* (2006), is not the rise of zombies but the destruction wreaked by San Antonio by a series of natural forces—hurricanes. The focus is on neither the hurricanes nor the subsequent hordes of zombies—neither of which could have been predicted—but on a single individual and his desperate quest to save his family. The specifics of the two natural disasters are alluded to but rarely explored in depth; hurricanes and zombies parallel each other, one kind of devastation complementing another but neither at the core of the story.

A subsequent novel, the Bram Stoker Award® winning *Flesh Eaters* (2011) alters a number of specifics: it is set in Houston rather than San Antonio; he focuses on a wider range of characters. But like the earlier book, it diminishes the importance of the zombies and writes instead about how their physical presence, their unanticipated *reality* alters the lives of several individuals. As I noted in an early review of *Flesh Eaters*,

> McKinney moves from one sub-genre to another with seamless facility, balancing each against the other, so that in the end, readers focus on the individual struggles of people they have come to care about. He shows characters faltering beneath the weight of the struggle, succumbing to their greed and pride, allowing themselves to become less than their potential until, eventually, they destroy themselves and each other. And he shows others rising to the occasions,

developing beyond what even they might have believed possible, giving their all to protect others, especially those they love. The three members of the Norton family go through the crucible of fire and flood, famine and disease…and zombies—only to emerge larger than they were, more aware of both strengths and weaknesses in themselves and in each other. This growth, this development of potential makes feasible—and acceptable—the final pages of the novel.

"…And zombies"—and that is the sum of the monsters' importance to the storytelling.

In Michaelbrent Collings' on-going series, *The Colony*, a disaster has taken place, although by the end of the first volume no one know what it was or when it occurred. All that is clear is that within seven minutes the vast majority of humanity (something like 98.9%) is either dead, a zombie (through no known process), or struggling to keep from becoming one or the other. Whatever happened to disrupt global civilization is essentially irrelevant at this point; what *is* important is that one man travel four miles to where his family is—he hopes and prays—safe and waiting for him. Those four miles take up the entire first volume, and even at that, readers do not yet know anything about the state of the family.

Zombies appear everywhere in the novel; but rather than characters, they become part of the landscape—true, a part that is capable of clawing and severing and consuming—but they are no more and no less important than the other things barricading the way throughout those four miles. They are, as Michaelbrent said that morning at breakfast, "nothing more than a force of nature."

Shortly after I posted a previous essay, "Seventeenth-Century Ghosts and What They Can Teach Us," at *Collings Notes* (michaelrcollings. blogspot.com), one of my Facebook friends commented that it had reminded him of being in a Graduate seminar. I thanked him and noted that the next essay would probably discuss zombies.

"No," he write, "those I don't remember at all from my Milton seminar."

No, I realized, he wouldn't. The seventeenth century had a boatload of problems, but zombies weren't one of them. Inescapable forces crushing individual volition and action are the obsession of the twentieth and twenty-first centuries. We live in the shadow of world-destroying bombs, of incurable diseases that could wipe out all of humanity. We fear the consequences of our own technology…of robots that ultimately realize that they can do *everything* more efficiently than humans can. And we fear the consequences of events that our technology is incapable of controlling…of zombies that rise from the grave for no demonstrable causes and destroy everything they encounter.

Robots and Zombies are, for very similar reasons, uniquely *modern* monsters. Their essence and their existence require a specific view of man and—and *in*—the universe, and the complex, multifaceted, kaleidoscopic relationship between them.

⚜⚜⚜

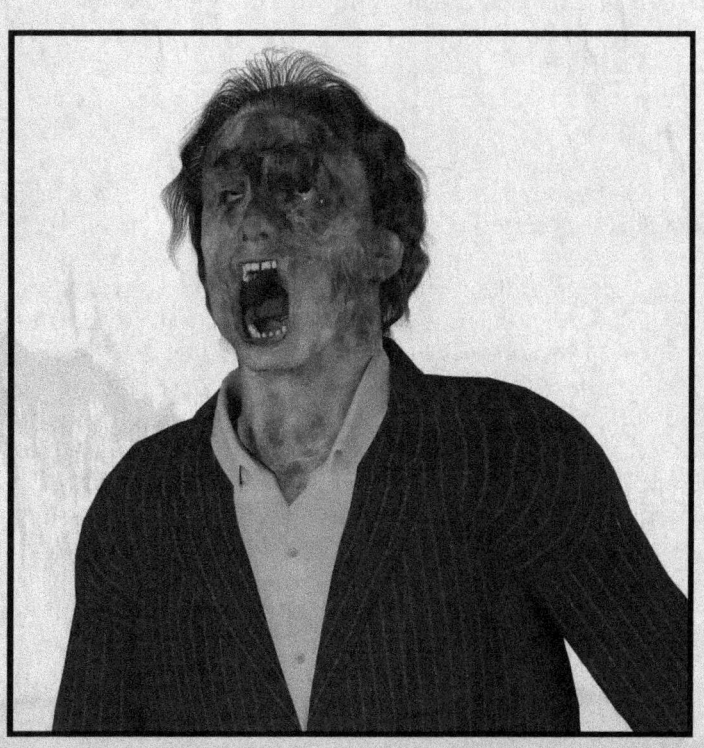

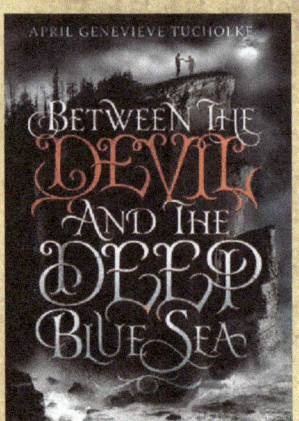

Between the Devil and the Deep Blue Sea
April Genevieve Tucholke
Dial Books
ISBN 978-0803738898
Hardcover, 368 pages,
young adult

In the haunted, sleepy little town of Echo, a visitor comes, washing the town with a twisted and terrifying mystery…

Violet lives in the boring seaside town of Echo, a small town structure where everyone knows your name, your family, as well as your family's secrets. Where the echoes of the past, haunt your todays.

Violet and her brother were brought up by eccentric and artist parents who abandoned their kids to study art in Paris, leaving them to fend for themselves in a rundown sea-side mansion. Once dignified and elegant, it now stands sea-bitten, overgrown and severally neglected. Although it seems like every child's dream to live alone, the reality of it quickly comes crashing down on Violet and her brother Luke.

When faced with the fact that they are quickly running out of money, Violet puts out an ad to rent the guesthouse, and that's where charming, handsome and enigmatic River West comes to stay. He brings with him an air of wonder and enchantment, masking the sense of fear and impending doom. Before anyone knows it, the town's legend of kidnappers and monsters comes alive, where children sleep in the cemetery waiting in the sea-misted fog for the devil himself. While gruesome murders start to occur in nearby cities, no one is safe as the murders finally creep into Echo. Fear claws its way to the surface as murderous blood begins to pour down the city streets, from crimes so sinister only the devil could be blamed.

Before Violet realizes, she is pulled into River's manipulative lull, swept up in love, leaving her open and vulnerable just like River wants. Enamored by this illusion, Violet ignores his lying, distrustful nature, falling for the blissful promises that his alluring *glow* can offer, throwing Violet into a blinded lust that washes away any sense of danger. Taking her on a journey that slashes through the deepest part of her heart, forcing her to decide if love can reside where there also is evil—and if so, could that make her wicked as well?

April Genevieve Tucholke seduces you with a chilling storyline, which gently rocks you back and forth, lulling you in. The story back-builds like a wave, which crashes before you, dragging you under with its power.

Between the Devil and the Deep Blue Sea is a gripping gothic horror unlike any other. From beginning to end it doesn't disappoint. Only once it's too late do you realize you are in the book's undertow, tumbling head-over-heels, throwing you into a world filled with mystery, magic, horror, and pure wickedness.

—Reviewed by Amy Shane

Anna Dressed in Blood
Kendare Blake
TorTeen
ISBN 0765328674
Paperback, 324 pages, young adult

Athame in hand, Cass slices through the neck of the hitchhiker; black blood pours from his thick wound spewing over his vintage jacket, up over his face and into his eyes. He doesn't scream as he shrivels up, and within a minute, he disappears…

Cass Lowood hasn't known anything in his life but killing things that are already dead. Coming from a long ancestry of ghost hunters, he has been given the power that very few have had the ability to yield, contained in the blade of his athame. Since his father's death, the weight has fallen upon his shoulders to continue the family tradition, sending him and his mother to the shadowed and sinister places that call for him.

However, the one thing Cass was not prepared for was the parchment paper letter with the blood-etched inscription: Anna Korlov murdered 1958—and the horrors that would follow. Anna Dressed in Blood is a horrifically violent local legend, notorious for dismembering and tearing the limbs from twenty-seven people who dared cross the threshold into her house.

Once Cass's eyes fall upon Anna, everything changes. She captivates him instantly with her midnight black hair and black-pool eyes. She wears a white dress saturated in blood that drips along the floorboards when she approaches, adding to the horror of the legend.

Every bit of normalcy quickly falls away, and Cass loses himself in the whirlwind that would be Anna. Finding himself surrounded by friends, he soon learns that this time the power within him and his athame will not be enough. For the power of Anna is one that is bound by deeper roots, where the only way to discover her true strength is to unleash the power that binds her, spinning Cass into a world he is not yet prepared for, while he attempts to unlock the dark recesses that lie below and tie Anna to her home.

Blood pours from the pages of this classic horror tale, pooling up and staining the words red. *Anna Dressed in Blood* is as gorgeous as it is gory. Perfectly gripping as it hurdles you into the world of Anna, spinning you into the dark abyss inside the author's mind.

ndare Blake not only captures your heart with a truly mesmerizing story of a boy, a legend, and the discovery of a love that was never meant to be, but she also captivates you with writing that entangles you in a blood-soaked adventure, leaving you with this ultimate question: Can a ghost have a soul?

—Reviewed by Amy Shane

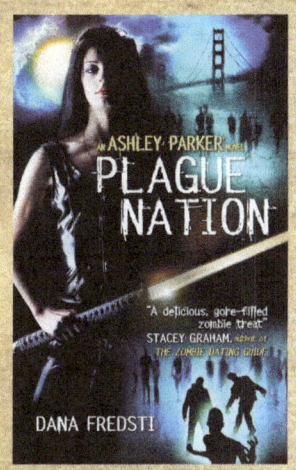

Plague Nation
By Dana Fredsti
Paperback, 336 pages
Published April 9th 2013
by Titan Books
(ISBN 13: 9780857686367)

I was (and still am) a huge Buffy the Vampire Slayer fan; like Joss Whedon, I greatly enjoy a strong female heroine who is just as fragile as she is tough. For this reason, I decided to give author Dana Fredsti's PLAGUE novels a try. I'm glad I did, too… the heroine, Ashley Parker, is not your typical college girl. She's a bad-ass zombie killer that would give Peter Parker a run for his money in the quip-while-fighting department.

If you are not familiar with PLAGUE NATION, here is the plot synopsis courtesy of Titan Books:

The undead have been defeated in Redwood Grove, but reports of similar outbreaks are coming in. What seemed to be an isolated event is turning into a pandemic. The last thing Ashley Parker wanted when she went to college was to become a zombie hunter. But she is one of a select few who are immune to the virus. Gifted with enhanced speed, strength, and senses, she is recruited by a shadowy organization that's existed for centuries, its sole purpose to combat the zombie threat. Dark secrets begin to emerge, and when an unknown enemy strikes, Ashley and the other wild cards embark on a desperate mission to reach San Francisco. If they fail, the plague will sweep the nation unchecked. And the person she cares for most may die. Or worse.

When I found out Fredsti worked on Sam Raimi's ARMY OF DARKNESS as an armorer's assistant and sword-fighting Deadite, I knew immediately that I had to give her work a shot. Raimi is one of my idols, not to mention a horror icon, so just the fact that she was on the set of one of my favorite movies of all time was enough merit for me to give her a look.

I have to commend Fredsti for introducing a riveting zombie series into a saturated market. I was curious when I first started reading the first book, PLAGUE

TOWN, wondering if this would be another rehash of what had already been done. But Fredsti skillfully blends light humor with dark zombie horror, and the result is an excellent series that is worthy of any horror fan's consideration.

PLAGUE NATION is a perfect continuation of the story, picking up very close to where the first book ends. And like its predecessor, it is written well and flows at a nice pace. The action scenes are not bogged down with unnecessary exposition and there is never any over-emphasized description.

The characters are pretty well fleshed out and believable, although there are one or two that some readers might consider over-the-top. Still, they all mesh well in the story and help to create the vivid, nightmarish world in which the series is set.

If I were forced to find a flaw with this series, I don't think I could. I tore through books one and two within the period of a week, and now I'm eagerly awaiting book three. I highly recommend giving these books a look. They are quick and enjoyable reads that zombie fans should love. Both books are available now.

—Review by Matthew Scott Baker

Fractured Spirits: Hauntings at the Peoria State Hospital
By Sylvia Shuts
Dark Continents
ISBN: 978-0984893119
Feb. 2013, Print $14.99
eBook $3.99

This book was not at all what I expected it to be. I was under the impression that it was a book of ghost stories about the residents of the Peoria State Hospital over the years. Instead, it was more a collection of tales about the various ghost hunting expeditions that the author was a part of over the years.

Reading this book I learned a lot about what both amateur and professional ghost hunters use for equipment and how they go about their investigations. To be sure, Ms. Shults does mention several of the ghosts by name, Rhonda Deery and Bookman, and gives their stories as well as those of a few other unnamed spirits. This non-fiction book is more about how the Asylum has been perceived over the years and today.

She does make special mention and tells the story of the doctor who turned Peoria State into a modern institution. Doctor George Zeller revolutionized patient care and worker stress during his years as the director of the hospital, making it the premiere facility of its kind. Its residents included both the super-rich and the poor, as no one was turned away because of lack of funds. This is in contrast to many institutions in the United States at the time, such as Danvers State Mental Hospital in Massachusetts.

At Peoria State, inmates were treated with dignity and

respect, no matter if they were insane, epileptic, depressed or simply unwanted by their families and therefore committed. The story of Dr. Zeller and his compassion makes the book worth its price. It is the real human story of this book.

Of special interest is reading about the ghosts in the Men's Ward and in the four cemeteries. Although they are not named, nor do we know their stories – their interactions with the investigators are sometimes chilling and sometimes downright humorous.

So, not the book I was expecting, yet overall a really great read. Ms. Shults does become a bit redundant in places, but that doesn't really detract from the stories she is attempting to tell. If you love history, if you love spooky, and if you'd love to know how these paranormal investigators (ghost hunters) go about their job – then this is a book you will definitely want to pick up for yourself.

—Review by Kat Yares

Sean MacRoibin that brings the book to the close. Saving the best for last? Well I'll let you decide that for yourself. I'll just say that I really liked it. I can easily say the same for Don D'Ammassa's "Farm on the Down" which was a delight if just for that playful title alone, as was the little slice of crazy that was "Box of Rocks" by John F.D. Taff. There are other winners to be found in the *Box of Delights*, but I've said enough. Nice surprises are always welcome and this book is full of them.

So if you're looking for a Whitman's Sampler of terror tales then you should really give this Irish import a try. You can get it directly from the publisher's website here: http://www.albedo1.com/aeonpress.html or at your favorite online bookstore like Amazon for your favorite eReader. That is, as long as it can read Kindle books. It's well worth the price and a refreshing breath of chilly darkness sure to *Delight* any horror fan. Consider it recommended.

—Reviewed By Brian M. Sammons

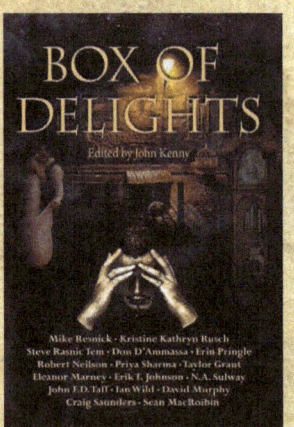

Box of Delights
Edited by John Kenny
ISBN 0953478483
Publisher: Aeon Press 2011
224 pages

I love the short story format when it comes to terror tales and so I'm always reading a lot of horror anthologies. Usually they have a theme behind them: vampires, zombies, psychos, the Cthulhu Mythos, future horror, past horror, etc. So I was quite surprised by a little book I got in for review called *Box of Delights*. First, because I just wasn't expecting it. Now normally I don't cover books that arrive to me unsolicited as I just simply don't have enough hours in the day to read them all. But this one stood out after I looked at the back cover synopsis because it sounded like a collection of horror stories and that's all. No theme, no premise, just seventeen horror stories and that's it. And hey, I like horror stories, so despite all my other reading commitments, I added this one to the queue.

And I was not disappointed.

To be sure, not every story hit home with me. In fact there was one I didn't like at all. But that's to be expected with a mixed *Box of Delights* like this. Thankfully I did find the majority of these tales yummy, so for me that puts this book solidly in the win category. As an added nice surprise, some fine stories were by authors I was not familiar with before, and I love finding new writers for me to keep an eye open for. While there were many good selections to choose from in this *Box*, favorites of mine included Steve Rasnic Tem's "The Ex", one of the shortest stories in the book and yet one of the best. That's a rarity for me, as I usually like my horror with more on the bones, but this tiny treat was very satisfying. Another quick hit of horror that I really dug was "The Horizontal Door" by

Future Lovecraft
Silvia Moreno-Garcia &
Paula R. Stiles, Editors
Prime Books
ISBN: 978-1607013532
July, 2012; $15.95 PB

What is the future of Lovecraft? Although they don't express the intention explicitly, the editors of *Future Lovecraft* have not only produced a quality collection of Lovecraft-related science fiction, but have done a fantastic job of selecting stories that raise that very question. Interest in Lovecraft is flourishing, and may now be greater than at any prior point in history. The iconic elements of the Mythos have moved beyond cult status into popular awareness, becoming cultural touchstones with a life of their own. But despite the explosion in interest, Lovecraftian fiction is arguably in crisis. There is some danger that "Lovecraftian" will lose its meaning and become a catch-all for any work that includes tentacle monsters, forbidden texts, or other popular tropes, while ignoring the underlying core philosophical concerns of the genre. Yet, those philosophical concerns themselves do not resonate today as they once did, and must be re-examined. In particular, Lovecraft's use of the Other as a source of horror and his sense of awe at the vast indifferent cosmos are increasingly problematic.

The idea of beings or knowledge so alien that the mind cannot encounter them and remain intact is an essential theme in Lovecraft's work, and this was expressed in part through the portrayal of various foreigners, savage tribes, and degenerate miscegenated hybrids. His views on women, homosexuals, minorities, and eugenics, found in his correspondence and stories, are likewise out of step with most modern readers. There is a notable lack of forgotten backwards tribes and barely repressed vagina monsters in *Future Lovecraft*, which is necessary in the evolution of the genre. Is it an obvious point? Perhaps, but there is probably a reason that I still see calls for Lovecraftian fiction in which the editors specify that they do not want to see the racial stereotypes common in the original. Otherness cannot legitimately be defined as "anyone who is not an educated straight white male" in a global multicultural society. The editors of *Future Lovecraft* propose that the future of Mythos fiction is very much international, with authors from North and Central America, Europe, Africa, and Asia included in the anthology. Several of the stories were translated from the original French or Spanish specifically for this volume. The editors thus make a statement about the genre with the selection of pieces for inclusion: going forward, the Other must be truly alien, not merely different.

But even then, the existence of alien races is not even horrifying in and of itself. The possibility that they may be hostile and more technologically advanced than we are maybe, but the probability that life exists outside our solar system is increasingly accepted. So what do you do as a writer of Lovecraftian fiction? We could normalize the Mythos – the aliens and others become simply races we were not familiar with, strange, but essentially just other people with their own concerns. They become potential members of the Imperial Senate or the Federation of Planets. But when we do this, they lose some of their power as agents of horror. There is no sanity check when you enter the Cantina on Tatooine, simply discomfort. This may be fair, given the way in which Lovecraft has entered global popular culture. I have purchased cuddly Cthulhu plush toys and wished people Mythos-related holiday greetings. There's even a Japanese light romance series with titles including *Nyarko-san: Another Crawling Chaos*. Is normalcy and harem anime the future of Lovecraft's vision? I hope not. If it is, it would be unsatisfying. The stories in *Future Lovecraft* that attempt to normalize the Mythos and its creatures or use them as a source of humor do not work well. They are at best amusing, and aren't philosophically Lovecraftian fiction, even if they include characters or elements. However, their inclusion does make a point about Lovecraft as horror versus something else, and so the addition of a couple of stories in that vein serves to strengthen the anthology overall.

A second major theme of importance to Mythos work is Lovecraft's sense of cosmic emptiness or scale. It may have filled him with a sense of awe and horror, but people are increasingly aware of the vastness of the universe – that the stars we see may well have died millions of years ago. And the idea that the universe does not care about us as individuals or as a species is no longer shocking to most. Obviously, it does not. We at least believe that we have come to terms with the void. Several stories in the volume deal very effectively with cosmic isolation, reminding the reader that intellectual understanding does not equal the experience of the endlessness of space or the existential dread that accompanies an authentic experience of the abyss, or encounters with impossible geometries and broken time. The anthology is at its strongest in this territory, dealing with the horror of the incomprehensible, and the sanity-rending power of cosmic experiences.

Overall, this is a fine collection of short fiction, including works that integrate essential Lovecraftian ideas into science fiction with great skill. The quality of prose is consistent, and there are several pieces that are of exceptional quality. In general the authors do not fall prey to the needless thesaurus browsing that writers sometimes inflict upon their readers when Lovecraft is the inspiration. There are two stories that lack any clear Lovecraftian element, and seem shoehorned into the volume. This is not to say that every piece needs an appearance by a named Mythos being, but if these represent the future of Lovecraft, then the future is diluted, and at risk of becoming an empty descriptor. Their inclusion does highlight this essential concern, which may have made them worthwhile additions.

There is a liberal quantity of poetry in the volume, which seems like a risky editorial decision. The strength of the volume is in the fiction. There are probably not very many successful volumes of science fiction and horror poetry on the market today compared to story anthologies, and, for people who do not care for it, poetry can feel like filler. There was certainly nothing in the poems that grabbed my attention, but this may reflect my personal tastes more than the work itself. I would suggest a second opinion from reviewers who enjoy the form and can better compare the quality of these works to other genre poetry.

I enjoyed the volume a great deal and found the way in which the editors probed the future of the genre with their selections intriguing. Even if I did not care for all the stories, the selection of them made me think about what Lovecraft has been, and may become, in ways that were intellectually stimulating. *Future Lovecraft* is very successful as an editorial effort and contains some wonderful stories that I would recommend to fans of both horror and science fiction.

—Reviewed by K. H. Vaughan

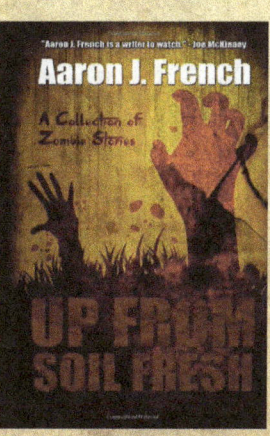

Up from Soil Fresh
Aaron J. French
Hazardous Press,
June 2013
ISBN 978-0615825496
Trade paperback, $5.39;
eBook, $2.99

In general, zombie stories are not directly about zombies. There are exceptions, of course, such as Patrick Freivald's engaging zombies-in-high-school novels

Twice Shy and *Special Dead,* which depart from the 'traditional' narratives in a number of intriguing and entertaining ways (both are delightful reads, by the way), even to the extent of giving readers a vivacious, if mostly dead, point-of-view character.

More usually, however, zombie stories accept the basic fact that zombies, no matter their origin, are in fundamental ways no longer human—they show little if any intellectual ability, they are driven by purely irrational and irresistible urges to devour human brains (and other body parts as available), and perhaps most tellingly they are indisputably *dead.*

For these reasons, zombie stories tend to use the creatures more as a backdrop than as fully functional (or dysfunctional) characters. In Joe McKinney's award-winning *Dead City* novels, for example, the stories gain their power by juxtaposing the everyday and the horrific: Ordinary people must suddenly confront the unbelievable as zombiism strikes. It is *their* conflicts, however, that make the novels work, not the mere presence of the walking dead.

In Aaron J. French's short (but highly readable) collection, *Up from Soil Fresh,* his eight tales of zombies-run-amok attempt something unusual—they range from stories told explicitly from a zombie's unique and rather unpalatable perspective ("Up from Soil Fresh") to something approaching the darker boundaries of high fantasy, in which the focal creatures are mostly relegated to the background while most of the emphasis falls upon the Grandmaster Wizard and his endless struggle against the Light ("The Shadow of Light and Dark").

These bookend pieces frame tales that explore the endless possibilities of life, death, and everything in between…and beyond—perhaps my favorite being the evocatively and highly appropriately named "—Rot—Rot—Rot—," in which the title wonderfully encapsulates the essence (malodorous and gooey) of the story that follows. "The Viewing" and "Mother" touch as much upon the psychology of the living—in both cases sons of deceased mothers—as upon sudden grisly horrors. "The Carpetbagger" incorporates not only the walking dead but an apparent immortal capable of transporting through time and space…along with such Old West staples as saloon girls with hearts of gold and vicious locals looking for—and finding—trouble. In the remaining two stories, drug dealers and hypocritical ministers take center stage. But no matter the story, zombies hover persistently around the edges of humanity, eager for their moment in the light and their mouthful of human brains.

French has done a good job in crafting mostly short, often jarring, always interesting stories. His writing is solid, never distracting from the stories. His shambling abominations are tinged with just enough humor to keep the collection from sinking to a depressing sameness but not so much as to overwhelm the essential horror of his subject. Freshly imagined, freshly told, the tales are indeed *Up from Soil Fresh.*

—**Reviewed by Michael R. Collings**

Detritus
S. S. Michaels and
Kate Jonez, editors
Omnium Gatherum Media
ISBN: 978-0615587684
2012; $12.99 trade paperback,
$2.99 ebook

DETRITUS is an anthology of short stories about collectors and collections. Because it's a horror-themed anthology, I don't think I'm ruining anything by telling you that these stories all focus on the obsessive, dark side of collecting, often exploring the ways that such obsessions can become destructive or terrifying.

I myself am a collector. I have a number of collections, though I primarily collect books. With nearly 6,000 books, not to mention thousands more comic books and magazines, my wife – and visitors to my home – would probably describe me as an obsessive collector. But I'm not a hoarder, and my house isn't (yet) collapsing under the weight of all my books. I don't just buy books and forget about them. I've electronically catalogued all of my books, and continue to spend time maintaining my collection, and the records of the collection. I am not happy when I'm on vacation if I can't visit a bookstore (or two, or three….) I also care about books as physical objects, as artifacts. I'm interested in the physicality of books almost as much as I'm interested in what books have to say. I like to hold books, open them, examine them, smell them. I enjoy being surrounded by books, preferably my own, but I have spent a considerable chunk of my life in libraries. Books comfort me in a strange way that I find hard to articulate. And I am continually on the hunt for new books, despite the fact that I own several thousand books I have not yet read. Many of these, I must be honest with myself and with you, I will likely never read before I die. Even so, I continue to acquire new books. So that's a very long way of saying that I have some understanding of the kinds of collectors and collections depicted in the fifteen horror-themed short stories in the collection DETRITUS. They each share the common theme of obsessive collectors and the sometimes unfortunate or even horrifying consequences of people getting too caught up in the act of collecting.

Mild plot spoilers for a few of the stories follow.

Not all the stories were extraordinarily memorable, but I will note a few of my favorites in the collection.

"Mrs. Grainger's Animal Emporium" by Phil Hickes: A very naughty little boy (we all know the type) has a run-in with the eponymous Mrs. Grainger who owns the new taxidermy shop that has just come to town. Delightfully creepy, it reminds me of the classic EC comic storylines in "Tales from the Crypt" and "Vault of Horror."

"Candy Lady" by Neil Davies: This begins as a story about a woman who collects creepy dolls in an old house infested by a strange kind of black mold and becomes a story about the end of the world, or at least human civilization. A very powerful tale, I'd actually have liked to see this one expanded. As is, it was almost too terse; I wanted to see it fleshed out even more.

"Heroes and Villains" by Michael Montoure: The unhappy tale of two comic book collectors who have the terrible fate of coming into possession of all the comic books they had ever dreamed of acquiring. A very dark piece about the lengths that the obsession with collecting and possession can take the collector.

The final story in the collection, "The Room Beneath the Stairs" by Kealan Patrick Burke, is also a fun one. Andy visits his Grandma after the death of her husband and discovers that Grandma is just a little creepier than he had imagined.

Collecting was a great theme for a collection of horror shorts. These stories make clear that the fetishization of the objects being collected, the collection as a whole, and the process of collecting can all take the collector down dark paths. A warning that should be heeded by all of us collectors, I suppose. I wish that the collection contained a few more stories I loved, but there are few real clunkers here, just some that are forgettable. I recommend the collection – despite the fact that, like most anthologies, not all the stories were winners – because it has an interesting theme and some stand-out stories. If you consider yourself a "collector" and enjoy horror, you'll enjoy adding this anthology to your…collection.

—Reviewed by Andrew Byers

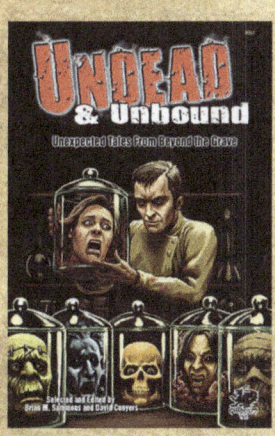

**Undead & Unbound:
Unexpected Tales
From Beyond the Grave**
**Brian M. Sammons &
David Conyers, eds.**
Chaosium
ISBN-13: 978-1568823683
August, 2013; $17.95 PB

Undead & Unbound: Unexpected Tales From Beyond the Grave is an anthology of horror stories about the living dead, released as part of Chaosium's expanding line of fiction. Chaosium, best known for the iconic *Call of Cthulhu* RPG, has been increasingly visible in the anthology community, producing some books that are specifically Mythos-based, and others that are more general in theme. This is the first of their non-RPG products I have read, so I can't comment on the line as a whole or how typical the volume is related to their other fiction products. The book itself is nicely bound and formatted, with attractive cover art by Steven Gilberts that evokes the classic era of horror film.

The first question one might ask about an anthology like this is "do we need another collection of zombie stories?" First of all, *yes*, but let's eliminate any misimpressions right away: *Undead & Unbound* does have its fair share of zombies, but the nineteen stories within cover a broad range of things from beyond the grave, both familiar and more obscure. A strength of the anthology is that the editors have worked to include a variety of living dead, including some from other cultures (the penanggalan of Southeast Asia) and unique interpretations of the tropes of Western horror. They also span historical periods and geographic locations, from the American Old West, to the North Pole, to future Mars. The contributing authors have been given the freedom to re-interpret and reinvent in ways that keep the usual suspects of undead fiction from becoming stale, and also produced some new forms strange and delightful. The tone of the stories varies significantly as well, with some written with dark sensibilities and others more comic. Overall the material skews dark, with some graphic violence and mature content not appropriate for the young. There are no sparkly vampires or the like within.

The table of contents includes a range of established and upcoming writers, who hail from the U.S., U.K., South America, and Australia. I do like to see this international flavor as some diversity of cultures enriches the anthology overall. There is a high proportion of authors who are involved in the horror genre as editors, publishers, and literary critics in addition to being writers themselves, and I think this shows in the frequency of nods to other sources, both popular and obscure. As a reader, I have the sense that the authors know and love their undead well, and would be a formidable team on Horror Jeopardy.

As for the stories themselves, the writing is generally very effective, and several of the stories are really remarkable. Although I don't like to name names in anthology reviews, there are some that have a very resonant emotional impact in the way the characters live with their dead, or struggle to understand and survive the nightmare of the supernatural. There are, at most, one or two that I took issue with based on writing issues. Because the stories do not share a common tone, they may not all be to the taste of individual readers. Some people don't like comedy mixed with their noir; some like their horror broadly apocalyptic, some more personal. However, readers who like the undead and know something of the history and classics of the genre will find stories here that they enjoy.

[Full disclosure: I have two stories contracted for future Chaosium anthology releases. This does not affect my opinion of the current work.]

- Reviewed by K. H. Vaughan

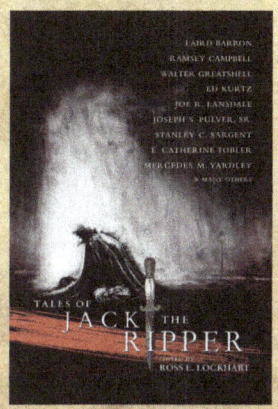

Tales of Jack The Ripper
Edited by Ross E. Lockhart
Word Horde
ISBN: 9781939905000
August 31, 2013 Paperback $15.99
eBook $5.99

Chances are if you are reading this review, you are asking yourself if it is really possible to offer up any new insights into the Whitechappel murderer. Any new theories, any new stories. The answer is an unequivocal YES. Just like Jack captured my imagination as a child, it's obvious the various authors in this anthology have thought quite a bit about him also.

In this collection you will find 18 solid stories and a poem, at the beginning, to set the mood. As with all anthologies, some stories struck a chord with me better than others. But, that's just me. I'm not fond of 1st person, and my favorite author of the group, Ramsey Campbell, chose that POV for his story, Jack's Little Friend. Termination Dust, by Laird Barron (another fantastic writer) felt more like a novella than a short story.

So what were my favorites? A Host of Shadows by Alan M. Clark and Gary A. Braunbeck tops my list. Absolute wonderful speculation of where the Ripper went after the murders, turning his life around, only to have it return to bite him on his deathbed.

The Truffle Pig by T.E. Grau is a wonderful take on the story adding in a mythology of its own. Ripping, by Walter Greatshell has an ending I didn't see coming and that makes any story nigh on perfect in my estimation

The stories that really blew me away were the ones written by women. They captured the victims (or at least how I see them) so wonderfully faithful to what is known, that the stories - while brutal - were honest and real. Something you don't see in short fiction often.

The bottom line is these are all excellent stories, all about Jack. Who he was, who he became and all sorts of speculation in between. Many of them will haunt you with the what-if they are right. If you're a Ripper fan (is that the right word, probably not) you owe it to yourself to get this book. You won't go wrong and you will be entertained for hours and be thinking about what you just read for days after you are done

—Review by Kat Yares

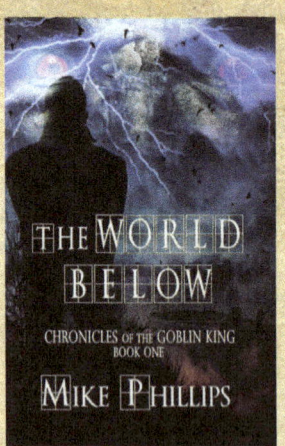

The World Below: Chronicles of the Goblin King Book One
By Mike Phillips
ISBN 9781615728862
Damnation Books, 2013

Let me first say that this book is not horror: I don't believe it was written to frighten the reader. *The World Below* is more of a dark fantasy-slash-modern fairy tale. While there are horrible things that occur, they aren't scary.

The opening chapters were a bit heavy on description, which slowed the story for me. Once the story gained momentum though, it was an enjoyable read with fantastical characters and some great one-liners. Phillips also has an amazing imagination: some of his incidental characters are uniquely unusual in their descriptions, actions and rituals, making them that much more memorable.

In keeping with the dark fairy tale, there is a damaged hero and a magical queen. But Phillips is able to bring a fresh perspective to the usual tropes of magic and mystery, while keeping a touch of humor. The heroine is relatable and—dare I say it—cool and the hero is sympathetic in his bewilderment as he is dragged into a world that he never could have conceived of.

I would have liked for the final battle scene to last longer. I think that with all the effort Phillips took to create the bad guy and all the hero's trials to locate him, the ending encounter only took a short time to resolve. But as this is Book One, there may be more "big bads" yet to come. Phillips ended *Below* in the right place, giving a satisfactory ending but leaving enough frayed ends on which to base the rest of his series.

There were also punctuation misuses and other typographical errors that if fixed, would have made this a more polished work.

Even so, it is worthy of a read and a good start to an epic dark fantasy tale.

—Reviewed by Eden Royce

High Stakes: A Vampire
Anthology
Various Authors
Evil Jester Press, 2013
ISBN-13: 978-0615786452
ISBN-10: 0615786456

Vampires. Can you really re-create them, mold them differently? Is it possible to present the blood drinkers in a fresh, yet believable style?

I wasn't sure before reading this anthology, but Evil Jester has done it.

The anthology opens with an intro by the great grand-nephew of Bram Stoker, Dacre Stoker, who takes us on a journey of his research into his ancestor's life and most famous work.

"The Contest of Inescapable Misdirection" by Linda Addison is a unique piece of game instructions in poetic form. It reads like a stylized "Choose Your Own Adventure" book. Only here you have to choose whether you begin the game fully alive… or not. Either way, the rules of the dead are not set in your favor.

Standout stories were:

As an MMA fan, I enjoyed "The Things that Live in Cages" by Jonathan Maberry. The story sympathetically dealt with an athlete, a master of his art, past his prime but unwilling to give up the lure of the cage. Descriptions were tightly written, the martial arts styles and combos well researched. Most impressive were the characterization of vamp involved and the method of blood sharing; it was a refreshing take on what can at times be stale tropes of the genre.

Horror and erotica blend so well together that there can be a fine line between the two. Joe McKinney's gut twisting "She Grew a Pair" was horrotica done radiantly well. He captured the emotions and reasoning that many women in abusive relationships use in these situations. In what world does a woman fear the wrath of her husband over an infuriated vampire? The actions of the husband were so vivid and so cruel that I cringed for the female lead. Horrifying for reasons beyond the undead.

Add in the multiple tragedies of "Bonesong" by Rain Graves. This was an eloquent story with a fresh point of view character and an inventive way of the villain gaining immortality. Visceral, heartbreaking action that doesn't stop hacking at you until the very end.

Evil Jester has managed to find authors that are keeping the vampire mystique new, interesting, and scary. *High Stakes* has stories that will satisfy the most bloodthirsty fan of the evil tortured nosferatu.

Recommended.

—Reviewed by Eden Royce

Dark Roads: Selected Long Poems 1971-2012
By Bruce Boston
Dark Renaissance Books, 2013
ISBN 13: 978-1-937128-90-6
ISBN 10: 1-937128-90-3

It's rare that I come across the opportunity to review poetry. Even rarer for me to find: the dark, moody sort that transports you to a lonely house on a hill. Where it's raining. And you're alone. With this collection.

Where do I begin with *Dark Roads*?

The stunningly realistic artwork by M. Wayne Miller dotted throughout this collection is such an asset to this poetry. It gives an added depth to each poem that is fortunate enough to have visual accompaniment. The image that opens this book "In the Darkened Hours" is reflective, in both image and mood. And it mirrors the balance of light and shadow that Boston presents to us in this collection.

The poems are presented in chronological order from the oldest to the newest. And I could see a progression, a morphing of Boston's style and theme. Don't worry, this isn't the poetry you had to read in school and dig out the symbolism.

u won't need to dig or decipher. It's there, waiting for you to notice its seductive manner.

My favorites:

"The Walnut Dark Sea is Blooming Swiftly": Undulating, swaying, sloshing words reminded me of ocean waves. Gentle repetition like water lapping at the shore. Reminding us that the sea is always there, watching the blood and bones and destruction we create.

"The Stardrifter Grounded": The tale of a space traveler past his prime. It appeals to the sci-fi geek in me.

"The Lesions of Genetic Sin" and "Pavane for a Cyber-Princess": Darkly sexual imagery

Oh, and there are a few poetic studies in Dark Roads as well. Apparently, not only are there "Thirteen Ways to Look at a Vulture", but also "Thirteen Ways of Looking at and through Hashish."

Something I have always done with poetry (even in school) is choose the best line in the collected works of a poet. The one that resonates with me the deepest. In Dark Roads, that line can be found in "The Mutant Lovers" – *So come my beauty, my horror, for us the night will hold.*

Because well… I'm a romantic.

Recommended for lovers of poetry, imagery, and quick dark reads.

—Reviewed by Eden Royce

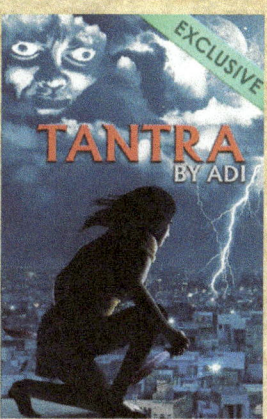

Tantra
By Adi
Apeejay Stya Publishing
ISBN: 978-8190863629
2013; $14.99 trade paperback;
eBook currently free

Stories about tough-as-nails women who hunt vampires and other things that go bump in the night are not exactly new. Indeed, there's practically a cottage industry of such fiction. But how many of those are set in India? TANTRA is certainly the only one I can think of.

Mild plot spoilers follow.

Anu Aggarwal is a young Indian woman who has been living in New York City for the last several years with her fiancé Brian. Anu isn't exactly an ordinary emigrant though; she fights vampires for a living using the mystical powers that an international organization trained her in. One night a vampire kills Brian, and the killer's trail leads Anu back to Delhi, so she returns there and lives with her over-protective aunt while hunting Brian's killer. Anu's return to India is a kind of culture shock for her, as she has been away long enough to become Westernized. Not surprisingly, she resents the social and cultural constraints on what a young unmarried woman can do in Indian society. Anu's family wants her to go on arranged, chaperoned dates and meet a man to marry; she just wants to kill the bad guys. Anu's vampire hunting quickly gives way to a very different kind of threat (possibly too soon; I'd have liked to see a new, Indian-centric take on the vampire). Anu quickly becomes embroiled in an even larger confrontation than she had imagined with an evil guru who has mastered the black magic of the tantric arts and plans to murder hundreds of kidnapped street children to become even more powerful. Anu herself must learn new mystic/psychic arts if she is to succeed since brawn, reflexes, and quick wit alone will be insufficient to win the day.

TANTRA is a kind of paranormal romance thriller. There's plenty of action, car chases, brawls, and mystic duels, alongside flirtation and romance. There is no graphic sex, nor does the romance descend into mushiness. I suspect that a comparison between TANTRA and Buffy the Vampire Slayer is inevitable. Indeed, TANTRA is essentially the story of Buffy with the serial numbers filed off and transported to India. In that sense, TANTRA is not an entirely original premise, but it's entertaining nevertheless, and the Indian setting and culture makes this a memorable read. I don't know much about India, its culture, mythology, folklore, religions, etc. In fact I think the only fiction I've ever read that was set in India – other than a couple of the Flashman novels – was Dan Simmons' SONG OF KALI (if you have not yet read that, I recommend seeking out a copy immediately after you finish reading this review). As unfamiliar as India was to me, at no time was I lost while reading TANTRA; indeed, it served as a gentle introduction to contemporary Indian culture.

Presumably, TANTRA is intended as the start of a series since – despite the initial premise – it's not really a book about vampire-hunting, nor is the murder of Anu's fiancé ever resolved. There's certainly room for the characters and setting to grow, as there are mere hints of many of the supernatural elements touched on in TANTRA. For example, what exactly is the organization that trained Anu? What are their goals and capabilities? What do vampires think about the fact that a group of humans is hunting them? What other supernatural elements exist in the setting of TANTRA? It seems clear that Hindu mysticism is real, and we know there are vampires, but what else?

I recommend TANTRA not because the premise is particularly original – it is not – but because it provides an interesting, fresh cultural milieu and set of supernatural powers that should be of interest to most Western readers. This seems to be Adi's first novel, but he's a talented writer and I look forward to reading more from him. And I certainly enjoyed the glimpse inside Hindu mysticism and beliefs about the supernatural provided by TANTRA.

—Reviewed by Andrew Byers

Hands of the Ripper
(Blu-Ray/DVD Combo)
Directed by Peter Sasdy
Synapse Films; July, 2013

Fitting for a "Women in Horror" special, Hammer's 1971 gory Jack the Ripper riff gets the Blu-Ray treatment from Synapse Films. Riding the Occult wave of the sixties, the film shows the protagonist Dr. John Pritchard (Eric Porter) debunking fake séances – only to come across Anna (Angharad Rees), a woman who turns out to be the daughter of Jack the Ripper (and who is supposedly possessed by his spirit). Pritchard, a student of Freud, uses various techniques to explore the violent outbursts of Anna.

The settings are quite convincing as usual for Hammer and Hands of the Ripper is one of the more graphic films from the studio (much in effort to keep up with the increasingly gory and violent US cinema Hammer originally inspired in the late 1950's/early 1960s). The film still holds up well and the performances are quite good. The early Seventies was definitely the time for the ladies with the Karnstein trilogy, Countess Dracula, Dr. Jekyll and Sister Hyde and Hands of the Ripper.

The transfer on the disc looks great and is Widescreen. There is a great documentary with the director, actress Rees, Producer Aida Young and others (including Joe Dante). Also included is a slideshow of violent highlights from Hammer's catalogue ("Slaughter of Innocents: The Evolution of Hammer Gore"), an international stills gallery and trailers and TV spots. Highly Recommended!

- Reviewed by Trever Nordgren

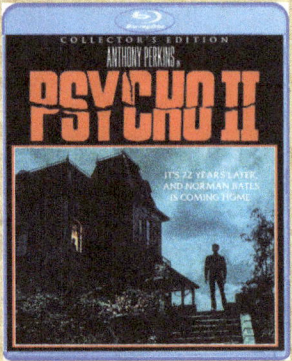

PSYCHO II (Blu-Ray)
Directed by Richard Franklin
Scream Factory
September 2013

On September 24th, Scream Factory releases the collector's edition of Psycho II on both Blu-ray and DVD – and by collector's edition, they deliver and do not disappoint. This transfer to Blu-ray is absolutely stunning. The picture is practically perfect and clear, the colors crisp and the 5.1 HD DTS is amazing. DTS is my favorite format for sound, and I have the system to showcase it – and I must say it blew me away; the mixing is perfect and incredibly impressive considering the film is from 1983. All of the dialogue is easy to hear and the soundtrack and Foley effects do not overpower it, giving the visuals a considerable companion.

This is the very first release of Psycho II on either Blu-ray or DVD format that has ANY special features whatsoever. The 2005 and 2007 triple feature from Universal have absolutely zero special features, and if you're like me – that's a big deal. The collector's edition from Scream Factory is filled to the brim with excellent goodies.

First impressions grabbed me right away; the main menu is realistic and gorgeously striking, has a long loop and is also mixed in 5.1 DTS! A real treat for those who are particular with their extras. The treats do not stop there – the disc contains an excellent and intriguing 35 minute feature from the Electronic Press Kit that has interviews with Janet Leigh (who reflects on her fear of taking showers!), director Richard Franklin, Anthony Perkins, Vera Miles, executive producer Bernard Schwartz as well as short outtakes from the master himself, Alfred Hitchcock. The special features also have 2 original trailers, 4 TV spots and a still gallery with 77 pictures (which have candid shots from the filming, behind the scenes stills, original posters, VHS display boxes and many lobby cards). Also, there is an audio commentary with the screenwriter, Tom Holland as well as another audio interview that plays over the film that contains previously unreleased interviews from The Electronic Press Kit. As you can tell – this is *THE* definitive version of Psycho II and is a *must have* for any fan of the series.

As far as the film itself goes, it's surprisingly good. Perkins picks up his role as Norman Bates perfectly, despite it being 22 years since the original. There are several twists and turns and a striking revelation to the franchise in the final scene. Director Richard Franklin does a nice job of replicating Hitchcock's style and pays a proper homage to him.

In short, Scream Factory has done it again and brings to us easily the best version to date and gives it the proper treatment that this often overlooked film deserves. Do yourself a favor and order a copy today.

Pick up yours at:

www.shoutfactory.com/screamfactory

- Reviewed by Anthony Dluzak

The Conjuring (2013)
Starring Vera Farmiga,
Patrick Wilson
Director: James Wan

The Conjuring is notable for many things, some of which add to the cinematic experience. The merits of the movie will be the first discussed. As a horror film, *The Conjuring* succeeds in its aim of frightening the audience. The mechanisms of fright are varied, and unlike so many films in the genre, empathy on the part of the audience is rewarded. Good horror requires a feeling of dread, and that is almost impossible without empathy for the characters.

We are introduced to the Perron family, who are then just moving into their new home in Rhode Island. It does not take long for the creepy shenanigans to start, (and this is where the parents in the audience were cringing) culminating in an unseen force grabbing one of the daughters by the leg. This motif of the infernal attacking the innocent is repeated throughout the film, but it is skilfully done.

The audience is introduced to Ed and Lorraine Warren, real-life paranormal researchers, in small glimpses, until the Perrons approach them for help. One of Ed Warren's eccentricities is a safe room in the family home, in which are stored cursed, possessed or ritual objects. When a writer asks him why he does not destroy them, Ed replies, "The spirits are bound to the objects. They're not going anywhere."

As the story unfolds, we find that the Perrons bought the house at auction, without knowing its history. As we might have guessed, the house has been the site of awful rites, among other things. Without giving away too much plot, let us discuss the craft involved in the movie.

As mentioned earlier, the demonic attacking the weakest is always present. All of the Perron children are *female*, and this is a key piece of the puzzle. Another well-thought out aspect is the pervasive use of childrens' toys as cursed objects. Dolls, music boxes and mirrors all become sinister when viewed in the dimming light of the Perron house.

Director James Wan does a fine job with the surface scares, such as hands appearing out of nowhere, and close shots of a person holding a single match, surrounded by oily darkness. Of more import is the mood that he manages to convey: A pair of loving parents have moved their five daughters into a home that might as well be an antechamber to Hell. Against the spectral forces, the parents are powerless, for all their love. That idea alone is liable to give parents nightmares.

In this, Ed and Lorraine Warren are dutiful members of the Church, but tire of the Church's balking at the idea of an exorcism, because, we are told, the children weren't baptized. Eventually, Ed must make the decision to break either with Church dogma or his own humanity.

We learn that Ed and Lorraine Warren, while being open about their researches, have never revealed the events surrounding the Perron house, until now. As someone who has read their books, I can say one thing: it was understandable.

- Reviewed by Jim Smiley

❀ ❀ ❀

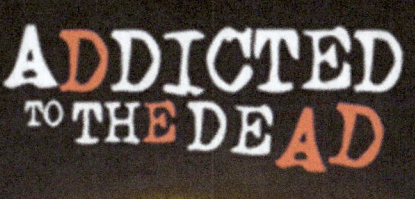

UNSETTLE... EDIFY... INVOLVE...

DARK DISCOVERIES

SUBSCRIBE and never miss another issue of...

www.darkdiscoveries.com

FEATURES:

Weird Fiction & Film, Extreme Horror, Comics & Pulps, New Blood, Dark SciFi, Twilight Zone, H.P. Lovecraft, Horror in Rock, Forgotten Horror & SF TV...

INTERVIEWS:

Ray Bradbury, Bruce Campbell, Christopher Lee, Joe R. Lansdale, William F. Nolan, EC Comics Al Feldstein, Brian Keene, Jack Ketchum, David Cronenberg...

FICTION:

Richard Matheson, Ray Bradbury, Thomas Ligotti, Richard Laymon, John Shirley, William F. Nolan, Ramsey Campbell, Joe R. Lansdale, Lisa Morton, Edward Lee...

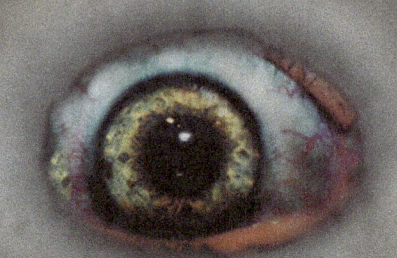

"Dark Discoveries is a very handsome publication..."

--Dean Koontz

"A bright new force in Dark Fantasy."

--William F. Nolan

"Dark Discoveries is a high quality mag... and it keeps getting better..."

--Horror Fiction Review

PRINT SUBSCRIPTIONS

4 issues (1 year): US ($37.95) Canada ($46.95) Overseas ($69.95)

8 issues (2 years): US ($74.95) Canada ($92.95) Overseas ($139.95)

(*Shipping is included on print subs)

ADVERTISERS!

Inquire via E-mail for rates!

Please Note: Future content subject to change without notice. All rights reserved.

DIGITAL SUBSCRIPTIONS

4 issues (1 year): $19.95
8 issues (2 years): $39.95
Payment accepted via PayPal: christophercpayne@journalstone.com
Also by Check/M.O. (Payable to)

JournalStone Publications, 1261 Peachwood Court, San Bruno, CA 94066, USA

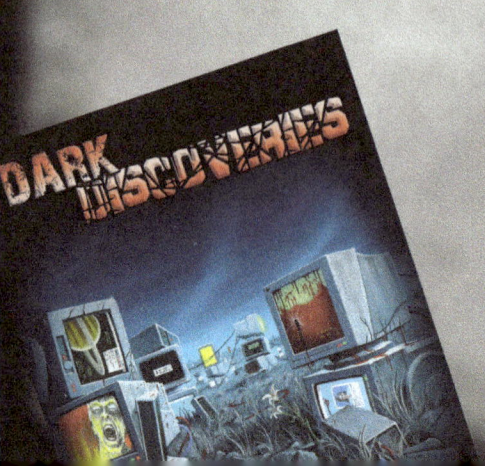

JOURNALSTONE
YOUR LINK TO ARTISTIC TALENT